UNDER WEDGERY DOWN

BOOKS BY ERNEST RAYMOND

NOVELS
A London Gallery *comprising*:

We, the Accused
The Marsh
Gentle Greaves
The Witness of Canon Welcome
A Chorus Ending
The Kilburn Tale
Child of Norman's End
For Them that Trespass
A Georgian Love Story
Miryam's Guest House

Was There Love Once?
The Corporal of the Guard
A Song of the Tide
The Chalice and the Sword
To the Wood No More
The Lord of Wensley
The Old June Weather
The City and the Dream
Our Late Member

OTHER NOVELS

The Bethany Road
The Mountain Farm
The Tree of Heaven
One of Our Brethren
Late in the Day
Mr. Olim
The Chatelaine
The Visit of Brother Ives
The Quiet Shore
The Nameless Places
Tell England
A Family that Was
A Jesting Army

Mary Leith
Morris in the Dance
The Old Tree Blossomed
Don John's Mountain Home
The Five Sons of Le Faber
The Last to Rest
Newtimber Lane
The Miracle of Brean
Rossenal
Damascus Gate
Wanderlight
Daphne Bruno I
Daphne Bruno II

BIOGRAPHIES, *etc.*

The Story of My Days (Autobiography I)
Please You, Draw Near (Autobiography II)
Good Morning, Good People (Autobiography III)
Paris, City of Enchantment
Two Gentlemen of Rome (The Story of Keats and Shelley)
In the Steps of St. Francis
In the Steps of the Brontës

ESSAYS, *etc.*

Through Literature to Life
The Shout of the King
Back to Humanity (with Patrick Raymond)

PLAYS

The Berg
The Multabello Road

Under Wedgery Down

A NOVEL
By

ERNEST RAYMOND

Who shall say which is greatest, Isidora,
Who shall say which is least?
That is my Master's business.

after KIPLING

CASSELL✳LONDON

CASSELL & COMPANY LTD
an imprint of
Cassell & Collier Macmillan Publishers Ltd
35 Red Lion Square, London WC1R 4SG
and at Sydney, Auckland, Toronto, Johannesburg
and an affiliate of The Macmillan Company Inc, New York

474279699

First published 1974

ISBN 0 304 29368 7

Printed in Great Britain by
Northumberland Press Limited,
Gateshead
F. 674

Contents

Author's Note

Lest any geographers, downsmen, or local historians should seek to identify the little town of Wedgery in this novel or the little estuary at Grayling Bottom let me say at once that many townships within the laps of the Sussex Downs and many ports (if that's not too large a word) at their feet have played their parts in the composing of these places, which are thus purely creations of the author's fancy. Though the last and Indian chapters are alike fictitious, and involve no direct quotations from published works, they could not have been written without the instant and willing help of the Rev. John Copley Winslow (who graciously allowed me the impertinence of attempting a fictional portrait of him), Bishop William Lash, late Bishop of Bombay, and Father Denis Marsh (friend and old Pauline like me, though, alas, of very different years), of the Society of St. Francis, Cerne Abbas, Dorset. While I thank all these for their splendid help I must ask their forgiveness for having, in places, assumed a dramatist's licence, disguising some names and compressing time, so as to bring closer and more sharply together the occurrence of dramatic events.

E.R.

PART ONE

At 'Slings' in Wedgery

I

Noon on Wedgery Beacon and the sun at its zenith. An Easter-tide sun spreading goodwill on the whole range of the South Downs so that it seemed to be immediately over the head of any-one, anywhere, on their long swaying run. And that is a run of seventy miles, heaving and drooping, from the marches of Hamp-shire to the round summit of Beachy Head which abruptly swings southward to present a scornful and haughty white face at the sea—and there end the South Downs for ever.

From Beacon Hill and Bury, Washington and Chanctonbury, Edburton Hill, Ditchling Beacon, Blackcap, Firle Beacon and Wedgery Beacon, solitude seems always sovereign at this noontide hour, though here and there a lonely figure may be seen walking, or a group standing to stare at great views, or an old shepherd dreamily following his sheep. Beacons? But so round and smooth are these green hills that perhaps breasts might be the apter word—comforting breasts of good old Mother Earth. In all our England there is nothing like them; they run alone for their seventy miles, so silent, solitary and separate that, in whimsical mood, and in modern terms, one might ask if these silent bulwarks that buttress Sussex from the sea didn't, once upon a time, declare an Unilateral Declaration of Independence from the rest of the Island. In nobler language does not a South Saxon poet speak of them as 'the heathen kingdom Wilfrid found', still dreaming and dwelling apart?

To gauge the apartness of these mountains—for mountains they may be called since they can top eight hundred feet—you have only to compare their smooth and welcoming repose with the tormented tops, all rocks and stones, all storm and stress, of our Cumbrian mountains in the north. They even differ, since they are unwooded and unpeopled, from the parallel chalk Downs in Surrey and Kent, which they face like a row of Chieftains with Wolstonbury Hill standing out like a captain in front of his array.

'The King has come to marshal us.' If you think like this you will certainly regard Leith Hill in Surrey as captain of the opposing host, standing as it does well in front of its North Downs and eight hundred and sixty feet high.

The South Downs are surely the best place in all England to know the sky. From any of their beacons you can see the whole firmament touching the world all round. Yonder it encompasses all the wooded hills on the farther side of the Weald; hither it bends down to the last horizons of the sea.

Lonely and apart they may be now, best known as ideal ground for easy walkers who say they can walk for ever with such turf beneath their feet, or as ideal ridges for gentlemen and lady riders in the full gaiety of canter or gallop; but almost every summit, however empty now, is printed with history. Standing on Chanctonbury or on Wedgery you can see about your feet the traces of a fortress 'camp' with its enclosing fosse, but whether shaped by Roman legionaries to command the great forestland of Sylva Anderida below, or by the ancient Britons before them, or by the invading Saxons after them, our scholars are not always in happy agreement. So if you have a talent for fantasy you are entitled, as you look down on these grassy earthworks, to imagine the ghosts of the legionaries with their helmets and shields, dead men in steel like the ghost of Hamlet's father, pacing their ramparts, or Saxon sentries sitting by their watchfires and gazing down upon Anderida, which they then knew as Andreasweald. The great forest of Sylva Anderida was already beginning to be known as the 'Sussex wold' or 'weald'.

Through all their length these hills have their combes and hollows, and such a one under Wedgery holds the little township of Wedgery with its stream, the Grayling, twisting down hill to the sea at Grayling Bottom. It was Wedgery Beacon, Wedgery's combe, and Grayling Bottom that saw our story happen.

Wedgery's combe—known locally as Wedgery Dip—has its charms, but the Devil is reputed to have played a mischievous hand in others of these gaps. Naturally he has little love for the beauty of the Downs which may engender a tendency to worship in good men; did he not in his malice attempt at the Devil's Dyke above Brighton to drive a gully that might invite the sea to rush inland and swamp the churches of Hangleton, Poynings, and

Edburton—where, nonetheless, they are still intermittently worshipping. The legend goes that his attempt, on a night of great wickedness, was a failure because he saw a light in an old crone's cottage and mistook it for the dawn—wherewith he hesitated because he likes to work in darkness. But if he didn't get the sea on to those southern slopes he did in time get the monstrous vulgarities of Brighton and its seedy back-streets which might still be gently rising sheep-tracks on a down. So perhaps we may think he achieved a second-best. Even in Wedgery old downsmen say that his abominable finger has left its print in Grayling Bottom where the Grayling stream shakes hands with the sea and so provided a sterling port for the sins of the smugglers.

On this Eastertide morning, it being early in the day, and early in the year, one might have said there was no one in sight on the Downs. There were sheep, of course, in the distance, those unaware artists who by cropping and taming the chalk-hill turf make of it the sweetest carpet in the world for human feet—and horses' hooves—and so happy an abode for harebell and scabious, thyme and tormentil, thistle and cats-ear, and flying above from flower to flower, the chalk-blue and Adonis blue butterflies. Over Wedgery Beacon and Beachy Head gulls came screaming and swooping as if to welcome this southward switch of the Downs and to greet the magnificent, if frowning, white cliff-face that defied their sea. Shadows slanted along the cheeks of the hills whenever a skein of white cloud drifted across the sun; but of human movement—nothing. Or so it seemed. So it seemed till a solitary figure came up from the lap below Beachy Head and, wandering over Wedgery's crown, descended the slope towards Wedgery Dip. It was a small figure and when seen more closely, in this holiday time of 1911, plainly a schoolboy from some preparatory school. This was revealed by his knicker-bocker suit, his woollen stockings reaching to the knicker-bocker buckles, and his green school cap, now crumpled and fading. His head drooping a little, and the thumb-nail at his mouth suggested that his thoughts were wandering far away while his body came wandering heedlessly, in lost and listless fashion, down the hill.

His thoughts were indeed far away. Nearly five thousand miles away, across continents and seas. They were in the Indian city of Gondapore on its breezy Deccan tableland. For much of this walk down the hill they were wandering in his parents' fine bungalow and garden compound, or they had left the British area with its wide tree-lined avenues and here and there its ancient palaces of the Mahratta Peshwas, and were visiting the old city down by the river which was there before ever the British came. Here the streets were narrow and treeless and might house lower-caste labourers and further down the river the ragged and ramshackle huts of the untouchables. Strange the difference between this native district and the Europeans' habitat up above where, as well as the broad avenues there was a cool and shady park of rare trees, the Empress Gardens, a Kew in British India. He visited also the handsome Brahman quarter, but most of all his mental eye was seeing, not the hill slope beneath his feet nor the long range of heaving hills beyond, but the lofty range of the Western Ghats which ran parallel with the Malabar coast and buttressed the heart of India from the Arabian sea much as these Downs buttressed the heart of Sussex from the English Channel. These Ghats, of course, were bulwarks as much higher, and their range as much longer, as the continent of India is larger than an English county. But it was their function of walling Central India from its ocean which caused this youthful expatriate, born in British India, to love these Sussex Downs and to stroll about them alone and think of them as junior Ghats.

Gondapore lies under the lee of the Ghats and many of their spurs intrude upon the Deccan plateau, so that soon this boy—whose name, by the way, was Conal Quentin Gillie—was remembering how his father loved to climb those spurs for the sake of their forest scenery and mountain views, and to take him by the hand (when at six and seven he was old enough) on to one of their peaks, or let him come happily toiling behind. It was his father who had loaded him with the love of hills and of Gondapore's hills above all. It was he who on many a day had made a child see and wonder and thrill, when the hot Indian sun, after floodlighting for a second the vast Deccan plateau went down in glory behind the Ghats, to be followed by a brief Indian twilight, and then the stars and a sudden coolness in the night.

Conal's father was now the Collector, or chief administrator of his Gondapore District, and that he was a kindly, just, and popular administrator Conal was thinking now, though vaguely enough at eleven years old, as he came down the hill. He could hear him speaking—perhaps on a slope of the Ghats or in an Indian train when he was bringing him home to England at eight years old for education at prep-school and public school; and what his father was saying would go something like this:

'Don't believe, Conal, more than a quarter—no, let us say more than a half—of what you hear about us poor Anglo-Indians trying to do our job in India. Perhaps a half of it is unfortunately true—and even a shade more than half—but—' here he would shake his head—'people say that because the Sahibs exclude the Indians from their clubs it means that they treat them with contempt as an inferior race. I don't know if this was ever really true. Clubs are for people of like interests, and two races can be quite unlike. That'll pass for some justification, but I've never been able to see, and never shall, any justification for banning all Indians from the clubs as guests. Still, I'm afraid this is the attitude of far too many of us and, alas, of most of our memsahibs—but, Conal, the word "sahib" means "friend", and it was first applied to us by the Indians themselves. What do you make of that? Oh, dear, oh dear, we're very far from perfect but I'm sure the more sensible of us now realise that India is the Indians' country, and that our business there is not so much to dig profits out of it as to give unity and order to a whole continent of fifty fiery religions, all quick to riot, as well as hospitals, colleges, universities, libraries, and, most significant of all, I suppose, the railways to knit together a continent that is a mass of mountains and rivers, valleys and tablelands, to say nothing of what is still but forest and jungle and desert. I'm pretty sure the wiser of our "downtrodden" subjects acknowledge this, and are content to await the future, while the less wise just accept it because they can't do anything else, and unless they are hotly anti-British give us their friendship. I sometimes think our good brown Aryan cousin is more capable of affection and courtesy than far too many of his European masters. You've seen how we've loved our servants and how they've loved us. Dammit, Conal, I can't imagine our achieving on the continent of Europe, which is incomparably less primitive and incomparably smaller, anything like the unity and order which we, with all our faults, have achieved in British India. I want you to be sure, Conal, because I know it's a truth, that when the worst has been said about the British in India, the simple fact remains that they've put more into a vast continent than they've taken out.'

Thus Conal's father, Mr Henry Quentin Gillie, the Collector, after eighteen years' service in India.

Ten years, all told, Conal would be here in England, away from his parents and his well-loved Gondapore; ten years from eight to eighteen at prep-school and public school; thirteen if haply he went on to the university. Meantime he lived with foster parents, Elizabeth and Gilbert Sheridan, in their Chelsea flat and during school holidays came with them to their rustic cottage in Wedgery. The Sheridans had a daughter, Marjorie Jacqueline, only six months younger than he, so that they ought to have been happy playmates together, and sometimes were, but more often were not. They were children of a different temper; she, in the modern tongue, a lively little extrovert, happiest with people about her, whereas Conal, having no great love for Mrs Sheridan and only a little more for Mr Gilbert Sheridan, and less than a little for Marjorie, was at his least unhappy when he was introverted and living with private thoughts and dreams. This morning furnished an example: Marjorie had no desire to 'fag up' to the top of Beachy Head, and Conal was grateful for this unwillingness because it meant he could wander up there alone and remember the Ghats.

Conal was allowed to call Gilbert Sheridan 'Uncle Bertie' but never Elizabeth Sheridan 'Auntie'; only 'Lizetta'—which, being a lady of affectations, she liked to be called by everybody. 'Lizetta' yes, but, most emphatically, never 'Liz'. Now, at eleven years old and approaching twelve, Conal had a faint perception that Lizetta, while ready to tolerate him as a son of her husband's friend, a source of more income for her household, and a companion for her daughter, really felt—possibly without full awareness—a distaste for him, a kind of submerged hostility, which Conal, also only half aware of it, often reciprocated. It was significant that she never called him anything but 'Conal' while Uncle Bertie was more likely to call him 'Young-fellow-me-lad' or, jovially punning on his name, 'Colonel'.

Lizetta was nearer fifty than forty, and in these early nineteen-hundreds this meant, in her case and as in many others, that she was a woman of large, roomy, matronly figure sternly enclosed in steel and whalebone which seemed to enforce a waist at the cost of hips below and bosom above.

Conal had been born early in the first year of the new century or in the last year of the old; for no one had decided then—and is the question decided yet?—whether the twentieth century began in 1900 or 1901. Conal would plump vigorously for 1901, maintaining that a century must be ten tens and therefore finish on a nought and begin with a 'one'; for which contention he would be snubbed and squashed as an ignorant child by Lizetta, a well-meaning but quick-tempered and rather silly woman (as he was beginning to assess her, from ten-years-old and upward).

'Of course the century began with the number nineteen,' she insisted, her voice lifting. 'Don't be silly and argumentative. You're for ever arguing something or other.' This was not far from the truth. 'For your age it's just ridiculous, arguing with people twenty—' she hesitated on the number—'twenty and more years older than you. Thinking you know better than anyone else.'

'But it *can't* begin on the nineteen,' Conal, the arguer, insisted in his turn. 'A century doesn't die in its ninety-ninth year but on its hundredth, and the new one must begin on its first year, which was 1901. And that means that my age runs with the century: I was nought in 1900, one in 1901, and now eleven in 1911. So far as I'm concerned, that's how it goes.' To himself he argued, 'And anyhow, "Auntie Liz", it isn't necessarily silly of someone to differ from you. It's you that's silly to think so. I'm sure that's what Daddy would say. He always says that chaps, whatever their age, ought to be allowed to say whatever they think.'

No sense in uttering these latter sentiments aloud. Conal's ripening intelligence was half in possession of the knowledge that there was no convincing Lizetta against her will; that the adult was not yet born who could do this, and it was certainly not within the compass of an 'ignorant child' of eleven.

The most remarkable house in Wedgery's tumbling street was the half-timbered Brotherhood Inn, called everywhere 'the smugglers' inn' because the legends said that it had once, by virtue of an ordinance from the Lord Abbot of Bellingham, been a place of sanctuary for refugees from justice and Wedgery's abounding smugglers could sit there with ease when the revenue men were abroad. It had then been the Rose and Crown, a most unsuitable name for a smugglers' venue, so a merry landlord long ago had changed the name to 'The Brotherhood', submitting with a wink or two that this nicely expressed the local fact: that the villagers took pride in their smugglers and were pleased to welcome them into his parlour, to hold them there in safety, and so do their duty by them, not as sinners but as neighbours and brothers. Possibly, too, this humane landlord had once been a smuggler himself and thus had a yet stronger reason to account all such gallant freetraders his brothers.

Not a hundred yards down the hill stood another eye-attracting half-timbered house, 'Slings'; this was the Sheridans' holiday cottage, long, low, and thatched, greatly to the family's pride. Long and low, but it had three floors, or, as you might say, two and a half, because the third was but an attic floor with tiny dormer windows, diamond-paned, peeping through the thatch. All its doors, like those of the Brotherhood Inn, belonged to an age of smaller Englishmen than now, so that Uncle Bertie, a tall man, a bald man, and a forgetful, often crashed his head on the lintels and swore to heaven. He would say that he'd done this so often that the crown of his head was almost callous, though still sensitive enough to justify a string of blasphemies if the contact had been unusually impressive.

To Slings on this morning of an Easter holiday Conal returned from his half-happy, half-despondent vagrancy on the Downs, bringing to his mid-day meal an appetite which held no trace of despondency.

'Where on earth have you been all this time?' asked Lizetta, carrying yesterday's cold joint into the living-room.

'I've been all the way to Belle Tout Lighthouse on Beachy Head and wish we lived in it instead of in Slings.'

'Well, for heaven's sake don't go near the cliff-edge and fall over. That'd be the end of you.'

'I'm not quite such a fool as that,' Conal retorted, not unirritably; and ever anxious to parade his knowledge, added, 'It's five hundred and seventy feet high.'

'Well, what's the sense of wandering off alone like that for hours and hours? You must have walked nearly four miles.'

'Nearer five,' he bragged, stretching the truth. 'But I've got back in time for tiffin.'

' "*Tiffin!*" Do call it lunch, not "tiffin". You're in England now, not India. Nobody here knows what you mean with your "tiffin" and your—what is it you call breakfast?'

'*Chota hazri,*' he supplied very willingly since it reminded him of India. He knew well that *chota hazri* suggested less a stout English breakfast of bacon and eggs than a first cup of tea and a biscuit in bed, but he was not above using it in this way chiefly to annoy Marjorie. And possibly at times to impress any hearers with his quality as a traveller.

'Yes—*chota* something,' said Lizetta, 'but that was hours ago. I see you've managed to arrive very promptly for lunch.'

'Heavens, yes! I can walk four miles an hour. Three uphill, perhaps.'

'But why go off alone when you could stay here and play with Marjorie? She was left all alone to play in the garden.'

'Marge wouldn't come.'

'I should think not,' said Marjorie, now in the room and as eager for food as Conal.

'How often have I told you not to call her Marge? I think it's hateful.'

These were days when margarine, as distinct from butter, almost symbolised the lower rungs of the social ladder. Only common people ate margarine and cooked with it.

'Yes, I wish he wouldn't too,' said Marjorie. 'I refuse to be likened to margarine.'

'It's made out of vegetable oil and fats,' said Conal, an unwise offering to a plump little girl if he was conducting his defence, but he could never resist the desire to display any depths in his scientific knowledge. He quickly saw an unwisdom in it, and quickly explained, hardly more wisely, 'I'm sorry but it often comes out like that because I always think of her as Marge.'

'Well, *don't* think of her as Marge. She's Marjorie Jacqueline. "Jacky" I'll tolerate but not Marge. I hate any mention of margarine or marge.'

At this inconclusive stage Uncle Bertie came in from his midday visit to the Brotherhood Inn, and once again crashed his head on the lintel: it was a warm day and he'd had two pints at the Brotherhood. 'Lord Jehoshophat in hell!' he swore, with a hand to his bald head. 'Jesus Christ and God Almighty, it can hurt. God blast all the saints and——'

'Really, Bertie,' Lizetta protested. 'Remember the children.'

'Remember the children? How can I remember children when I've been knocked silly by an almighty crack on the head? You none of you know what it amounts to, and you don't care a damn about my sufferings. And you never will because you're not tall enough—unless perhaps the Colonel grows as tall as I am. I hope he will, and then when this impact happens—as I trust it may once or twice—he'll remember his poor Uncle Bertie and understand. Why can't you all yell out when you hear me approaching and remind me of this blasted doorway? Yell out "Mind the door". What's for lunch? Oh, that old bone?'

So entered Uncle Bertie, and Conal noticed that he was neither questioned where he had been nor sneered at for arriving promptly. Better to be a grown-up and master of the house than a boy lodger from abroad. 'Phew!' Uncle Bertie sighed as the ache on his head subsided, and he sat with the others at the table. 'The sun's hot. A proper heat-wave in April. Never heard of anything like it.'

This was Friday, but Uncle Bertie was with them. Normally during these spring and summer holidays in Wedgery he went on five days of the week to town and worked, not over-strenuously, in the offices of his firm, Robbins, Waite and Sheridan, Chartered Accountants, Grosvenor Gardens. But there were days in April or May, and many more in August, when, if the sun was in high and merry mood, this daily attendance was not too rigidly observed.

'Oh, couldn't we bathe, Daddy?' Marjorie rushed in with this question.

'Oh, yes,' Conal begged. 'Oh *yes*. Yes, please. It's almost May.'

'Of course not,' Lizetta forbade. 'Bathing in April. I've never heard of such a thing.'

'Oh, let 'em bathe. Their holiday's almost over. Let's make some hay while the sun shines.'

'Don't encourage them, Bertie. You always encourage them when they want to do something ridiculous. Can't you support me sometimes when I'm trying to do my duty by them?'

'I'm only encouraging them to be plucky. *I'll* bathe. I'll go in first and make sure it's warm enough. Then we'll all go in quickly and come out and dry in the sun. It's blazing.'

'It was blazing hot on the Beacon,' Conal endorsed. 'And hardly any wind at all.' An overstatement and an understatement, but both of them were somewhere near the truth.

'You be quiet,' Lizetta suggested. 'You know nothing about it. One hot day isn't enough to warm the sea. You'll catch your death.'

'They'll catch nothing of the sort. You haven't been out yet. You don't know how hot it is in the sun. Conal's perfectly right.'

'I tell you I'm not having my daughter catch her death.' No one present, not even Conal, noticed that it was only her daughter's death to which she alluded.

'And I've told you I'll see that she comes out of the sea alive. Even if it's cold, what harm can a cold bath do to anyone? Some people have cold baths all the year round. I used to, and wish I had the guts to do it now.'

'All right. If you want to kill your daughter, do so.' Lizetta liked her quarrels with her husband or anyone else to be as dramatic as possible. She liked to work them up into a 'scene'. 'Because a great strong man like you can go into a bitterly cold sea without harm, it doesn't follow that a child of ten——'

'Of course she can. And she's nearly eleven. Children of eleven are as strong as mules. They're at their best. Probably much better than a poor old dodderer of fifty like me.'

'You're not fifty. What's the good of telling a lot of lies in front of the children?'

'It's not a lot of lies, my dear. It's only one. And barely that.'

'Well, I've said what I have to say. I leave it to you. You must do what you like. I retire from any further say in the matter.' By now she was enacting happily the tragic resignation of a king's mere consort; and the two children, turning their faces from one to the other, watching the mounting drama with pleasure and anticipation; they were used to Lizetta's 'scenes' and enjoyed them. 'All right,' she was repeating now. 'Kill your own child if that's your fancy. It's not in my power to stop you. And, anyhow, we shall have to get out the tent from the store-room where we packed it away last September. And it's a mile and more to walk on a hot day.'

'Those are totally different points,' her husband emphasised, liking to be specific. 'I thought we were talking about death. Let us stick to Marjorie's death.'

This really worked up the scene to a grand finale. 'Of all the wicked things to say . . .'

'But, my dear, it was you who introduced the interesting topic.' Just as Lizetta rejoiced in a resounding storm so he liked to display a masculine reasonableness, calm and humour; than which nothing could more exasperate Lizetta; if her scene was to be different from his she would play it with all the more bravura. 'Your own daughter! Treating her death as a matter for joking! Our only child. Perhaps you'd like to see her lying dead.'

'Yes, naturally I'd love to. That goes without saying. On the other, and perhaps smaller point, there'll be no great difficulty in getting the tent out of the store-room. That presents no obstacle. Conal and I'll have it out in no time.'

But Lizetta wasn't going to have her scene downgraded and brought to an end like this. She got up, crashed down her knife and fork, picked up her plate, remembered she'd need the knife and fork if she was going to finish her lunch in the kitchen, recovered them both, and announced, 'I'm not going to be insulted in front of the children. I'm not going to listen to facetious joking about my daughter's death. I happen to love her.' With her plate and the necessary cutlery she left the room.

'*Au revoir*,' said he. And '*Auf Wiedersehen.*' And '*A rivederla.*'

Both children were sorry that the performance was over and the leading lady gone from the stage.

'I think we shall need a bathe after that, Conal,' said Uncle Bertie. 'Come, let's dig out that tent.'

'Hurray, hurray,' cried Marjorie.

3

The little township of Wedgery overran part of the narrow Grayling river as it went wandering in serpentine coils to the sea. Leaving Wedgery behind, it wound for a mile through the broad green pastures of Grayling Vale, where, as far as eyes could reach, there was little to be seen but the cattle grazing; then it passed under its last and lonely bridge at a point called Tideway Gate, because, somewhere here, it accepted the flood tide and went out with the ebb.

That afternoon, when the stormy luncheon lay behind them, the Sheridans and Conal crossed the bridge and went down the eastern bank to the delights of Grayling Bottom. The various parts of the bathing tent were under the arms of Uncle Bertie and Conal. It consisted of a big umbrella (once white) and a tall pole in two parts, and curtains to hook all round the umbrella spokes and conceal disrobers—women especially—from any public gaze. Women? Yes, despite Lizetta's fuming and boiling outburst over the luncheon table she as well as Marjorie was walking with the others for the bathe. Normally it was about half an hour before Lizetta, having thoroughly enjoyed her high dudgeon, and her dramatic withdrawal from the company of those who had offended her, was ready to admit that the play was over, the curtain down, and she in circulation again. A fact of which her husband had been aware when he said his ‘*Au revoir*’ and ‘*Auf Wiedersehen*’.

Before reaching Grayling Bottom they had to pass through a small forest of tamarisk, that feathery and gentle plant that so loves the sea. Indeed as they took their winding path through it they were welcomed by the fresh, salt, sea-weedy breath of the sea.

At Grayling Bottom they saw that the tide was well out; too far out as yet for a bathe. The sea lay flat as a dance-floor, not a wave in it, or a lift, from the beach to the blue horizon. The rocks of tumbled chalk, long fallen from the great cliff and long mantled in sea-weeds of every shade—dark sage, grass-green, and rusty brown—went fingering out towards the sea as if to reach the red-and-white striped lighthouse which had lately replaced old Belle Tout on the cliff's top.

It must have been the very moment of the tide's turn because the river, instead of racing between its banks with the ebb, was now sluggish and grey-green and waiting.

Here where the Grayling met the sea there had been a village of some size six hundred years before this visit by the Sheridan family, but the Black Death laid it waste, so History says, and where the Black Death left the sacking incomplete, the raiding French pirates in after years finished its work. Today there were no buildings in sight between the dipping hills, except the few grey homes of a coastguard station, a trio of unexplained huts on the western hill-slope and a red farmstead in the widening meadows far away.

'H'm ... no bathe yet,' said Uncle Bertie. 'We must sit and watch the tide come in.'

'Oh, but let's go to Parson Screwby's Hole,' said Marjorie, and Conal endorsed this with a 'Yes, yes!'

'All right,' Uncle Bertie agreed. 'Parson Screwby let it be.'

How many times the children had visited Parson Screwby's Hole it would be impossible to say; it had the inexhaustible fascination of a cave. To reach it they had to walk beneath the towering and angry chalk face of Beachy Head, over stones and beach and rocks. Here the beach in parts was nothing less than mound after stippled mound of multicoloured stones, ash-blue, buff, flint-grey, and dead white. Not that Uncle Bertie would ever allow that the name, Beachy Head, had anything to do with the beach below. It harked back, he said, to the days of the Normans when it had been 'Beau Chef', meaning perhaps 'Chieftain' or 'Head' of all England's high white cliffs that front the sea from Tennyson Down in the Isle of Wight to Shakespeare's Cliff at Dover. And Parson Screwby's Hole: seldom did they visit it without Uncle Bertie rehearsing for them that it had been dug deep at the cliff's base by the Vicar of a village on Beachy Head above, the Reverend Jonathan Screwby, as a place of escape from his lady's tongue. As ever, he recalled this today, thinking perhaps of two hours ago. Though he did (as often before) offer the children a different interpretation. 'Some people maintain that it was a smugglers' kitchen or cellar where they stored their tubs and kegs at high tide so as to collect them when the tide was low and the coast clear and no revenue cutters in the offing; or possibly when the night had fallen to cover their deeds of darkness. Personally I surmise that the good Parson Screwby may have supervised the digging of it for them. After all, they were probably his parishioners, and some of them members of his congregation. And he, maybe, one of their company. Even the leader.'

'Oh, I'm sure he was the leader,' said Marjorie, who much preferred this idea. 'I always think he must have been rather a poppet.'

As they set off for the Hole Lizetta, now lying on the beach, called, 'Do be careful, Bertie. Don't get cut off by the tide. It's coming in. And it can reach the cliff sometimes.'

'My dear,' he called back, 'there are twelve hours' interval between high tides. That must mean that it takes six hours to reach the cliff, so I think we shall be safe. I doubt if we'll give more than four hours to the Hole.'

But this piece of satire, thrown back behind him, was not heard by Lizetta, or not listened to.

Once at the Hole, Conal, as always, pictured its pebbled floor covered with the casks and kegs and tuns of the smugglers, and the smugglers themselves at work among them; generally in his imagination the smugglers were dressed like the old salts in *Treasure Island*, like Long John Silver, the sea-cook and Black Dog and Blind Pew, with knee-breeches and buckled shoes and their heads swathed in scarves or wearing a rough red Phrygian cap, and perhaps a pigtail behind. One smuggler was generally out on the beach with a brass telescope at his eye, watching for any glimpse of a revenue ship far out at sea. As likely as not this watcher wore a tricorn hat and his pigtail swayed in the wind. All of which was nonsense because Wedgery's smugglers would have been farm labourers in corduroys or shopkeepers in shirts and trousers with sleeves rolled up.

When they returned from the Hole to Lizetta's side, the tide was still some way out, so they spent a little time erecting the umbrella-tent and holding its curtains to the beach by turning up their long hems and loading them with stones or sand. Then they lay down to wait, and Conal, lying supine with perhaps his hands behind his head since pebbles made a bad pillow, glanced often at the great wall of wrinkled cliff and thought of those who had so often used its five-hundred-foot fall to end unhappy lives on the beach he had just trodden. Or he stared out at the striped lighthouse on its plinth in the sea, wondering about, and even envying, the men who lived beneath its lamp and kept the beams swinging all night over miles of sea. But most often he recreated the activities of the smugglers on the very beach where he lay.

But at last the tide came shuffling in and its ripple of waves began to caress the beach near their feet, so Uncle Bertie gave the order for action: 'Now then, ladies and gents. "Ladies first". Into the tent'; and Lizetta went behind the curtains alone at first because she needed all its space, and not a little time, to get into her bathing costume. An elaborate dress it was when she emerged: braided bodice, sashed waist and quilted skirt which only just concealed the drawers beneath. Then Marjorie emerged in a dress hardly less elaborate, with its bodice, skirt and knickers, but less ornamental. Next Uncle Bertie and Conal got into their bathing suits, striped affairs stretching from neck to thighs and vested about the loins (in to-day's language) with a very mini-skirt to ensure the ultimate decency. Lizetta was already in the sea and for one who couldn't swim, quite far out. Let her say what she liked about an April bathe giving Marjorie her death, she loved bathing and was now bobbing up and down in four feet of water, or in nearly five feet with screams. The others swam well enough, though Lizetta called to Marjorie, 'Don't go too far, darling.' To Conal she said nothing but Uncle Bertie called out, 'Not too far, young-feller-me-lad; I'm not risking death to come and save you—at least I don't think I am. And Madam's no good. She can't swim. And Marjorie isn't interested.'

When at last Lizetta and Marjorie went back into the tent to dry themselves unobserved by males, even of their own household, Uncle Bertie suggested to Conal that they stripped to the waist and dried in the sun. This they did, and their swimsuits became no more than loin-cloths about them—*dhotis*, Conal called them, thinking of the loin-cloths he'd seen on *rishis* and *mumukshus* or other sages and holy men in Poona, perhaps in a procession winding along to the home of Vithoba, their greatest incarnation of Vishnu.

Lizetta came out fully dressed and seeing them in these *dhotis* asked, 'Is that quite nice? I don't think it is.'

Uncle Bertie assured her it was very pleasant.

The sun, now falling, flung its beams on the crumpled white face of Beachy Head, so that the sea, so tranquil, mirrored them in what looked like long golden bars on its brilliant blue surface. In the distance the sea had melted into luminous haze behind which any meeting of sea and sky was no longer discernible.

4

Two days later, and the last but one of this Easter holiday, and Conal was again climbing Wedgery Beacon alone. He was climbing it to bid it goodbye. The sun was as lively as ever, pretending to be six weeks older than it was; and Marjorie might willingly have come with him on this sentimental journey, but she'd engaged herself to play with some newly found friends in a Wedgery garden.

'To the Hill' said the signpost by the church, and it pointed to a broad driveway which ran by the churchyard's southern wall, and tilted upwards after a hundred yards or so to become a white chalky track between the last of the hedges and the last of the fields; and finally to go perishing into the turf and become a beaten green platform, a natural starting place for ridge and summit. In short, the signpost by the church was unnecessary, a work of supererogation, because 'The Hill' stared you in the face, and it was its proximity which had given—since Heaven knew when—Wedgery's noble church its noble title of All Hallows-at-Hill.

Conal was half-way up the sloping ridge when he sat down to rest. Turning his head as he surveyed the great view of the Weald, he saw a figure climbing his way, the only other figure within sight. Curiosity caused him to remain seated till it should pass him and he might learn who it was. Soon there was no doubt. It was that ancient man, Dr Julius Balder, an eccentric archaeologist and antiquary, with a deep cravat of white beard and a scanty crown of white hair. He was coming bareheaded beneath the warm sun of mid-afternoon. Conal had never met him to speak to but knew much about him because he was much talked about. He knew that he was in his eighties and had come to Wedgery three years ago to live in an unimpressive terrace house, stucco rendered, which he had named, being then eighty-one—and the name was painted in a generous arc over his door—'The Last Lap'.

By profession he was a doctor—a profession which he declared he hated, so he had soon exchanged his 'general practice' for the practice of archaeology and his needs as a scholarly bachelor being few, earned a sufficient income by accepting locum-tenens-es. Then in his seventies he was left a handsome legacy by a devoted elder sister, who had been no less than the first principal of St Ethelred's College, Oxford. And medicine lay for ever behind him in a murky past.

When level with Conal, he stopped, stood still, and stared down at him as an archaeologist might at some phenomenon in the downland turf which was not without interest.

'Who are you?' he demanded.

Conal did not know how to answer this; it seemed absurd to say, 'I'm Conal Gillie.'

So the white beard demanded again, 'What are you doing here?'

'Don't know,' Conal said. 'Just walking to the top.'

'You like walking alone?'

'Sometimes.'

'Then we're brothers. Never mind if I'm a hundred years older than you: we're brothers. Why do you like walking alone?'

'Don't know. Because nobody wants to come too, I suppose. And I think it's wonderful up here.'

'You couldn't be more right. That being the position, I'll walk to the top with you. I dare say I could tell you a lot that's more wonderful than you know. Would you like that?'

'Oh, *rather*!'

'Come along then, mate.'

'It's frightfully decent of you.'

'Perhaps. Yes ... I suppose it is.'

And together they walked towards the summit, Dr Balder's feet, though now eighty-five years old, being no less active than Conal's.

On the summit he halted and said, 'Now then, mate. Look around.'

And he indicated the earthworks of a Roman camp and the traces of a sunken pathway which the legionaries had made 'so that they could march down unperceived and bully the ancient Britons who'd be scratching a living in some clearing among the trees of the vast and limitless forest, the Romans' Sylva Anderida and the Saxons' Andreasweald'.

These two magnificent names, at a touch, turned for Conal the whole Sussex Weald into a wonder. There it lay below him, no longer an endless forest between two chalk-hill ranges but a patchwork of scattered woodlands, hedge-bound pastures, spired villages, and arable brown from the plough.

He said only, 'Gosh!'

'Yes, there, instead of a mighty forest,' said Dr Balder, 'is the whole of Sussex with some impertinent intrusions of Surrey and Hampshire and Kent—England's loveliest county once you're quit of the Brighton, Eastbourne and Worthing roads and those disgusting resorts that befoul our coastline. Where do you live?'

'In Slings. A cottage in Wedgery.'

'Lord, boy, I know Slings! Who doesn't? That's the proper sort of house to live in. Nothing like thatch, good honest thatch, for keeping out frost and rain and cold and heat. Far better than my miserable slates.'

'It's not our home. We only come there for the holidays.'

'Who're your father and mother, and what do they do?'

'They're in India——'

'Jesus Christ! Where in India? It's rather a big place.'

'Gondapore for the most part.'

'Hell!'

'No, I love Gondapore and especially its mountains, the Western Ghats. I used to climb the Ghats with Daddy.'

But Dr Balder was thinking of other things. 'What's your old man doing out there?'

'He's a Collector now, a sort of chief magistrate.'

'God help him. And who looks after you, then?'

'Lizetta and Uncle Bertie.'

'Lizetta and Uncle Bertie. I see. And who the hell are they?'

'A Mr and Mrs Sheridan. Uncle Bertie was a friend of Daddy's, and I came to live with them three years ago so that I could go to school in England.'

'Poor child. One of the sacrifices to this Moloch we call the Empire. I trust you know that Moloch, or Molech, was the God of the Ammonites, who burnt their children as an offering to him— a doubtful habit but at times I think there's something to be said for the practice. D'you like these people, the Sheppertons?'

To this unforeseen and improbable question Conal gave the answer that seemed necessary. 'Oh . . . yes . . .'

'Doesn't sound convincing.'

So Conal improved it. 'I like Uncle Bertie.'

'And cordially dislike Auntie Lizetta?'

'Oh, I wouldn't say that. . . .' (But it was next door to the truth.)

'Have they no children you could play with?'

'Only Marge. And Marge isn't as keen on climbing as I am.'

'Do I take it Marge is a girl?'

'Yes, six months younger than I am.'

'Oh, well, girls are not much use. Not for any worthwhile stuff. Pretty things, but limited. Slings. Lucky boy; and I live in an unlovely stucco house built at a time when English architecture was reaching its lowest—about 1850. If you'd care to come back with me I'd show you a few things that ought to interest an intelligent creation like you. But don't expect tea. I never drink the muck. I might dig you out a piece of cake.'

'It's frightfully decent of you, but Lizetta——'

'Damn Lizetta. Don't tell her where you've been. Let her think you've come straight back, and meanwhile live your own life.'

So down the hill they went together, one lonely and brooding ancient and one lonely and brooding child. 'Enter,' he said at the door of The Last Lap. Conal went in and found the entrance hall and living-room were a museum of antiquities. They hung from the walls, stood against the walls and lay arrayed on shelves. The living-room, once the drawing-room of a house built in the ample mid-Victorian days, was long and lofty with wide, tall windows. On a table under glass lay flint arrow-heads, axe-heads, spear-heads and other palaeolithic implements.

'Yes,' said Dr Balder, as Conal looked down on them. 'Instruments from the Eolithic, Palaeolithic and Neolithic ages.'

Conal stared, having no idea what these heavy words implied.

'Yes, you're right,' Dr Balder said with a nod and a smile. 'Those are just our cocky words for the Old Stone Age and the New Stone Age.'

This Conal understood so he said 'Gosh!' Pointing to some roughly shaped axe-heads and arrow-heads he asked, 'How old are they?'

'Anything from a thousand thousand years B.C. to two thousand B.C.'

'Gosh!' exclaimed Conal again; and since that seemed insufficient added 'Golly!' He pointed to some which looked neater and more polished. 'What about these?'

'You're a bright youth, Mr—"Conal"—was it? Those clearly belong to a time when the prehistoric boys were getting cleverer. Let's say the last of the Stone Ages. About two thousand B.C. they started messing about with bronze.'

'The Bronze Age,' said Conal, showing off at once.

'Good boy. And what came next?'

'The—the Iron Age,' said Conal, more doubtfully.

'Quite right. Go to the top, though you weren't sure of it. Iron Age about a thousand B.C. But move on. Come here.'

Resting his hand on Conal's shoulder, he led him to another table with its treasures under glass. Here were bracelets and tools and weapons cast in bronze. 'You see, we've moved about three feet along the floor but about a thousand years in history. We've successfully emerged from the Stone Age into your Bronze Age. We're getting on. Seen those? Well, come on. Let's walk another thousand years. Into the Iron Age. And when we talk about Iron, we've really come to Sussex.'

'Why?'

'Look about you.'

His eyes, smiling, led Conal's eyes to this thing and that thing and another thing, standing against the walls: firebacks, fire dogs, and irons, and even a sixteenth-century cannon on its wheeled carriage. 'All made in Sussex which was the ironmasters' great county. Once the ironmasters' furnaces were ablaze in most of that forest country we saw from the Beacon. I imagine they drove all the charming wood-nymphs away—Heaven knows where—but now, thank Heaven, we've long driven the ironmasters away to their filthy Black Country in the North, and I've no doubt the wood-nymphs are back again—in Worth Forest, perhaps—yes, surely. That's a constable's staff, and that's a Pyecombe crook. All the best shepherd's crooks in England come from Pyecombe just under the Downs. Now what about that piece of cake I offered you? Sit down.'

There were plumply upholstered chairs and a long Chesterfield sofa in the big room. Conal sat on the sofa's edge. Evidently the old gentleman desired to rest easily during his 'Last Lap'. While he abstracted his cake from a bureau Conal looked at a parade of pottery on the Victorian chimney-piece, both on its wide mantel and on the shelves of the overmantel above: jars, urns, cruses, crocks. 'Are those old?' he asked.

'Well. . . .' Dr Balder shrugged dubiously. 'Some may go back to Babylon—those glazed ones—but there are others from Nineveh which are nothing—nothing at all—quite modern—two-thousand-seven-hundred years old, perhaps.' He was cutting a slice of cake.

In this lofty and rectangular room fireplace and mantel seemed a long walk away, so that Conal did not at first distinguish one vessel that differed from all the others. In the centre of the array, it was a rounded vessel, some six inches high, with rounded base and lips and a low ornamental lid. There was no patina of age about it; it looked to be made of some golden marble rather than earthenware.

'Is that middle one old?' Conal asked as he was handed the cake.

'Gracious, no! Dear boy, you've got an eye. That's only about six years old.'

'Then why is it among the others?'

'That's right: always ask questions and never be content with inadequate information. Probe the depths and don't let older people get away with anything just because they're older than you. Don't spare 'em. Many of them are probably much sillier than you are, especially the women, because their minds are finally set and yours isn't. I've a suspicion that this is particularly true of that Auntie Lizetta, and I'm not at all sure that it isn't my business to save you from her. What were we talking about? Oh, that urn. Unfortunately I can't give you an exact date; it only came into my hands six years ago. It's a cinerary urn.'

Proud of his new character as a ruthless questioner, Conal demanded, 'What's—what you said it was?'

'A cinerary urn. An urn made to hold the ashes of the dead.'

This aroused all the morbid interest in a child. 'But are there—are there ashes in it *now*?'

'Of course there are. That's why it's there.'

Conal stared at it, fascinated more than ever.

'But ... whose ashes?'

'Those of a very dear friend. My best friend of late years, she was. Thank Heaven they've at last had the sense to legalise cremation. It was universal in Greece and Rome till all the nonsense of Christianity arrived, with its twaddle about the resurrection of the body.'

These words were an instant shock; they were like a shot from a gun. In all Conal's young life he had never been hit so sharply. Plainly being clever and 'probing deep' carried risks of sudden deaths like this. At home—whether in India or England—all believed in the resurrection of the dead, or said they did in church. Not wanting to expose his dismay lest he lost his reputation for cleverness, he ate his cake in silence. Dr Balder seemed undisturbed by what he'd said and so had nothing more to offer. Instead of eating cake he was mixing himself a drink: an inch of golden liquid and two inches of water.

Recovering from the shock—or nearly so—Conal decided to be clever again and seek further information. Hadn't his new mentor told him never to rest content with inadequate information? 'Was she ... was she your wife?'

This appeared to strike Dr Balder as funny. 'Oh, no, dear boy. I've never been married. I'm not the marrying sort. But she was my very good friend, my best ever; and I don't see why I shouldn't keep her ashes in a place of honour. At times I think I might do something else with them, but I never do. One of my notions is to have them thrown into the sea along with mine, shortly. Or dispersed with mine on the top of the Downs. Let's say on your Wedgery Beacon. I don't know that I care a hang about what happens to us after death, but in silly moments I sometimes like to think of ourselves up there. She was only my housekeeper for a dozen years but I grew very fond of her. Don't imagine she was anything more than a housekeeper: hell, she was no mistress.' Apparently there was nothing Dr Balder shrank from discussing with intelligent youth. 'Good lord, she was older than I am, and that's saying a lot. And she had a husband somewhere—at least I suppose she still had; he'd been much younger than her and, deciding that he'd made a mistake, he disappeared to the Antipodes and no more was heard of him—and thank God for that. It was a good day when I found her because some of my housekeepers before her were no good—no good at all. I've no one to look after me now as she did. Only an old beldam who comes four days a week—if it suits her. So why shouldn't we be thrown to the wind together—"earth to earth, ashes to ashes", as you Christians say.'

You Christians—these words gave Conal the courage to ask, no longer in a desire to shine, but in curiosity, 'But aren't you a Christian?'

'*Me* a Christian! Great Glory, no. Whatever made you suppose that?'

'I thought everybody was. At least everybody respectable.'

'Not me. And I like to think that an intelligent boy like you'll soon be quit of all that superstitious nonsense.'

'But the Bible?' Conal submitted—out of the heart of his dismay. 'Don't you believe——'

'Not one word of it—though I rejoice in some of it as poetry. To be thrilled by what a poet says is not to agree with him; it's only to be thrilled to the bone by a perfect expression of some sincerely held belief. I read old Job again and again—though I can't go along with him when he surrenders to a God bellowing to him out of a whirlwind, "Where were *you* when I laid the foundations of the world ... when the morning stars sang together and all the sons of God shouted for joy?" Glorious words, but not all the whirlwinds in Heaven would have made me shut up. Which was practically what God said, "Oh, *shut* up, Job." ' He drank from his glass and wiped his lips with the edge of one palm. 'Ecclesiastes is my boy. "Vanity of vanities, saith the Preacher, all is vanity and vexation of spirit and there is no profit under the sun"— though I don't know that I agree with "vexation of spirit"; I've enjoyed it all. Or that "in much wisdom there is much grief, and he that increaseth knowledge increaseth sorrow"—dammit, that's exactly what I'm trying to do for you now. I like you, you see, I like you, and I like to think I'm helping you to be quit of all this supernatural rubbish one day. Dear lad, you can't deal in things nine-hundred-thousand years old and believe that something which happened only nineteen centuries ago is of any great importance. Why, devil take it, I've nearly completed my century—and eighty-five years seem like nothing—so it's only nineteen times the years I've lived since the thing happened. Besides, why should you believe in something supernatural happening then if it hadn't happened in the millions of years before? Be yourself. Never mind Lizetta and company. I've no use for Lizetta. Begin to think for yourself and to live your own life. Be yourself. Have another slice of cake.'

5

Dr Balder, in one hour, had worked an earthquake in Conal's life; he had overturned the whole surface of his thoughts. Or, as Conal liked to phrase it years afterwards, 'Dr Julius Balder flung a stone that put all my stars to flight—and all Lizetta's and all Marjorie's too.' Clearly Dr Balder must be one of the most learned men in the world, knowing all about everything from ten thousand B.C.; and he didn't believe in Christianity but called it superstitious nonsense. Conal was at an age to receive and even welcome a stone which dispersed all the stars in the bowl of night. To many it may be a troubling experience to break away from the beliefs of childhood, but not so to Conal. To him it was a thrill. As he walked homeward to Slings he felt inspired to think differently from Lizetta and Marjorie and Uncle Bertie—perhaps especially from Marjorie. Though, come to think of it, it was possible that Uncle Bertie didn't believe in Christianity either. Conal had never heard him say so, but it was only Lizetta and Marjorie who went regularly and with enthusiasm to church. Another reason, this, to strengthen his desire, as a male and therefore a superior thinker, to separate his views of the universe from theirs. Even so, walking from The Last Lap to Slings, he wondered if he would have resolved on this distinguished and fascinating apostasy if he had been living in Gondapore with his sadly missed parents; they regularly and dutifully obeyed the church bells and set an example of religious behaviour to the King Emperor's deeply religious subjects.

Here was Slings, and he must enter, carrying his exciting apostasy. He did not purpose speaking of it to Lizetta with some such words as 'I've been thinking a lot and decided that I no longer believe in Christianity'. Not that this would have been a stab; rather would it have given her the chance for one of those righteous outbursts of ever-heightening indignation, and ever

her, and there'll be the most horrific row. And I shouldn't be surprised if God *did* strike you dead. Nor awfully upset, come to that.'

This again was not in harmony with his declared superiority to all superstitions but he knew Marjorie to be as superstitious as her mother—or as cautious about superstitions, which is much the same thing—and he had hoped it might halt her in her tracks. Not that he thought her fool enough to suppose she might be struck dead, but rather that God might visit her with some lesser chastisement, if she wilfully betrayed a confidence.

It did not halt her, but it made her mark time. She said nothing at the dinner-table, because Lizetta was too busy with dishes, and Uncle Bertie might only let loose a roar of laughter on hearing that Conal no longer believed in God. He was a frivolous man. Marjorie had all of her mother's feeling that a good row should be enacted in a setting suitable, silent, and promising. She waited till the three of them, Lizetta, Conal and herself were together in the room behind rain-spattered and wind-rattled casements, with Lizetta, who'd completed the packing, knitting a scarf in silence.

Then Marjorie opened fire. She scattered the silence. 'Mummy, have you heard the latest from Con?'

Lizetta was so little interested that she didn't look up from her knitting. 'No.'

A disappointing opening for Marge. So she made her next words loud and clear. 'He no longer believes in God.'

'Dirty sneak.' From Conal in a whisper.

Whether or not Lizetta had dropped a stitch at these clearly spoken words, she certainly dropped her scarf and her needles to her lap. '*What* did you say? *What?*'

'I said he's told me he no longer believes in God and that it's all a lot of super-spicion.'

Lizetta turned to Conal, the knitting on her lap forgotten. 'You said *that*?'

Not unafraid of the coming row, Conal mollified his answer. 'I said I was beginning to think like that. That I didn't——'

'That you didn't——?' Her eyes pierced him.

There was no dodging it. '—believe in God, really....'

'Or in Jesus,' added Marjorie, pouring more good oil from her cruse on to embers already brightly glowing.

33

Obviously Lizetta didn't at first know how to cope with an hitherto unimaginable situation. 'How dare you say things like that,' was all she could utter at first. 'And to Marjorie. I won't have you saying wicked things like that to her. I won't have my daughter's mind poisoned with that sort of talk. You at your age! I've never heard such nonsense. You'll believe in God if I tell you to.'

'And in Jesus,' Marjorie reminded her, not wanting her important contribution to be neglected.

'*And* in Jesus. Of course. Certainly. It's my duty to see that you believe properly. Your parents would have wished it. They entrusted you to us to bring you up as a Christian and a God-fearing little boy. And that I shall do. Make no doubt of it. Mark my words. You'll believe everything a Christian should, so long as you stay with me.'

Though still afraid of the trouble that threatened, Conal managed to grumble, 'I don't see how you can make me think what I don't think. You can only make me pretend to, and that'd be a lie.'

'Will you stop talking to me like that——'

So far from stopping, Conal thought of something else to say and got it in quickly. 'I'm sure Daddy and Mummy wouldn't make me tell lies. Daddy certainly wouldn't. He'd tell me to think for myself, and *be* myself.'

'All right: you're saying that I ill-treat you. I see. You consider yourself misunderstood and ill-treated. After all I've done for you. Taken you in at eight years old, a little boy from India who needed a home—' an incongruous savour of pathos here amid the mounting indignation—'taken you in and tried to take the place of your parents and do all that they would do—and please remember they were not my friends; they were my husband's. *You* thinking for yourself at *your* age. You at eleven years old declaring that there's no God. The whole thing is so idiotic that it'd be laughable if it wasn't so shocking.'

'It's blast-pherming, isn't it?' said Marge, happier with this interposition than she knew.

Lizetta turned towards this helpful child. ' "Blaspheming", darling,' she corrected. 'Yes, that's what it amounts to, and I——'

But Marge, not greatly interested in this amendment of her

pronunciation, pursued, 'Cissie Powell says you can go to hell for blastfurnacing.'

However accidentally appropriate this new mispronunciation might be, Lizetta had no desire to deal with Cissie Powell's views, and pursued her own course. 'I tell you I won't have blasphemies in this house. Understand that, Conal. Once and for all. This is a Christian household, and I'll——'

The fury was rising to the boil, and she ready to rejoice in it. But of a sudden there was an interruption; the gas, let us say, was suddenly turned low beneath a splendidly simmering pot. She had looked out of the window and seen a white horse. A white horse drawing a hay wain. Instantly she swung her eyes away from the horse lest she saw its tail. And lest she saw the tail of the wagon.

Lizetta's attitude to superstitions was precisely her daughter's, and when Uncle Bertie ridiculed them, she would get angry and say that, as a religious woman, she was ready to allow that they might, or might not, be absurd but you never knew; there was far more in life than Uncle Bertie allowed, and it was as well to be on the safe side.

To see a white horse was lucky; you could make a wish and expect it to be granted, but not if you saw the horse's tail. And not if you saw the back of a hay-cart. In both cases the good luck became bad luck, and your wish would be withheld. The Sussex wain passing the window carried no hay—the hay harvest being weeks away—and this was a pity because to see a load of hay on the roadway brought a promise of luck—always provided you averted your eyes from the hay-wain's back. So there was a double risk of misfortune in this vision: no hay, and the danger of seeing the empty wain's back.

Fortunately old Sussex wains were long, and Lizetta was able to close her eyes for two seconds till all danger was passed.

Having seen the white horse and the wain, and avoided seeing the tail of either, she could return to the current business which had been exciting and pleasurable—what was it?—oh yes, the arraignment of Conal which offered the chance of a 'scene', hot, loud and dramatic. She was about to resume her most justified impeachment—she had begun, 'Where does he get these idiotic and bumptious ideas'—when yet another intervention stopped her. She had her work-basket on the table close at hand, and among its wools, threads and darning needles was a small square piece of looking-glass unframed; its provenance was forgotten but it lay there ever available if she should wonder whether her face was in disarray. She took it out now, half wondering if this heated altercation with Conal had worked any damage. Not displeased, apparently, with what she saw in the piece of mirror, she tossed it carelessly—and with undiminished, indeed renewed anger —towards its bed among the wools, but it struck the brim of the basket and fell to the floor.

Instantly, in a moment of despair, she cried, 'Oh, no! Oh, dear! It's not broken, is it? Oh, please not.' If it were broken this would be grossly unfair of God or Providence or Whoever dealt out the apportionments of luck, good and bad, because she had so piously forborne to see the tails of horse and wain. Anxiously she stooped to pick it up, saw that the rug had saved it from cracking, and exclaimed, 'Thank God it's all right. It's seven years' bad luck if you break a looking-glass. *Seven years!* I don't know that I'm really superstitious, but I must confess I never want to break a looking-glass. Things can be very mysterious. Only a few nights ago I dreamt that a serpent came into the kitchen, and the very next morning there was that bad news about Father.'

Conal had never heard about the logical fallacy of *post hoc ergo propter hoc*, but some sprouts of logic were breaking through the bare soil of his young mind, and he perceived, uninstructed, the substance of this fallacy. If something comes after something else, it doesn't mean that the first something has any connection with the second something. Still, since this episode—like the passing of horse and wain—had damped down the incipient blaze, he decided—but unwisely—to make his offering towards the prospect of peace and said, 'It isn't exactly that I don't believe in God, it's simply that I no longer feel sure about him. I'm not saying that other people shouldn't believe in him, but there are colossal arguments——'

'*You* to allow us who are years older than you to keep our beliefs! *You* to treat us with this kindly consideration!' Lizetta now went on where she'd left off. She resumed her knitting, and the needles increased their speed as her exasperation gathered pace. 'Where does he get these idiotic and bumptious and insufferable ideas from? I can't imagine.'

Marjorie had the anwer to this one. 'He's been talking to that old Doctor Julius Balder.'

'*That* terrible old man. Oh I see. Now I know. Now I understand. Of course. He's well known as a ranting atheist. So you've been talking to him, have you? That's where you get to when you wander off alone. Talking to an old man who goes about trying to poison the minds of everyone he meets. Where did you meet him and how often?'

'Once only. On the Downs.' He thought it better to add nothing about his consequent visit to The Last Lap, or about the Stone Age, the Bronze Age and the Iron Age. And the urn on the mantel.

'Once on the Downs. And you're a little fool enough to let one talk with an old man, probably senile, undo all the faith you've been brought up in. It's too simple-minded for anything. I'm surprised at you. Why don't you develop some brains and be above that sort of thing? After all, you're getting on for twelve, and I should have thought that at nearly twelve you'd begin to grow up. But you don't seem to. I forbid you ever to speak to that old man again. Never, never. Do you hear?'

'Yes.' It was a timid 'Yes', but Lizetta was not to know that it announced audition only, not assent.

'And I repeat that you'll kindly keep any mention of Doctor Balder's wicked and atheistic talk away from Marjorie. You're never, never, to say another word to Marjorie about being an atheist, even if you're stupid enough to imagine you are one. I tell you I'd rather see her dead than an atheist. I'd rather see my own daughter dead. Dead at my feet. There! I've said it.'

This was her magnificent conclusion to an enjoyable row. It was her finest moment. A climax whereafter she could rest. A happy triumph on almost the last day of their Easter holiday.

PART TWO

Warfare opens in Wedgery: the hostile forces assemble

I

Full summer again. Summer which in Conal's absence had been climbing the Downs as he would do, and, though its stride was invisible and its steps soundless, had spread all the velvety turf with blue harebells, with the lilac blooms of the lesser scabious, with pink clover and bird's foot, and, most generously besprinkled of all, the yellow stars of cats-ear. Full summer, which now, if the sea beneath the white face of Beachy Head chose to be reasonably tranquil, sprinkled its measureless distance with diamonds as far as eye could reach and made of the shore at Grayling Bottom a sun-warmed paradise of pebbles and beach and rocks for children.

A first day of August, and the Sheridans were in Slings again with Conal, his long school term safely done with and happily tossed behind him.

Conal's prep-school was St Jourdan's at Bath, merely because, under a different proprietor, it had been his father's school thirty-odd years before. Throughout the long term Conal had maintained (though very privily) the handsome cloak of Disbelief with which Dr Balder had invested him. It was hardly likely that Lizetta's fiery abuse of this new garment would produce any other result in a schoolboy who was savouring and sipping for the first time the wine of intellectual rebellion. Fortunately as a boarder at St Jourdan's there was no need to expound this Unbelief to the headmaster, or question whether in his present state he should attend church; the boys, seventy-two of them, were marched on Sunday mornings to St Wilfrid's Church, Bath, in their Etons and straw hats; and that was that. There sat Gillie C.Q. in a pew with others, and the headmaster had no means of knowing whether he was praying or refraining from prayer.

What attitude would need to be adopted at home in Chelsea or Slings was another matter. There were aspects of the Unbelief which Conal found very agreeable. It was a night of some significance when he realised he need no longer say prayers at his bedside but could hop straight into cosy bedclothes. But not all such new pleasures as these were untroubled. His mind—or his soul—was naturally a scrupulous one, even a punctilious one, so that even though this new Heathenism had freed him from the tedium of prayers and from other acts which hitherto his conscience had pronounced sinful—such as telling lies when it was prophylactic so to do, or when he wanted to brag of fine things he had done or wonderful things which had happened to him, none of which were true—his conscience did not spare him. It did not 'let him off' lightly. And, endowed with such a conscience he could see as clearly as any parson or preacher, twenty years his senior, that Unbelief begat immorality or at least a speedy depreciation of the old morality. Conscience stayed dominant, however much he set about disobeying it. In other words, we may say that his conscience reigned but did not rule. Like the Monarch, as he or she is understood in the British Constitution (if there is such a thing, or anyone can define it) conscience could exert a powerful influence. So powerful that there came times when he felt a longing, a kind of nostalgia or homesickness for the old morality, with its churchgoing and prayer-saying and guilty penitences and purposed amendments, and all. He could see it for a country where he had once been—and might be again—more at peace than he was now.

He might say no prayers in his church-pew, sing no hymns, certainly sing no psalms, and least of all attend to the Litany, but he enjoyed the long hour of peace in church, whether he was on his knees, seated for Lessons, or standing for interminable psalms, because he enjoyed day-dreaming. There, stamped on his hymn book, were the words 'St Wilfrid's Bath Not To Be Taken Away' (which amused him) and he dreamed of St Wilfrid who had converted the South Saxons long after the rest of Anglo-Saxon England had been won for Christianity. Thinking of Wilfrid widened his lips in a private smile because he knew why this conversion of the men of Sussex had been so late; it was because they were the most stubborn of all the Saxons and their universal vow was 'Oi woan't be druv.' Again, to think of Wilfrid was to see all his beloved Downs heaving and swelling along and to remember a verse which someone had quoted to him and he had never forgotten: 'Here the Old Gods guard their round And, in her secret heart, the heathen kingdom Wilfrid found Dreams, as she dwells apart.'

When he was under the spell of Conscience one of the hymns might suddenly seize hold of his heart and partly load it with an appeal that was the very opposite of Unbelief. St Wilfrid's, Bath, was 'High' and had recently abandoned *Hymns Ancient and Modern* for *The English Hymnal* and on a day in mid-June they were singing the praises of St Barnabas, Son of Consolation.

> The Son of Consolation!
>   Lord, hear our humble prayer,
> That each of us thy children
>   This blessed name may bear;
> That we, sweet comfort shedding
>   O'er homes of pain and woe,
> 'Midst sickness and in prisons,
>   May seek thee here below.

Touched by this, Conal found himself wondering whether he wouldn't like to be a saint, and visit those who were sick or in prison. And perhaps some lepers. Or some aborigines. Cannibals, even.

> The Sons of Consolation!
>   Oh, what their bliss will be
> When Christ the King shall tell them,
>   'Ye did it unto me.'

But such moments of wondering were rare and quickly over; he was content with his new freedoms.

Full summer now in and about the Downs; and this was the long holiday when all the things happened. Conal was always to look back upon it as holding the most critical experiences of his life, unapproached before, and unsurpassed later, till a bearded Anglo-Indian stranger from Ahmadnagar, eight years afterwards, came to visit him in the garden of his college at Oxford.

*   *   *

At his first opportunity, an early afternoon, Conal was passing the pleasant signpost, 'To the Hill', passing the churchyard wall of All Hallows, and beginning his favourite climb up Wedgery Beacon. He was only a little way up the hill when he saw a hatless white-haired figure ahead of him. Quickening his pace, he saw that it was old Dr Balder but that his walking was less brisk than it had been three months before. It seemed that in an old man well over eighty, three months could effect changes. The situation of three months ago was today reversed: he was climbing towards the Doctor instead of the Doctor climbing towards him. Conal's dress differed. Instead of the knickerbocker suit and green school cap with the school's crest above its peak, today he wore a green blazer with the crest on its left breast-pocket, and the grey flannel shorts ordained at St Jourdan's for cricket-wear—'shorts', as they would be called nowadays though they were scarcely short, since they decently covered his knees. Further, he now went bare-headed in deliberate imitation of his new friend, the Doctor. He climbed quickly towards this friend, inspired by an affection that was almost filial, partly because Lizetta had been so rude about him, even forbidding this encounter. Dr Balder heard his steps and turned towards him.

'Hallo!—it's my young fly-by-night again. What—finished with school and here on Wedgery again? You and I are certainly a pair. Good afternoon to you.'

'Good afternoon,' Conal echoed with a pleased smile that showed no memory of, or interest in, Lizetta down below.

'Whither goest thou, dear boy?'

'Don't really know. Perhaps as far as Beachy Head.'

'Well, you can't go further than that or you'll pitch into the sea. Where's the little sister? There was a sister, wasn't there?'

'She isn't my sister, and she never *will* come climbing up here. She hates it as much as I love it.'

'Poor limited and unimaginative child. My heart bleeds for her—or it ought to. Could you tolerate an old man's company for part of your way?'

'Of *course*.' He said it emphatically. 'I'd love it.'

'Love it? Extraordinary youth. When I'm a hundred years older than you.'

'No, you're not. You're only seventy-four years older. You told me so.'

'Maybe, but that's the best part of a century,' said Dr Balder as they walked on side by side. They were silent at first, till the Doctor began to talk about the thousand things he knew; about the chalk, the turf, the plants, the butterflies and the birds, distinguishing in the course of their walk the gulls, the larks, the kittiwakes, the guillemots, and a pair of kestrels hovering. Not a word was lost on Conal because he delighted in it all, and asked question after question of this encyclopaedic scholar, till at last Dr Balder said, 'Mr—I've forgotten your name. What is it?'

'Conal.'

'O'Connel?'

'No. Just Conal.' Conal spelt it out for him.

'Well, that's Irish. You've obviously got some Irish in you with an outlandish name like that; and perhaps that accounts for a lot, because you're certainly the best listener in the world. The Irish may be a little mad, but they have some sense of wonder and mystery unlike the miserably practical Anglo-Saxons—unlike your little sister, I imagine. *I* am half-Irish. My mother was Irish, thank God.'

It was as they walked down into the Dip under East Dean and Beachy Head that they saw a flock of slowly grazing sheep, with their old shepherd seated upon a one-plank bench which some individual or corporation had set there for the help of the elderly. He sat there with his Pyecombe crook between his knees, an old crumpled felt hat on his head, a long soiled overcoat hanging about his body (though it was summer) and his Sussex sheep-dog lying at his feet.

'There now!' Dr Balder exclaimed. 'There's someone who'll interest you. Old Jem Cafful.'

'Old who?'

'Jem Cafful. His name is really James Canfield but in Sussex we don't pronounce names according to their spelling but in ways we prefer. To all Wedgery he's Jem Cafful. I'll introduce you to him. He's about as old as I am, and there's nothing he doesn't know about smuggling. He pretends only to have seen it all in his boyhood, or been told about it, but don't take any notice of that. He was deep in it with his mates. They were all in it, fifty years ago:

whether shepherds or shop-keepers or ostlers or farm-labourers—pretty well all of 'em. 'Morning, Jem—I mean afternoon.'

'Marnin', Mus Balder,' said Jem, equally indifferent to the day's hour. He spoke in the slow, lingering, almost unwilling drawl of old Sussex men.

'How are you, Jem?'

'Me? I be middlin' well and purty. I be'ant as young as I was.'

'You? You're only a baby. How old are you?'

'Sen'ty siv'en, come next muck-spreading.'

'What's seventy-seven? I'm eighty-six next muck-spreading—if muck-spreading's what I suppose. I want you to meet my very good friend, Mr—er—I've forgotten his name, but he's the best listener in the world, and he wants to know all about farming and sheeping and—er—about smuggling.'

'Yes, please,' Conal begged.

'A-done-do wid your smugglin'. I do'ant know naun about that. It was all dunnamany years ago.'

'Nonsense, Jem. You know quite a little about it and probably a good deal more than you ought to.'

'Danged if I do. I only know what I been telled.'

'Get along, Jem, I'm too old to be bamboozled by you. But this young gentleman isn't. Anyway, tell him some of the things you've merely been telled.'

'The little lad's yourn, ma'aster?'

'Mine? Didn't I tell you I was nearly ninety? How could he be mine?'

'Could be,' Jem grinned. 'Reckon he could be in *your* ca'ase. Be he your gran'son?'

'No, as I told you, he's just a good pal of mine and an unnaturally good listener. So tell him all you know.'

'There's no' so much to tell.'

'There's all the world to tell, Jem.'

Jem turned his eyes towards his grazing flock. 'I got mi ship to look ah'ta.'

'Stuff. They're looking after themselves well enough. Besides—' Dr Balder glanced down at the shaggy collie lying peacefully at Jem's side, while Conal was stroking it—'there's Toby, and he'll see that they behave. He can do all that's necessary.'

'That he can when ness'ary,' said Jem, proudly. 'He can see the who'al pack of 'um, all five hundred of 'um, through the ship-dip wid-out me bein' there. I sometimes reckon they're more his nor mine.'

'Have you put them to the tups yet?'

'Tups? No. We'll ha' to bide a tidy wik or two before that. Then I'll let the rams into 'em.'

'Can Toby see to that too?'

'Surelye. He'll round up all the ewes that are justabout un-willin'.'

'You both of you know your trade, don't you.'

'I niver learned no trade. All I done was to watch mi farder, and he niver said naun. Shipherds be'ant talkers. Nohow. Too much al'an. But I like to git 'em lambin' all at sa'am time, early in the year, say Febrary; I ha' to be there all day and all night then to help em drop.'

'Kind of midwife?'

'Yes, mid-wif. Surelye.'

None of this made any sense to Conal who continued stroking Toby's head and fondling his ears. But he forgot the dog's ears when he heard the Doctor saying, 'Well, granted, Jem, that you, as a law-abiding citizen, took no active part in this villainous trade of smuggling, this gross defrauding Her Majesty, Queen Victoria, of her legitimate revenue, but you must have seen a lot of it going on when you were young. Just seen, you under-stand; not aided or abetted in any way. And you could tell young—young——'

'Conal,' Conal provided.

'—tell young Conal what, in your innocence, you happen to have watched.'

Jem conceded, 'Well, I reckon I could tell un what liddle I sin. Surelye.'

'Yes, tell him that—and quite a little more you may be in a position to remember. He's terribly interested in smugglers. Keeps asking me about them. But unfortunately I wasn't here when they were going strong or I should have been one of the best.'

Here Jem grinned again and nodded his head sideways. 'Yes, I can see you as a tar'ble fine smuggler, Mus Balder, a clever gen'man like you.'

Copying Jem's language, the Doctor said, 'Surelye; and now

I've got to get home. I'm a working man while this young Conal's got all his holidays before him. I'll leave him with you, and you do him proud with your tales of the smugglers. Just you listen, young Conal, and you'll really hear something.'

With this Dr Balder turned, lifted a hand in farewell, and, rather slowly and laboriously for him, started up the slope of Wedgery again, leaving Conal seated on the turf with the dog between him and Jem Cafful. He played with Toby's ears again and stroked him.

'What d'ye want me to tell ye, young ma'aster?'

'Everything, please.'

'That's a tar'ble lot to tell,' Jem demurred and did not respond immediately. But once that very shrewd old doctor-gentleman was half-way up his hill yonder Jem was ready and even eager to tell plenty to a schoolboy lolling beside him. Even as he spoke, his dragging Sussex drawl quickened. 'Yes. Tar'ble lot. Ye'see, in them days there was this smugglin' all along the coast between us and the Frenchies, wheresumdever there were good high cliffs and a tidy, valiant liddle haven like we got here; I've heard it said that our Wedgery was justabout the best smugglin' place of 'um all. Yes, Grayling Bottom was justabout made for it and Wedgery had an unaccountable good lot o'smugglers.'

'Oh, I'm so glad,' said Conal, with a stir of local patriotism.

'Yes, and accordin' to mi farder everyone in Wedgery was on the side of the smugglers.'

'As I should have been,' Conal assured him. 'What were they smuggling?'

'What smugglin'?' Jem seemed surprised at such ignorance. 'Why, good liquor, o'course. Tubs o' brandy, kegs of this spirit and that; butts of Frenchy wine; tea; tobacca. And lace for the wimmen. Mind you, I only know what I been told. The wimmen were unaccountable fond of lace. Leastways so I been told.'

'But how did they do their smuggling? How did they set about it?'

'Set about it? Oh, I can tell ye that. I ca'an't pretend I niver sin 'um at it.' Jem stressed proudly his strict loyalty to truth. Happy with the staring Conal for an audience on an empty hillside, he belied his previous assertion that 'shipherds be'ant talkers'. 'Set about it? Why, the ship'd be anchored, bow and stern, at no great distance away and when the ship's ma'aster knew that all was safe and there weren't no coastguard boat nor revenue cutters in sight he'd give us—I mean he'd give the lads on the shore his signal. He had to be tedious careful because if the revenue men got wind o' what he was up to, they could forfeit the who'al ship and git him fined five hundred pound. When our lads on the beach were sure that everything was all right around 'um, they'd signal back and hurry out in their boats, rowin' tar'ble quick to the ship's side; and the ship'd lower its tubs or its kegs till each boat was full. Or mebbe if the ship's ma'aster suddenly suspected summat—excise men or summat—they'd throw all the casks into the sea all tied together—just dump 'um overboard wid somethin' to float above 'um and show where they lay—like they do wid lobster pots. Then, when all was clear, our lads'd haul 'um up. Mind you, there were dunnamany people on the beach, most of Wedgery, in fact, to help 'um carry the tubs to safe hidin' places.'

'Where did they hide them?'

'Oh, they had their well-kno'an places. The church and the churchyard, p'raps. There was an empty tomb in the churchyard which was a valiant place for hidin' a powerful lot. Or Parson'd be going to church next mar'nin and be surprised to find tubs and barrels in his tower, or even in his pews. And plenty in his pulpit, like as not. That's to say, surprised if he hadn't bin helpin' the lads on the beach hisself.'

'But did he allow them to use his church?'

'Surelye. He knew he'd git a keg o' brandy or a tun of wine or a tub o' Hollands left on the Rectory doorstep as a kind'a "thank-you-ma'aster". Ah'ta all, as I telled ye, he'd like enough done his share. . . . But y'understand this was before my time; it's just what I've heard tell. Then they had their special hidin' places in houses along the road like Cutler's Cottage and Slings——'

'*Slings!* That's *our* cottage.' For the first time Conal saw the long thatched cottage flooded with a new and admirable light. Not till this moment, at Jem Cafful's side on an empty Down, did he fall in love with Slings.

And Jem, full of a subject which was delighting him as much as his listener, went drawling on. 'But the lads what had the mo'ast tedious-dangerous job were them what had to git the stuff from Wedgery to Lunnon. Mar'cy lad, if they were caught shiftin' it they were fined dunnamany times its value; three times its value, mebbe. And that'd be money. That'd be the ruin of 'um. I remember once—I remember hearing once that there was a tedious gurt crowd of customs men settin' and drinkin' in the Brotherhood before it got dark and we—I mean the lads'd want to be at it—which was reckoned to be tedious unfair of 'um because in the o'ald days, when it was the Rose and Crown, it was reckoned to be a kind of sanchery.'

Conal nodded. 'Yes, I knew that. My Uncle Bertie goes there regularly.'

'Do 'ee now?' was the whole of Jem's comment; and thereafter silence.

2

Excited and possessed—perhaps one might say 'diabolically possessed'—by the tales of law-breaking smugglers, Conal wandered that evening into the outhouse and attics of Slings (one of which was his bedroom) and stood in these places seeing *Treasure Island* smugglers at work with their tubs and butts and tuns (new and charming words to him) and the next morning immediately after breakfast he set off for the churchyard to see if he could guess which of the many table-tombs were used as caches for the contraband; and then, were it open, to prospect in the church itself.

All Hallows-at-Hill was (and is) the largest and noblest of all the ancient churches at the feet of, or between the knees of the Downs. Seven hundred years old, it was obviously built for a congregation much bigger than the little town could now provide. Either Wedgery was much bigger then, three times as big, or the faithful were three times as many, or the hopes and aspirations of the builders were exalted indeed. Nave and transepts are Norman, with perhaps here and there a 'perpendicular' window replacing the round-arched windows of these first aspiring builders. The chancel, except for its lower stages, is later than the body of the church; this much is clear from its flying and pinnacled buttresses. But the superb crown of the whole grey building is the huge square lantern tower. It is a tower which required no steeple to add to its total confidence; it finishes proudly with its own square ornamental cornice. Splendidly square and solid and stubborn it stands; like a statement that neither the winds nor the storms from beyond Beachy Head, nor the gates of Hell, shall prevail against it. It rises square and sturdy and righteousness itself, and as sure that its Faith, once delivered to the saints, is infallible and everlasting.

All around this great gift of our Norman conquerors to a downland valley were the listing headstones and the tabletombs standing in the silence of a 'God's acre' between yew trees and church. Here seven centuries of Wedgery's squires and townsmen lay sleeping.

And into this silent enclosure, seven hundred years after Norman hands had worked upon those stubborn walls and round-arched windows, came Conal Quentin Gillie, not alas to meditate on the eternities or to pray for the souls of the righteous, but to wonder where the smugglers had stowed their brandy.

It was difficult to decide which of the altar-tombs could have been a temporary wine-cellar; all seemed too massively built to be opened up and unlidded like a chest or a coffin. He visited all he could see but they yielded up no secrets. So he left them, no wiser, and turned towards the church, remembering that, according to Jem's recollections, either of what he had been told or of what he had personally experienced, the contraband had sometimes sought a passing 'sanchery' in its pews or, perhaps better still, in its pulpit.

With his green school cap crumpled reverently in one hand he walked nervously into the open church, looking into the pews and imagining the unholy stuff there. He did not know that less than forty years before this visit the pews had been roomy stalls with walls almost shoulder-high, rather like loose-boxes, and that some of them, if rented by the wealthy, had even held their private stoves to warm their occupants or induce a sleep if Parson's sermon was prolonged. Nor did he know that in the same years the pulpit had been a three-decker with seats one above another for parson and clerk. Still less did he realise that in the sanctuary the Lord's Table had been narrow and naked and bare, with the Ten Commandments in an arched panel above it and the Lord's Prayer and the Creed in smaller arched panels on either side of the Decalogue. Yet higher than the Tables of God's Law had been the royal coat-of-arms, lion, unicorn, crown and all, to proclaim the Queen's ecclesiastical supremacy in the land and shame all impious lawbreakers. But luckily for the smugglers it would be at night when they hurriedly hid their spoils here and there so it was unlikely they would have had either the light or the time to consider this rebuke hanging on the wall.

Conal was wrongly imagining that it was into these new Vic-torian pews, or yonder Victorian pulpit that the jolly smugglers rolled their casks or heaved up their tubs, perhaps by the light of a hurricane lantern. A pity he knew nothing of this earlier furnishing, for it would have been pleasantly amusing if he could have thought of the Decalogue, and the picturesque symbol of royal authority watching all this nefarious behaviour from the East Wall.

Having wandered and dreamed as he gazed up into a most innocent and religious-looking pulpit, he let his eyes stray towards the altar. Instead of the one-time narrow and sternly undecorated 'Lord's Table' he saw now a wide altar with an embroidered frontal and four riddel posts embracing it to hold dorsal and side curtains. On the altar stood a cross and two ornamental candlesticks. There were also decorative candlesticks on the tops of the four riddel posts. No panelled Decalogue or royal arms hung from the wall behind. He had of course never, in All Hallows, Wedgery, seen any other altar than this, but today for the first time, alone in a large, empty echoing church, he thought it beautiful and was surprised by a sudden grip of disappointment to think that he was now an atheist. But the rebel in him, while Lizetta's contemptuous vituperation remained unforgotten, was not disposed to step down from his new and distinguished rostrum. His platform now was by the side of a new friend, Dr Balder, who always spoke to him in language both kind and flattering.

Footsteps behind him. Starting alarm within him because the church had been so empty and silent. He swung round from looking at the altar and saw, appropriately enough, that it was Dr Julius Balder, the prophet of atheism and its begetter in him, who was coming up the nave.

'My dear Conal Quentin,' exclaimed the prophet. 'What, pray, are you doing here? In this temple of superstition? I thought I had divested you of all childish and semi-savage beliefs.'

Conal did not lack some talent for quick repartee and, smiling, asked, 'But why are *you* in here?'

'History, my dear Conal. I'm interested in all history, say from the pre-Cambrian era of seventeen-thousand million years ago to—' he waved a hand around the church's walls and chancel—'all this temporary and transient business here—this mere Norman stuff of yesterday. It will have been quite an interesting episode in history but not, in my view, a very important one.'

Conal, anxious not to appear to have lapsed back into childish and semi-savage beliefs, and perceiving that he also could claim history as his excuse, explained, 'I only came in to look at the places where Jem Cafful said the smugglers hid their stuff.'

'I believe it was all quite different in those days,' said the Doctor, 'different pews, different pulpit—all much better suited to barrels of rum than these new contrivances. Listen, boy. Stand still and think. Can't you imagine the unquiet ghosts of the smugglers all around you visiting their old haunts?'

'No,' said Conal, very much wishing the answer could be 'Yes', and trying hard.

'Nor can I. A pity, because I must confess that I incline to have more sympathy with the smugglers' use of these places than the use of your Auntie Olivetta—'

'Lizetta,' Conal amended.

'—your Auntie Lizetta and your sister, Margo, make of it. Or his Reverence the Rector.'

'Lizetta isn't my auntie.'

'Yes she is, surely? Your Auntie Olivetta?'

'No.'

'Sure?'

'Quite sure. And her name isn't Olivetta.'

'Oh, well, whatever her name is, she's probably a silly woman. And I gather her daughter's no better. But I must say I'm glad it's only a historic interest which brings you here and not a superstitious one.'

'Yes, Lizetta says it's a real historic church and terribly old.'

'Terribly old? Nonsense. Only of yesterday. What on earth—and "earth" is the right word—are some seven hundred years? Why, the Downs where I had the good fortune to meet you are over a hundred million years old. That's about the date we assign to their cretaceous period. The whole of the business they celebrate here isn't yet a couple of thousand years old. And infinitely more transient, I suspect, than your beloved Downs.'

'What is "transient"?'

'Temporary, impermanent, passing, my dear Conal. Destined to disappear in a few hundred years like so many other religions of the immature hominids on the face of this earth.'

'But Daddy always says the religion of the Hindus, which he admires, goes back ever so far B.C.'

'And he's right. The origins of Hinduism and the Vedic hymns are way back in the mists of pre-history. They had a Trinitarian doctrine years before Christianity, with their Brahma Vishnu and Seva, and Incarnations too, with their avatars of Krishna. Say three-thousand-five-hundred years B.C. What's that? What's that, compared with Wedgery Beacon's hundred million years?'

Conal had an answer to this. 'But they're still there and Wedgery's still there,' he said. 'After a hundred million years.'

Dr Balder nodded. 'Bright child.'

So Conal, encouraged, continued, 'And Daddy always says that the philosophy of some Hindus is terrifically noble.'

'And he's right again. I begin to have an admiration for your father. Personally, I prefer the philosophy of Hinduism at its loftiest to anything poured out from that pulpit up there.'

Encouraged again, Conal persisted in his partly successful contention. 'And they show no sign of disappearing.'

'Nor,' submitted the Doctor, 'do your beloved Downs.'

'No, and they're still there,' Conal triumphed, 'after all these millions of years.'

'Still there? Still there? Yes, but how long? Child, our chalk hills were laid down under the sea and they are composed either of the shells and other calcareous remains of tiny sea animals or, more likely, derive in the main from sea algae—sea-weeds to you—and are therefore a vegetable more than an animal deposit. Given time enough—aeons of time—and the highest of them will have been worn down by rains and streams and water-action till they're on the level of the sea; and the steeper they are the quicker they will be brought low. While the valleys and sea-beds are being exalted, why shouldn't the seas come washing over them again?'

By this Conal was silenced, defeated, his brain standing still, so he returned to the easier subject of the smugglers. 'Do you really believe the smugglers came and hid their stuff in here?'

'Certainly, if Jem says so, and he probably helped them do it, whatever the old liar pretends. I hope they did. You see, this extraordinary building—splendid, I grant you—in which we're standing has probably seen your smugglers, not only coming in by night to hide their tubs but on Sunday mornings as well, to pray. And why not? Mostly they chose to believe themselves guiltless and God-fearing types properly outwitting a shameful law that taxed abominably an honest man's liquor. Free traders they called themselves, seeing it all as an honest game by night against the revenue boys, and I should say that most of the congregation who'd come to pray agreed with them.

'Moreover I suspect some of the revenue men had a bit of sympathy with them and looked the other way or steered their cutters in the wrong direction, especially if they knew they'd get a complimentary keg or two for this courtesy. It was a merry and prosperous game because a keg of brandy could be got for fifteen shillings in France and sold for fifty in London. That's why quite a few Wedgery men in the daylight might be dressed as plough-boys in corduroys or fishermen in oil-skins but the only fields they ever ploughed were the wet ones beyond Beachy Head, and the only fish they ever caught were the casks dumped on the sea's bed. Or, of course, these excellent fish might be caught under the decks of a French ship, for the customs officers had the right to search any suspicious vessel, so you can be sure the captain kept his decks looking as clean as kingdom-come and as innocent of any contraband as his face was innocent of any sin.'

'But why is there no smuggling now?' asked Conal, as if sad that this amusing occupation should be a thing of the past.

Dr Balder shrugged, not sure of his answer. 'Well ... the import duties were lowered, so I suppose the game was no longer worth the candle. A pity, I agree.'

'When did it stop?'

'1860 or so. Fifty years ago. That'd make Jem Cafful a fine young man in his twenties and well able to lend a hand in rolling the casks up this aisle.'

'And did they really hide the casks in the tombs?'

'Oh, yes.' The Doctor was not above exaggerating a story to add to its charm. He turned his eyes towards the round-arched windows which looked out upon the tombs. 'And themselves too, sometimes, whenever the tombs were spacious enough, so that when all danger was past there would be a small resurrection of the dead, in our churchyard.'

Conal did not believe this. Having looked at the many altar

and table tombs in the churchyard he had decided that most of their tops would be much too heavy to lift like lids. But the Doctor thought a General Resurrection in All Hallows' churchyard, as at the Last Day, made an elegant picture with which to conclude a discourse, so he laid a hand on Conal's shoulder and said, 'Well, dear boy, I'll leave you to your contemplations. You have the makings of an intelligent hominid, and I want you to be one. Don't forget that the root of all real intelligence is scepticism——'

'Is *what*?'

'Scepticism. Doubt. The refusal of all credulity. The refusal to give total belief to anything till it's proven. The refusal to believe just what your mums and dads try to make you believe. And certainly to weigh with the utmost care anything an almost palaeolithic old archaeologist may tell you.' The sun was now pouring its sparkling moted beams through the south windows. 'Fare thee well. The sun is too bright to stay here considering ephemeral phenomena like this when one might be out on the hills which have endured for millions of centuries and may endure for several more.'

With a parting smile he turned, strolled down the nave, and went out through the West Door into the sunlight. Conal was left in the church standing near the chancel steps, vaguely remembering and vaguely impressed by all that he'd heard. Certainly he would aim at a high intelligence and begin to doubt, deny, and refuse acceptance (even if only behind a silence) of all that Lizetta insisted he must believe. He even felt some pity for Lizetta in her inferior state of intelligence—and a little for the rector of this church in his similar plight.

It was while he was thinking this, by the chancel steps, that a door opened within the chancel—which is to say a door opened at the opposite end from that through which Dr Balder had gone out into the sunlight. A singularly tall and slight figure in a belted black cassock stepped into the chancel. He saw Conal and came towards him between the choir stalls: a clergyman, as his collar showed, with fine-boned features beneath thin greying hair. The features might be sharp, the brow lined, and the grey hair scanty, but the expression on his face and in his eyes looked bright and youthful: Conal put him as no older than his father.

He came towards him with a most friendly and welcoming smile on his lips, but before those lips could speak Conal guessed who he was. From Lizetta and Marjorie he had heard much about the coming of a new rector to All Hallows. They had talked excitedly about his 'Institution' next Friday when the Bishop and the Archdeacon and all the clergy for miles around would be present. Here almost certainly was this Rector designate.

The kindness in his eyes was almost paternal as he looked down upon a schoolboy visitor who was standing and staring at his chancel. 'Interested in this beautiful church?' he asked.

'Yes, *rather*!' said Conal with some fervour, though omitting to mention that his interest was in smugglers rather than in architects.

'And you are a churchman?' A smile for this grown-up word.

'Oh, yes.' Not altogether a lie since 'officially' he was no less; was he not compelled by Lizetta to go to church?

'Well, so am I interested in it because it's going to be my church. I shall be its rector from about six o'clock next Friday.'

'Oh, I know. That's your "institution", isn't it? We're all coming.'

'Institution *and* Induction.'

Conal frowned in some bewilderment. 'What does that mean? Are they different things?'

'Yes. I shall be instituted by the Bishop and inducted by the Archdeacon. D'you do Latin at school?'

A nod. 'Worse luck.'

'Well, translate *Accipe meam curam et tuam.*'

Conal, who would have been unable to translate a difficult piece was delighted that he could manage this easily, and would seem like one of the dazzling scholarship candidates in the 'special' at St Jourdan's. 'Accept my care and yours,' he provided instantly.

'Perfect. You'll hear the Bishop read those words in English from the Deed of Institution while I kneel before him holding its seal between both hands.'

'Is the Bishop really coming?'

'Of course. Of course. No bishop, no institution.'

'Oh, I'm longing to come and see it all. I've never seen the Bishop. I'm longing for Friday,' said Conal, indulging in no lie this time and leaving aside for the moment—or forgetting—his distinction as an intellectual and an atheist.

'It's always rather a wonderful service in these days because it's done wholly in church before the people.' And this new rector began to expound it all to the staring Conal like a gifted teacher telling a tale from history to an enraptured class, or a parent a bed-time story. 'In the old feudal days, you know, I should have had to do little more than find the bishop somewhere—on his horse, perhaps—and get accepted by him as my feudal lord, and then go chasing after the archdeacon—quite likely also on a horse—that's why bishops and archdeacons still wear gaiters—and tell him I'd got a mandate for induction. After that I'd have been taken to my new church which would be sternly locked against me and the archdeacon would lay my hands on the keys of the church as the signal that I might enter. I'd then have gone quite alone into the empty church, and they'd have shut the doors on me, leaving me there alone while I tolled the bell to tell the whole parish that I'd entered into possession. I was now a vassal owning fealty to my feudal lord, the bishop, and through him a liegeman of my Sovereign Lord the King.' Here he considered his young visitor with the friendliest smile. 'On the whole I'm not sure things will be so very different next Friday. Ever heard of George Herbert?'

'No.' Conal's distinction drooped.

'I'm sorry, because he was one of the loveliest of our seventeenth-century poets and vicar of a church in Wiltshire——'

'Please, what's the difference between a rector and a vicar?'

'Quite simple. The rector gets the tithes of a parish and a vicar doesn't. He's just somebody else's salaried substitute. Heard of Izaak Walton?'

'Oh, yes.' The distinction revived. '*The Compleat Angler.*'

'Good. Well, he wrote a life of George Herbert in which he tells us that, after George Herbert had gone into his new empty church and tolled its bell, someone looked through a window—an inquisitive type—and saw him prostrate before the Holy Table. That was the sort of man he was.'

This picture so appealed to Conal that it left him yet more dissatisfied with the intellectual necessity to be an atheist.

And the new Rector was proceeding, 'Nowadays it's all done as a religious service before a congregation. What happens now is that archdeacon and clergy proceed to the church's west door where the archdeacon lays the new rector's hand upon the keys and says something like this—grand old words—"By virtue of this mandate I do induct you into the real, actual, and corporal possession of this parish church, with all the rights, dignities, and appurtenances thereunto belonging." And the rector tolls the bell.'

'Gosh, I'm longing to see it all.'

So the Rector, encouraged, even as Dr Balder had been, by so fascinated a listener beneath his eyes, told him of all the traditional ceremonies that would be performed in procession around the church—at font, at chancel steps—'Here where we're standing now'—at lectern, pulpit and sanctuary; to all of which Conal listened with such open-mouthed interest that the Rector concluded, 'I shall love to have you there. Bring all your family.'

'They're not my family. My family's in India. I only live with them so's I can go to school in England.'

Plainly the Rector had trapped some sadness in this prompt answer. 'And when are you going back to your family?'

'Not for years, I'm afraid. Not for about another nine years if I go on to Oxford. But I don't suppose I shall ever get to Oxford. I should have to get a scholarship and I'm not clever enough. I'm not even in the Scholarship Class at school. So I might go back in seven years. I've been here three years already.'

'Won't your parents come home on furlough soon?'

'Oh, I hope so. But they'll have to go back again.'

'Where do they live in India?'

'In Gondapore mostly.' And just as he had told Dr Balder he had to tell this new friend, 'Daddy and I used to climb the Western Ghats,' and many of the other things that here in England he missed.

'You're longing to go back to India?'

'Oh, yes, yes, I love India. I was born in India.'

'Well, I know that at your age,' said the Rector after Conal had poured out more about India and Indians, 'nine years seems an eternity, but really it's not very long; it'll pass quickly.'

All this time the two of them, Rector and Conal, had been standing at the chancel's three steps, the Rector on the top step,

Conal on the pavement of the nave. Now, plainly moved by what he had heard, the Rector came down one step and rested a pastoral hand on Conal's head, 'I'm so very, very glad to have met you, even if you're only one of my parishioners at holiday times. Bless you.'

Since this seemed like a dismissal, Conal turned and went quickly to the door through which Dr Balder had disappeared. He was now feeling an affection for this kindly man at least equal to that which he felt for the Doctor. This new affection was making him doubt whether he would really be able, or would really want to sustain himself on the Doctor's high intellectual pinnacles. In the porch he turned round with some idea of waving a goodbye, but he saw that the church's new Rector was now kneeling in the front pew, one pace from the chancel steps, with his head pillowed on his arms. He remembered the picture of George Herbert and slipped quietly away.

Returning punctually for lunch, he reported over the dining-table his encounter with the new Rector—'He's the most frightfully decent sort'—and became at once the target for all eyes and all questions. 'What's he like; what's he like?' demanded Lizetta; and 'Gosh, what's he like?' Marge echoed. Even Uncle Bertie, though a churchgoer of notable infrequency, lifted interested eyes from his knife and fork.

'Ever so tall and thin,' Conal told them, 'with hair quite grey, though he doesn't look all that frightfully old.'

'How old?' asked a spell-bound Lizetta. Marge's eyes asked the same. So did Uncle Bertie's.

'Fiftyish,' Conal suggested, and then dropped a hodful of bricks from the high position he was occupying on this ladder that led to information. 'I should say about as old as you and Uncle Bertie.'

'I'm nowhere near fifty,' Lizetta sharply rejoined. 'Nor am I anything like as old as your Uncle Bertie.'

Uncle Bertie flung back his head to laugh with his mouth full. 'Don't spare me,' he said, 'though I *am* only a few years over fifty. But I'm quite content to be sacrificed for any woman's happiness. Conal, old boy, you dropped a hairy old clanger then. "Fiftyish" will pass for me all right, but it's no word to use about your auntie. "Fortyish", perhaps.'

'I'm not his auntie,' Lizetta interposed, her temper frayed.

'Oh no, of course you're not. I always forget. But go on, Conal, about the new vicar.'

'He's not a vicar; he's a rector,' said Conal, proud of this correction.

'Rector, is he? What's the difference, Colonel?'

A welcome question: Conal was able to stand again with some distinction on his ladder. 'It's quite simple. The rector gets the tithes of the parish, and the vicar doesn't. He's only a salaried substitute.'

'Almighty God in Heaven, where did you get all that from?'

'Don't swear in front of the children, Bertie. Please.'

'Yes, but does he even know what tithes are?'

'No, he's just showing off,' said Marge, feeling some jealousy of Conal's current successes.

No one explained what tithes were, because not even Uncle Bertie felt confident that he knew what they were.

'Never mind about tithes,' said Lizetta. 'And of course he's a Rector. But what's his name, Conal?' She never called him 'Colonel'.

'I've no idea. He didn't say anything about that.'

Here, curiously enough, Uncle Bertie did have the exact answer. He had learned it over his mid-day pint at the Brotherhood where there was plenty of talk about the 'new man coming to All Hallows'. 'Patrice,' he said. 'Stephen Patrice. "Reece", not "rice". And what's more, he's a canon. A canon and all! Canon Patrice. He must be a man of some prominence if he's a canon at his age. He's a wonderful preacher, they say.'

'Where did *you* get all this from?' asked Lizetta.

'From old Toby Hudson, one of the many gardeners at Drood Place. He was there in the Brotherhood and he told us that Sir Harman Drood, who has the gift of the living, was hugely bucked at having secured a canon and a preacher with a big reputation for a comparatively small parish like Wedgery— though the church, of course, is one of the grandest anywhere around. He's been talking to Toby and all his other old gardeners about it. You're going to hear sermons far more remarkable than anything the old vicar—or rector—or whatever he was—gave you. I might even come to hear some of them myself.' Liking to glean superlatives from any sort of soil, as most people do, he repeated, 'Yes, you're going to hear some wonderful preaching, according to Sir Harman.'

' "Canon Patrice",' Lizetta mused. 'What a lovely name.'

Marjorie endorsed this enthusiasm, though not very logically. 'I'm sure he's going to be wonderful with a name like that.'

'He was frightfully nice,' Conal reiterated. 'He asked me to ask you all to come along on Friday for his Induction.'

'Of course we're all coming along,' Lizetta announced in her snubbing manner. 'Is it likely we shouldn't be there?'

Conal didn't submit that, as an avowed disbeliever, there was no obligation on him to attend. Indeed he had forgotten his dis-belief and was as eager as anyone to witness the thrilling cere-monies which Canon Patrice had described. So instead of opening a controversy about Belief and Disbelief he expounded for them the difference between Institution and Induction—though add-ing in modesty, when he perceived that Marge was 'looking snooty' at all this display of knowledge, 'He told me about every-thing. There're going to be terrific goings-on at the Service.'

'But what were you doing in the church when the Rector told you all this?' Lizetta asked, a note of reproof still in her voice.

'I went there to see where the smugglers hid their tubs of brandy and rum, and he came from somewhere just as I was looking up at the pulpit and seeing heaps of tubs there. He talked to me for quite a long time; he asked about Daddy and Mummy in India and when I was going back there.' Lizetta looked displeased at these words but made no comment. 'I told him all about Gondapore and Daddy's work. I suppose we talked for half an hour, and when at last I came away I turned round to sort of wave a kind of goodbye to him, but I saw that he was kneeling in the front pew and praying.'

'Gracious goodness!' said Uncle Bertie.

'Yes, he was praying like billy-o.'

Instantly Lizetta snapped at him, 'For heaven's sake don't use words like that about prayer. Have you no reverence? I don't like Marjorie to hear them.'

But now Uncle Bertie rebuked her for a change, 'Oh, leave the boy be. What's wrong with what he said? I'm sure God must be pleased when people pray like billy-o.'

'I was brought up differently,' she muttered, more to the tablecloth than to anyone in particular.

And there it rested.

3

In their enthusiasm Lizetta, Marjorie and Conal set out for the
church, on this hallowed Friday evening, a good half-hour too
early because they expected 'an enormous crowd'. Uncle Bertie
came with them, less to pray, Conal imagined, than to watch a spec-
tacle. The bells of All Hallows, a peal of six, were flinging their
chimes down the hill and grandly clashing them as a call for all
who would, to come and greet their new pastor. So early had the
Sheridans started that the church was but sparsely occupied
when they arrived and they were able to sit in a forward pew.
People came filing in steadily, but the great church, belonging to
earlier and believing centuries, was never much more than half
full, even though all the villages round about had sent their
faithful. The most of Wedgery was there. In fact, so deep was
Wedgery's interest in its new rector, after a previous incumbency
of thirty-three years, that Conal, for ever turning round to see
the people coming in, assessing how many they were, and longing
for a great crowd (which was strange in an unbeliever) chanced
on one of these enumerations to see, of all people, old Jem Cafful,
in a back pew. As Dr Balder had called him an old sinner Conal
could but wonder if this was the first time he'd come into the
church since the distant days when he came by lantern light with
his kegs of whisky and what-not, and if he was remarking the
difference between the high-walled pews which had held his
contraband and the natty little pew which was now holding him.

The clock struck, the organ introduced the first hymn on a
printed Order of Service in everyone's hand, the congregation,
rising, sang it willingly and loudly, 'Come, thou Holy Spirit, come';
and the procession entered from the vestries: crucifer, choir, the
Patron of the Benefice, Sir Harman Drood, the Rector (still only
designate), the Rural Dean, the Archdeacon, the churchwardens
with their wands and, majestic climax, the Bishop, in lawn-sleeved
rochet and scarlet chimere, his chaplain following behind like a

general's aide-de-camp. The Bishop had the advantage of being taller than anyone else; of his white crimped hair that fitted to his head like a casque and almost glistened in its whiteness; and of a straight-featured youngish face beneath. He had the reputation of being the handsomest bishop on the Bench. He was taller and certainly shapelier than the new Rector who was tall but slim to awkwardness. As a tribute to this downland parish in his South Saxon see, the Bishop bore in his left hand, not an elaborate crozier, but a Pyecombe crook like Jem Cafful's (only cleaner). His height made the crook look small, but Conal thought that Jem at the back must be pleased with that familiar pastoral instrument. As he was thinking this, he heard Marjorie whisper to her mother about the Bishop, 'Isn't he absolutely divine?'

The Bishop took his seat on a temporary throne just above the chancel steps, and Sir Harman Drood, the Patron, escorted by both wardens, came forward to present the new incumbent. Sir Harman, Squire of Wedgery, with his erect soldierly figure, crisp military moustache, and manifest London tailoring, looked every inch what he was, a retired colonel—and, moreover, a colonel of the Guards. To the seated Bishop he said, 'Right Reverend Father in God, I present unto thee this godly and well-learned man to be admitted to the Cure of Souls in this our parish.' The ancient words, though spoken loudly and formally in a voice accustomed to command, were loaded with history and did not fail to reach hearts in the congregation, not excepting Conal's, which was stirred by them.

The Bishop, making a slight inclination, demanded that the Oaths should be taken. To the congregation he said, 'Please be seated.'

Holding a Testament high, the Rector designate made his Oath of Allegiance, 'I, Stephen Patrice, swear that I will be faithful and bear true allegiance to His Majesty King George, his heirs and successors in all things lawful and honest.'

Then the Bishop enjoined the congregation, 'Dearly beloved in the Lord: in the Name of God and in the presence of this congregation, we purpose now to institute to the Cure of Souls in this parish our well-beloved in Christ, Stephen Patrice; and forasmuch as the charge of immortal souls, which our blessed

66

Lord and Saviour has purchased with his own most precious blood, is so solemn and weighty a matter, we beseech you to join together with us in hearty prayer to Almighty God that he would vouchsafe to give to this his servant grace to perform aright the duties which belong to so sacred and grave a trust.'

As instructed in the Order of Service all knelt 'in silence for a space to make their humble supplication to God'. Conal though kneeling with the others, and not a little thrilled by the drama of this Induction, knew that he was now in no intellectual position to pray, and he spent the silence looking at the mural plaques on either side of the chancel arch: 'Sir Aylwin Drood, of Drood Place, Died 1605', 'Sir Eudo Drood, Died 1771', 'Sir Jasper Drood...' 'Lady Aurelia Drood....' He knew that the Droods of Drood Place had been the lords of Wedgery for four hundred years. 'Sir Octavius Bredbury Harman Drood, 8th Bt., Died 1794.'

Notes from the organ ended the silence, and the choir led the people, still kneeling, in the next hymn, the *Veni Creator*, 'Come, Holy Ghost, our souls inspire'.

Then all in the church stood for the Institution—all except the seated Bishop and the new Rector kneeling at his feet. The Bishop read the Deed of Institution while the Rector, as he had told Conal, held its seal in both hands. Giving the deed into his hand, the Bishop said, 'Receive this Cure of Souls which is both thine and mine....' *Accipe meam curam et tuam*: Conal heard the Latin words in his mind and remembered his pride in translating them. Meanwhile the Bishop was blessing the now instituted Rector in further magnificent words, 'The God of peace ... make you perfect in every good work to do his will....' which Conal, thanks to an enthusiastic master of St Jourdan's, was well able to appreciate, even with a swelling of the heart. Indeed, the more appealing the old words the less he found himself desiring to be an intellectual and an unbeliever. But he held on to his high position, rather like a climber exposed on a high pitch of a mountain face.

'Whereas we have duly and canonically admitted our well-beloved in Christ, Stephen Patrice—' The Bishop was now addressing the Archdeacon—'we hereby empower and require you to induct him into the real and actual possession of this church and benefice and to defend him so inducted.'

So empowered, a procession of verger, Archdeacon, new Rector, Rural Dean and churchwardens passed down the nave to the church's West Door, while the Bishop went to his proper throne within the altar rails. All the congregation turned round towards the door.

There the Archdeacon laid the new incumbent's hand upon the key of the door and said the words of induction which Canon Patrice had rehearsed to Conal: 'By virtue of this mandate I do induct you into the real, actual, and corporal possession of this parish church of All Hallows-at-Hill, with all the rights, dignities, and appurtenances thereunto belonging.'

The Rector tolled the bell.

The Archdeacon's procession returned up the nave to the chancel, and here the Archdeacon, taking the Rector by the hand, led him to his stall, where he—alone of all in the church —knelt, as the Archdeacon said, 'The Lord himself is thy keeper, the Lord is thy defence upon thy right hand. The Lord shall preserve thee from all evil; yea, it is even he that shall keep thy soul. The Lord shall preserve thy going out and thy coming in, from this time forth for evermore.'

A loud and general Amen from all the congregation.

At this stage Conal saw that Lizetta who, if irritable, had a quick heart, was weeping with handkerchief visiting her eyes and resting under her nose. These tears were infectious and produced a similar uprising in his own throat. He looked towards Marjorie to see if she was in tears, but she was only gaping at the fascinating and kneeling Rector. What Uncle Bertie might be experiencing one could not know, but he showed no symptoms of emotional disorder.

Still kneeling, the new incumbent said alone—for the hearing of all—the Lord's Prayer.

This was the preparation for all to kneel while he prayed in the set words for his parish and people, after which the Archdeacon prayed for a blessing on him. 'Almighty God, bless, we beseech thee, this thy servant with the help of thy Holy Spirit; that he may worthily fulfil the charge now committed to him. Be thou his joy in worship, his support in his home, his comfort in sorrow, his counsel in doubt, his help in toil, his defence in adversity, his patience in tribulation. . . .'

All this was too much for Lizetta; it drew more than covert tears behind a handkerchief; she was snuffling audibly, and Marjorie was looking at her in some doubt and embarrassment. Uncle Bertie stretched an arm behind her for support and comfort. Marjorie now was clearly less attracted by the ceremonials and ritual of an Induction than by her mother's present lachrymose condition.

Meantime the Archdeacon's procession was returning with the Rector down the nave to visit, one after another, all the 'Several Stations of the Church': font, chancel, lectern, pulpit and sanctuary; and Conal was even having moments when he almost wanted to be ordained a priest of this Superstition and be inducted like this, at door, font, lectern, pulpit and sanctuary. For this procession the organ and choir led the people in 'We love the place, O God, Wherein thine honour dwells'.

At the font the Bishop from his high place in the sanctuary charged the new incumbent that it was his task to bring unbaptised people to the Holy Sacrament of Baptism: 'Wilt thou do this gladly and willingly with the help of God?'

And the answer came from the other end of the church, 'I will so do, the Lord being my helper.'

So the Bishop charged the people: 'Churchwardens, Church Councillors and people of this parish, will you fill your part in this duty by the grace of God?'

And all—or many—answered, 'We will so do, the Lord being our helper.' Lizetta could only mumble this promise through her handkerchief; Marjorie was too over-awed to speak aloud; Uncle Bertie was conceding no promises; and Conal could not feel justified in saying anything. He could only think that the whole service was beautiful. And 'rather tremendous'.

At chancel steps, at lectern, by the pulpit, and, most important of all, before the sanctuary, the Bishop charged the Rector with his duty and received always the answer, 'I will so do, the Lord being my helper': then charged the people and received again their promise. After the most solemn words of all at the sanctuary he rose and stood before the altar with his Pyecombe crook in his hand and yet again charged the Rector: 'It is the duty of the Minister diligently to set forward quietness, peace, and love amongst all men, to remember that he has to give account for their souls to the Chief Shepherd at his appearing, to use all diligence to help all those who are in doubt and anxiety, to recall those who have fallen into sin, and to train and fashion the hearts of all men to accept the blessed Gospel of which he is a steward.'

'Which all applies to me,' thought Conal, while he heard Marjorie whispering to Lizetta of the Bishop, 'Isn't he *too* glorious?' and the Rector, who was kneeling at the altar rails, giving his answer, 'I will endeavour myself to do all these things gladly and willingly with the help of God.'

Now the procession broke in pieces, the Rector returning to his stall, the churchwardens with their wands to their honourable pews, the Rural Dean and Archdeacon to choir stalls on the cantoris side.

There was no sermon, the Bishop having decided that enough had been enjoined upon people and priest. Only followed a recessional hymn before the Blessing. This hymn, thundered out triumphantly by the organist, was the famous Old Hundred-and-Fourth, 'O worship the King All-Glorious above'. Inspired by the organist, himself inspired, the congregation gave it the tops of their voices and their enthusiasm. 'O gratefully sing His power and His love, Our Shield and Defender, The Ancient of days, Pavilioned in splendour And girded with praise.' Lizetta and Marjorie and even Uncle Bertie were caught up in the enthusiasm and singing with fervour. It was likely enough that this was the first time in years that Uncle Bertie had sung fervently in church. Conal must not sing but he was enjoying this triumphant chorus. All the hymn's words delighted the poetry-lover who had lately been brought to birth in him by the enthusiastic master at St Jourdan's; but the verses which gave him most to think about were two:

> The earth with its store of wonders untold,
> Almighty, thy power hath founded of old;
> Hath stablished it fast by a changeless decree,
> And round it hath cast, like a mantle, the sea—

'Stablished it fast'? 'Changeless decree'? Dr Balder, Doctor Balder, what say you to this?—and the following verse:

Thy bountiful care what tongue can recite?
It breathes in the air, it shines in the light;
It streams from the hills, it descends to the plain,
And sweetly distils in the dew and the rain.

These words rang in his head when, blessing given and clergy gone, they all trooped out into the evening sunlight. Here was the church, All Hallows-at-Hill, on the slope of a down, and here through the last of the sunlight came a strong salt wind from the sea. The sky, little clouded, was flooded with a light both golden and faintly crimson from the lowering sun; herring gulls and other sea-mews were swept and drifted and called far inland, over church tower and hill-top, presaging, so the wise men said, rains and storm. Wedgery Beacon, Wedgery Band, Firle, Beachy Head—stablished fast by a changeless decree? Fast? Changeless? But Dr Balder had said, 'Time enough, and the rains and streams and water action will have worn them away to the sea's level, possibly to be overwhelmed once more by the sea.'

Strange that Lizetta and Marjorie, talking happily of all they had witnessed while Uncle Bertie admitted that an Induction was 'Certainly an impressive how-d'ye-do'—strange that they should have no idea, no suspicion of two worlds at war within Conal, trailing silently apart from them.

4

The Order of Service, given to all present at the Induction, had concluded with a Special Notice: 'The Rector's first sermon will be at Morning Prayer on Sunday next. He hopes that as many as possible of today's congregation will attend.'

Assuredly Lizetta and Marjorie would attend, with Conal, the apostate, trailing obediently after them. No less assuredly Uncle Bertie would not attend; he had his usual mid-day engagement at the Brotherhood. Lizetta was right in thinking there would be no need to hurry this Sunday morning and no difficulty about getting a foremost pew, because Wedgery would be less interested in hearing a first sermon than in watching a ceremony, with Bishop, Archdeacon, Rural Dean and all the clergy of the neighbourhood playing their parts.

If even at such a ceremony the great church had been only half full, this morning it was but a quarter full. It held only the faithful; for instance, there was no Jem Cafful there. But these faithful, after Morning Prayer had run its course, were rewarded —or disappointed—or shaken by an astonishing and even sensational sermon.

Word had been abroad that this Canon Patrice was a remarkable preacher, but no one had foreseen anything as strange as this.

Canon Patrice went up into the pulpit and stood there, leaving a silence in the church till the last of the people had seated themselves and achieved their comfort—a long and oddly pregnant silence it seemed before he spoke the words, 'Let the words of my mouth and the meditation of my heart be always acceptable in thy sight, O Lord my strength and my Redeemer.' He made no sign of the cross over heart and breast, as his predecessor used to do when he said these words.

He opened a book on the pulpit's lectern, fumbling its pages to find the desired place, and when it lay open before him he looked at the people for another few seconds of silence which seemed like a whole minute. In that pause the congregation had time to consider his long, lean figure, the fineness of his sharp features beneath the thin grey hair, the earnestness in his eyes and a kindliness in them, even, some may have thought, an other-worldliness in them that suggested sanctity.

He began, 'On Friday those of you who were present at my Induction heard my Oaths of Allegiance and Canonical Obedience, but none of you heard the Declaration of Assent which I had made in the vestry before the service. I would wish you to hear it. It runs—' he lowered his head to read—' "I assent to the Thirty-nine Articles of Religion and to the Book of Common Prayer.... I believe the Doctrine of the Church of England as therein set forth to be agreeable to the Word of God, and in Public Prayer and Administration of the Sacraments I will use the form in the said book prescribed and none other." ' He paused as if to leave those last three words echoing in the air; then repeated them as if underscoring them: 'And none other.' A silence in their honour. He knew the potent effect of a silence while he looked straight at his audience—before proceeding, 'I made this declaration with all my heart because it is an exact statement of all that I shall try to teach you. I therefore intend that this first sermon of mine should take, perhaps, an unusual form. It shall be no less than a reading to you very clearly many of the Articles and more than one clause of the Athanasian Creed. I do this because the first are very seldom, if ever, read and the second is most wrongly neglected today.'

People were turning to the Articles at the end of their prayer books. Seventeen pages of them! A reading of them! In the name of Heaven and of Christian compassion, what could be sterner or duller? And yet, though the operation, with the Athanasian Creed, lasted for three-quarters of an hour, it was far from dull. This for two reasons: firstly because the Canon had every gift of the platform or pulpit orator, modulating the pitch of a beautiful voice, varying the pace of his speech, and at major moments leaving a musical pause that his words might begin to haunt his listeners; secondly because probably not a single person in the church had ever read the Articles and all were interested to hear what they were about. And when they were so dramatically read, when, moreover, listeners were shocked, excited, shaken, and even

73

frightened by the things they said, tedium had little place among the pews. Of all in those pews probably none was so shocked and shaken as Conal sitting beside Lizetta and Marjorie.

Of this protracted, provocative but epochal sermon, which was to stir such contention in Wedgery, all that is of interest to us here is the fusillade of bullets, deeply wounding, that it shot into the heart of one child listening.

It was with a most friendly and engaging smile that the preacher shot the words, 'This your village—and mine now—is, I regret to say, greatly famous as a smuggling village.' Some suppressed laughter, but the smile on his face stayed merry and affectionate. 'I am even told that this hallowed church has in its day been used as a convenient place for hiding all manner of contraband. And this unhallowed fact, my dear people, amounts to saying that a house of prayer has been used as a den of thieves—for thieves they certainly were, robbing Her Majesty's Revenue. Well, this doubtless interesting fact that this your church made an excellent place for concealing liquor and tobacco and lace and so on seems to justify me in stating that these were not the only contraband which was smuggled into England, and into this church, from the Continent some sixty or seventy years ago.'

That 'sixty or seventy' tactfully evaded, in what he was about to argue, any reference to his predecessor in the benefice who had held it for only thirty-three years; but, despite this, there was an expectant silence in the church. To what was he leading?

'In those far-off days, contemporary with your celebrated smugglers, there was being smuggled into England, and into its national church—by ministers of whose sincerity and in some cases sanctity I have no doubt but only admiration, though I hold their actions to have been misguided—forms of religious faith and practice that were manifestly opposed to the Laws of our land and to the Protestant Reformation which is the glory of our English Church. It is for *that* reason that I want to declare before you uncompromisingly what our Law still is and what for four hundred years has been the faith of our beloved Church as by law established. Not one of you but has before you our Book of Common Prayer and in it you can read—on almost the last pages—' here again the engaging smile—'that the Articles were agreed upon by the Archbishops and Bishops and the whole clergy in a Convocation at London in the year 1562 "for the avoiding of diversities of opinion and for the establishing of consent touching true religion". Turn a page and you can read the King's Declaration ratifying and confirming the clergy's final decision and "prohibiting the least difference from the said Articles".'

That pause again, and the repetition of three words: 'The least difference.'

There was little to disturb an enthralled congregation in his dealings with the early Articles; they dealt only with Trinitarian doctrine and the Creeds. No one was troubled by these familiar and abstract things. But it was a different matter when he came to the Article on Predestination and Election. At first the splendid old words contained nothing but comfort, and no actor could have more splendidly recited them.

'Predestination to Life is the everlasting purpose of God whereby (before the foundations of the world were laid) he hath constantly decreed by his counsel secret to us, to deliver from curse and damnation those whom he hath chosen in Christ out of mankind, and to bring them by Christ to everlasting salvation, as vessels made to honour.... As the godly consideration of Predestination and our Election in Christ is full of sweet, pleasant, and unspeakable comfort to godly persons, and such as feel in themselves the working of the Spirit of Christ, mortifying the works of the flesh and their earthly members and drawing up their minds to high and heavenly things, as well because it doth greatly establish and confirm their faith of eternal salvation to be enjoyed through Christ, as because it doth fervently kindle their love towards God, so for curious and carnal persons, lacking the Spirit of Christ, to have continually before their eyes the sentence of God's Predestination is a most dangerous downfall whereby the Devil doth thrust them either into desperation——'

Conal, sitting there, his still childish heart beginning to throb with fear, was seeing Dr Balder who had said, 'I like to think an intelligent creation like you will be quit of all that superstitious nonsense one day,' and remembering his own instant resolve to be an intelligent and unsuperstitious disbeliever.

For a moment he thought some alleviation of his fears was coming, for the preacher was saying, 'You will notice that the Article evades—may I say "charitably dodges"—' a smile for all at this frivolous word—'the Calvinistic doctrine of Predestination to damnation; but it is here that we must remember how an earlier Article declares and insists upon our belief in the Creed of St Athanasius, which is nowadays so often and so shamefully neglected by those who don't want to hear its stern pronouncements. And yet if you will look into your prayer-books before you, you will see that this great Creed is ordained to be said or sung at Morning Prayer on all the great festivals and on the days of several saints. And what are its opening statements? What its closing statements?'

He so arranged his pauses that each of these statements, the opening and the closing, should be embraced by a silence. He read, 'Whosoever will be saved; before all things it is necessary that he hold the Catholick Faith. Which Faith except everyone do keep whole and undefiled: without doubt he shall perish everlastingly.' Silence. 'Such are the opening words. The closing words echo and stress them.' He read them. 'They that have done good shall go into life everlasting, and they that have done evil into everlasting fire. This is the Catholick Faith: which except a man believe faithfully, he cannot be saved.'

By now Conal's panting heart had almost stopped because he was breathless with fears. 'Except a man believe....' 'Everlasting fire....'

No word of comfort and easement came to him from the lips of that kindly, earnest, benevolent face; they were saying only, 'We are right to believe with joy in the love, the mercy, the total forgiveness for those who accept and act upon the Gospel's teaching and as such are God's elect, but I can see no escaping from the inexorable severity of Christ and the Church's utter condemnation of those who reject or deny his offer of salvation. We must not rejoice only in the comfortable words of the Gospel but also hear and fear the dark. They come straight from the Saviour's lips; terrible words for those who stand on his left hand: "Depart from me, ye cursed, into everlasting fire prepared for the Devil and his angels".'

It was not within the power of Conal's mind, nor perhaps within the compass of any seated in All Hallows church that day, to perceive that Canon Patrice, this good and deeply spiritual man, was looking down upon a world of sinners with what he conceived to be the God's-eye view; and that on this great and lonely summit, this Mount Sinai, it was a view that appalled him and called for nothing less than severe, complete, unsparing exposition.

On the words 'everlasting fire' he lapsed into a mood of quiet theological interpretation. 'The words are there and are repeated in other places by Our Lord. According to the universal opinion of the early Fathers the pains of hell are of two kinds, spiritual pain (*poena damni*: the pain of the everlasting loss of heaven) and physical pain (*poena sensus*: wrought by the undying fire). One and all maintain that the fire of hell is material. They offer no answer to the problem as to how material flames can torment immaterial souls, but affirm that such, beyond denial, is God's revelation through Christ our Lord. All we can do in these days is to take the scriptural words as undoubtedly they stand, and accept that, whatever the "fire" may be, it is something very terrible and everlasting.'

Some of this Conal heard, but not all, for a child possessed by horror, and breathless with it, has little place in his mind for the passing of distant words.

5

Conal lay sleepless and tossing in his attic bedroom at Slings. He was glad to be alone in this dark little room beneath the sloping thatch, because he would have hated Lizetta and Marjorie to see that he was crying, and could not stop crying, under the sheet pulled over his head. Somehow it seemed good that the sheet should curtain his tears even from the dark. He was crying because the weight of Dr Balder's unbelief was tightly lodged within him, and he could no longer make himself, force himself, to believe all that Lizetta and Marjorie so easily believed and that the Rector with his gentle, affectionate smiles so firmly believed and preached. He could not. *But—'everlasting fire'.*

Apparently neither Lizetta nor Marjorie had been the least troubled by the Canon's sermon. They must both suppose that, since they went regularly to church and never questioned anything they heard there, they were in no danger of eternal damnation. That applied to other people. But what did they think about Uncle Bertie who seldom went to church on Sundays, preferring the Brotherhood when they were at Wedgery and the Duke of Wellington when they were at home in Chelsea? Perhaps because he had never said aloud that he didn't believe or worry about the Church's teaching they needn't think he was in danger of the undying fire—or could it be that if Lizetta sometimes feared he might be in such danger, she was resigned to the fact that she could do nothing about it. As for Marjorie, Conal was sure she had no such critical powers as himself and never gave a thought to her father's fate.

So Conal lay there brushing tears from his eyes under the sheets and trying to imagine what everlasting fire was like. Everlasting. Never to stop through aeons and aeons. Never. A torment inconceivable; and he could not, by making himself believe, save himself from it. How could you believe if you didn't? And he didn't. Dr Balder had crushed his childhood belief to dust and flung it to the winds on top of the Downs.

Midnight. Conal heard the clock in the tower of All Hallows chime the midnight quarters, and later the single quarter, the two quarters, the three, the hour of one. And the chimes went on, sounding through the soundless hours, while he lay still awake and intermittently crying. Two o'clock; three; and he could only lie there, alone with the darkness and the small hours. He did not hear the clock strike four because he had come upon a sudden solace in the thought that if he didn't believe in the Bible he needn't believe in St Athanasius either. It was an unconvincing solace, and the menace still hung around him in that dark little room, because he could still think that he might be wrong in rejecting both Bible and Athanasius and, if so, then eternal damnation stayed as his sentence. But this half-comforting thought had been enough to enable a child to drop asleep.

He awoke to find himself staring again into the face of last night's terror. The terror was even sharper in the bright sunlight of morning. Excruciating pain for ever and ever ... and ever. From death for thousands and thousands of years, and even then it would still be only beginning. No escaping except by believing in Christianity as simply as Lizetta and Marjorie. But, strive as he might, he couldn't achieve this. Dr Balder's call to him 'to be himself, his own man, independent of all others' had captured his heart. And the Doctor's overwhelming assurance that not even the hills were everlasting, and that Christianity was a thing of yesterday which would go the way of a thousand superstitions before it, had captured his head—or at least had offered him an allegiance easier to accept than the merciless demands of Lizetta, the new Rector, and Athanasius.

Torment for ever and ever ... and still ever, ever, ever.... The terrifying idea was suddenly so powerful that, for sickening moments, he experienced it as fact—a fact in which he dwelt with heart sunken, weakened, and barely beating. Or beating so feebly that its timing was all awry. This imaginative experience was so complete that he, though not yet twelve years old, knew all about a total death-wish: better extinction for ever than a life which threatened such sickening emotions as these. He rose from the chair on which he was sitting in loneliness, because he must move, he must be doing something.... A little movement, a little looking out of the window and the ghastly thing died in him. A total horror had passed, and he was an ordinary child again; nothing remaining but a dread of its recurring. Forget it, forget it, try to forget that such moments were possible. He said nothing to Lizetta, knowing that she had nothing to give him but condemnation. Nor was help likely from Uncle Bertie: no condemnation from him, but in all probability only genial laughter, a pat on the back, and there an end. No solution here in Slings. No lifting of the burden.

It was while he spent the day with these incommunicable thoughts that, of a sudden, at about five in the evening, a new idea stood before him. It came so suddenly that in his present patchwork of muddled thoughts, half disbelieving, half wondering about this disbelief, he was able to wonder if God had sent this idea. *Could he not go to the Rector, lay his trouble before him, and hear what he would say?*

It was no easy step for a boy of eleven years old to set off alone, without a word to anyone, knock at a Rector's door, and ask if he might come and talk. But the Rector had been nice to him at the chancel steps; he had laid a hand on Conal's head and said, 'Bless you'; so Conal did, in the end, slip from the cottage unseen and walk towards the Rectory slowly, doubtfully, and ever more slowly as he drew nearer the house. Would he really touch that knocker or press a bell?

On the doorstep he stood at first doing neither. But at length the memory of last night and the dread of another such night— twilight was already threatening—forbade him to turn away with his mission untried. He pressed the bell nervously, drawing his hand away from it quickly. It rang within the house, and he wished he hadn't touched it. Steps approaching. Heavy steps like a man's. The Rector opened the door.

'Yes?' he inquired, neither surprise nor irritation nor welcome in his eyes. But he quickly recognised his visitor, and the kind smile appeared. 'Oh, we've met, haven't we? In the church. And we talked about smugglers. Did you want to ask me something?'

'Yes, please.'

'Well, come in, come in. This is a most welcome visit from one of my new parishioners. Only three days after my Induction. Absolutely my first visitor! The first that's paid me the tribute of a call.'

'I'm frightfully sorry to trouble you.'

'Trouble? There's no trouble. Only an unexpected pleasure. Come this way. I haven't got things into any sort of order yet. So you'll have to put up with a mess. But I daresay you're used to that. No one cares excessively about tidiness at your age.'

He led him into a littered study where only a knee-hole writing-desk with a swivel chair before it was empty of papers, cases, files, books, and clothes. There were two easy chairs on one of which lay an academic gown, a black cassock, and an academic hood, red-lined, which Conal, who had an interest in such things, identified as an Oxford M.A.'s. Canon Patrice cleared one of the easy chairs for Conal, sat in his own desk-chair, and said with an inviting smile, 'Now tell me all about yourself. I remember you told me a lot about your father and the Indians. It was most interesting.'

Conal, sitting nervously on his chair's brink, stuttered, 'It was your sermon yesterday; could I ask you something about it?'

'Why, certainly! That's absolutely the right sort of thing to do. I wish more people would do it. Go on.'

Conal stumbled on, trying to explain his recent loss of faith and his fear of eternal damnation. He stumbled, like some dim-sighted cripple in a tussocky meadow, over things that Dr Balder had said and things that the Rector had preached. Face flushing and sweat forming on his fiddling hands, he explained that he didn't want to disbelieve, he'd much rather believe simply like other people, but somehow he couldn't. All through the stuttering explanation he saw that the Rector was gazing at him with wonder in his eyes; and because of this he felt the more ashamed of what he was doing, and wished he was away from this room and back in his attic at Slings; or dead.

Perceiving the embarrassment, the Rector said, 'I'm so very, very pleased you've come to me like this. It was absolutely the right thing to do. Go on. Go on. Don't hesitate over anything.'

But Conal was now dumb. He could think of no more to say. And there was a silence between them both, he on the brink of his low chair, the Rector on his higher seat before the desk, with his eyes momentarily on the ground.

The Rector spoke. 'My dear boy, let me say first that I think it truly remarkable for you to have had the courage to come and see me like this. I've been a parson now for nearly thirty years and this is the first time someone of your age has come seeking my help. It delights me. I welcome you. I welcome you.'

But Conal knew that there was no courage in this visit; only fear; only a sickness craving relief. Silent, he sat fiddling with his fingers.

'I believe I know,' the Canon began, 'what to say to you, and it should be nothing but comfort. Great comfort and great happiness. You're young to have known such distress—or perhaps your intelligence is above the average——'

'They don't think that at school,' Conal laughed—or attempted to laugh.

'Schools can get their measurements very wrong. Exams measure memory and hard work much more than intelligence. Your intelligence may be just at the ripe stage to be experiencing these doubts and worries. Did you tell me your name? I forget.'

'Conal Gillie.'

'Well, Conal, I want you to rejoice in what has happened. I believe it's nothing less than the Holy Spirit convincing you that for those who know the whole Gospel there is sin in disbelief. And if I'm right then there's no question of your being condemned to eternal punishment but rather—on the contrary—that you have every reason to believe you are one of God's Chosen. One of his Elect. God is preparing you with the fire of his love for the salvation he has designed for you. Remember what the psalmist said, remember it again and again: "It is good for me that I have been in trouble, that I might learn thy statutes." You must see this troubling of the water in your young soul as a mark of God's favour.'

Conal was not without an answer to this, a troubled answer. 'But if I simply can't believe in God and his interest in me—if I can't *make* myself do it—supposing I never can—aren't I still, as you said in your sermon, kind of—sort of—condemned to perish everlastingly?'

'No, no, because you *will* believe. You must. The Bible is uncompromisingly plain, "There is none other name under heaven whereby we must be saved" and we have Jesus' own words, "No man cometh to the Father but by me". It's not for us to unsay one word that Christ has said——'

Conal's heart plunged into despair again; into his pit. Miserably he murmured, 'But if I don't believe in Christ...?'

'Hush! I hate to hear you even speak those words. Don't you see that God's ways are far beyond the understanding of poor limited creatures like ourselves? If He has ordained since before the beginning of the world that those who should believe in Christ would be destined to salvation and has pronounced a penalty on those who, after hearing the Gospel message, refuse to believe——'

'But it's not fair,' Conal began, daring to interrupt, 'not fair that one should be tormented for all eternity just because——'

The Rector interrupted. 'Dear boy, it's not for the very wisest of us to question one syllable of Christ's words. We must just accept with rejoicing that he has chosen to choose some of us. It isn't we who choose God. It is he who chooses us. The real glory and the mystery are that he has chosen any of us. It's for him to say what he intends to do with the others. Conal, I feel sure that he has chosen you.'

An impatience with this failure to answer his despair with anything but Biblical comments strengthened Conal again to submit his 'But if...' and 'Is it fair...'

'But I can't get it right,' he objected. 'I'm sorry, but it seems unfair—' now it was *he* trying to make things easy for his listener—'it seems rather unfair that those who can't believe it all are to be punished for ever and ever.' So he said, wondering if he sounded obstinate and silly. 'I'm sorry, but I simply can't believe this. I can't feel it's right and fair.'

'God has spoken.'

Firmly the Rector said this but rather to the opposite wall than to the boy sitting before him. It was as if he were asking of the wall how best he could comfort this young visitor without deserting truth. When at Oxford Canon Patrice had at first treated his Schools with some flippancy so that he had got only a third in Classical Mods, but then he had been 'converted' by an earnest undergraduate to Evangelicalism and the Lowest of Low Anglicanism; and, deciding to be ordained, he had studied like a hermit in his cell, like St Jerome with his lion, and taken a first in Theology. Since then he had always been liable, when discoursing, to tumble into theology—remember his *poena damni* and *poena sensus* in that first sermon—and now, even with a schoolboy he must speak a little theology, not in conscious self-display—he was too consecrated a man for that—but it was likely that, deep within him, lingered an unconscious drive towards this weakness.

'Let me try to help you, Conal. Some of the Fathers distinguished between a Visible and an Invisible Church, maintaining that some people who are separated from the Visible Church by what the Fathers called "invincible ignorance"—that's to say, an ignorance which has never been adequately or convincingly enlightened for them—can be, if they are devout and good, members of the Invisible Church and not really separated from the faithful. God must know his own. That is all I can offer you without being disloyal to God's written and spoken word.' He didn't sound quite convinced by the Fathers' magnanimous view, and quickly proceeded, 'But while telling you this I must also solemnly adjure you that, since the whole glorious Faith has always been laid before you by your parents, by the good people with whom you now live, and by your ministers in church, you can hardly claim to be in a state of invincible ignorance.' The affectionate smile was there as he said this. 'But you won't need to, Conal. I'm sure God is calling you. I think it's wonderful that so clear a call should have come at your age. Your ignorance is very "vincible", surely? Look, child, shall we kneel together and pray about it?'

He rose from his desk, knelt facing Conal, joined his hands, and looked upward. Conal, embarrassed, did the same, except that instead of pressing his palms together and looking upward, he continued fumbling with his fingers, while he looked straight ahead at the Rector's clerical collar. And also at his gold watch-chain which had a gold cross hanging from it.

Earnestly, eyes upward, the Rector prayed, kneeling in the midst of the litter in this untidy room. 'O God, Father and lover of us all, I yield thee humble thanks that thou hast vouch-safed to call this thy child to the knowledge of thy grace and faith in thee. Increase this knowledge and confirm this faith in him evermore. Help him to perceive without doubt or difficulty what are thy holy will and commandments. Help him to dread any breach of thy laws, and to remember the warning words of thy holy apostle, "Of how much punishment, suppose ye, shall he be thought worthy, who hath trodden underfoot the Son of God and hath counted the blood of the covenant wherewith he was sanctified an unholy thing. And hath done despite unto the Spirit of Grace. It is a fearful thing to fall into the hands of the living God." '

These menacing words inspired him to rise with the intent to lay a hand of blessing and forgiveness on his young supplicant's head, but Conal, copying him in all things, blundered by trying to rise too, till he perceived what was afoot. Then he kneeled down again, unhappy that by this blunder he had turned something which was meant to be solemn into an untidy affair in an untidy room. With the Rector's hand on his head he heard him saying, 'Defend, O Lord, this thy child with thy heavenly grace that in all his works, begun, continued, and ended in thee he may continue thine for ever.'

When Conal rose he saw that the Rector was smiling down upon him with a manifest love. Sure that this was the end of the visit, he could think of nothing to say except 'Thanks most frightfully. It's really frightfully decent of you.'

To which the Rector responded, 'I feel very, very happy for you, dear boy.' And he accompanied him to the door with a hand on his shoulder.

But Conal, as that door closed behind him, went out into the deepening twilight of the street, and back into the depths of his dread, not only unrescued but deeper immersed. 'There was nothing in all that for me. Not a single thing. If I don't believe and can't believe, I can't help it. They *won't* understand. They just *order* you to believe or get to hell.' The disappointment burgeoned into rebellion. 'I *don't* believe it all, and I *won't*, even if it has all been preached to me a hundred times. And if I don't believe any of it, I needn't worry about it any more. If you don't believe in the Bible, you needn't believe in everlasting fire. And I *don't*.' But that word of the Rector's addressed to the wall rather than to him: 'God has spoken'?

'God has spoken.' And suppose he, Conal Gillie, a nobody in a

village street, was wrong, and God, the All-Powerful, was right ...
then there was no comfort in rebellion; one was back again with
the old sick terror and despair.

6

Evening of the next day, and yet another night to come, a night like the last, a night of tossing dismay. So far from healing his fears the Rector had heightened them, because he was so obviously loving and good. Surely such a devout and holy man must have the *truth*. Evening; dusk foreshadowing the dark; he simply *must* seek comfort somewhere. No answers likely from Lizetta or Uncle Bertie; one voice only that might abate the fears. So Conal stole out from Slings and wandered slowly, hesitantly as on the evening before, towards the terrace of stucco-fronted houses, one of which held Dr Julius Balder. He came to the terrace, walking even more hesitantly now, and looked at the furthest of the ten houses, which was his friend's. There, arched over its doorway, elegantly and conspicuously painted, was the name his friend had given it: 'The Last Lap'. The cheerful acceptance of life and death expressed by these impudent words was not wholly lost upon Conal; it encouraged him—at last—to ring the bell. Quick footsteps, hardly those of a man on his last stretch, or were they those of a man putting on a special spurt for this last lap? They approached the glass-panelled door.

The Doctor opened it. 'Aha! Conal Quintus. Quintus ... um ... what comes next? A surname?'

'Conal Gillie. Conal Quentin Gillie.'

'Yes, of course. I remember. Very kind of a mere bambino like you to come visiting an aged and doddering old bore like me. Hardly anyone but me crosses this threshold. No friends now. Too old.'

'I wanted to ask you something about what you said, but I don't want to disturb you if you're busy. It's not very important.'

'Busy? What should I be busy about in these days apart from preparing for my end; for an orderly and dignified departure from this sorry scheme of things?' Words spoken in jest, and Conal was not to know how near to truth they were, though uttered with a laugh. 'Of course I'll tell you anything about what I said, if I've any recollection what it may have been. What I said—when? Pray, when?'

'About a week ago. On the Downs. And the next morning in the church. You said you didn't believe in Christianity, and that it was all superstition.'

'I'm sure I did.'

'Well, we all went to the Institution and Induction—' Conal was proud to be stating this aright—'of the new Rector.'

'Oh yes; there's a new prophet in Israel. I've heard about him. Canon Somebody, isn't he?'

'Canon Patrice. And he preached his first sermon on Sunday. It was all about Hell. And everlasting punishment.'

'Oh, he's that sort, is he? Heaven help you all.'

Comfort stirred in Conal's heart. 'Yes, everlasting fire.'

'God in his mercy! Come in and tell me all.'

He led the way into his large white living-room, so like an archaeological museum with its many specimens, historic and prehistoric, on tables and walls, in show-cases and in corners, and on all the many overmantel shelves. Conal's eyes shot instantly to that urn of ashes standing in its place of honour on the chimney-breast.

'Well, sit and tell me what absurdities the holy man proclaimed.'

Conal, after admitting apologetically and magnanimously, 'He seems an awfully nice chap,' poured out much of the Canon's sermon, quoting the exact words of the Athanasian Creed which he could do with ease since they'd been reiterating themselves in his head through the tossing nights. 'Perish everlastingly ... everlasting fire ...' and so on.

All that happened was that Dr Balder threw back his head and laughed loud; then said, 'Golly!' And inquired, 'But surely the holy man knows that his Athanasian Creed was never written by poor Athanasius, but in Southern Gaul early in the fifth century?' Was there anything that this astonishing old scholar didn't know? Conal didn't understand why, but he found some comfort in the fact that the Athanasian Creed wasn't written by Saint Athanasius.

It encouraged him to add much that the Rector had said so gently and uncompromisingly in his littered study. The Doctor listened with a patience no less amiable than the Rector's. It was easy to see that he too, whatever his cynicism and ribaldries, was touched that a childish schoolboy should come to his door for help. But there was more to his interest than this. He sat gaping at all that Conal was telling him. And when the boy had finished, he sighed, 'Good God in Heaven above—not that I believe in that Gentleman or that District—but, good God, is it possible that people can say such things? Is it possible?'

Conal said nothing, but waited for him to expound his amazement further.

'Will you tell me,' he resumed, 'or, better, will you ask his Holy Reverence how any decent man can love and worship a God who's going to spend all eternity tormenting poor creatures who were born with the primitive and savage instincts of the brute creation still lingering in them and have failed in their poor little seventy years or so—nearly ninety in mine—to get properly shut of them? A thousand years or so of hearty chastisement for some of the worst tyrants in history might be pleasant to contemplate, if vengeance is what the Reverend's Deity enjoys; but eternity! Eternity! And apparently, according to the creed foisted on poor Athanasius, a like vengeance is to be wreaked on all those who, try as they might, have been quite unable to believe that the Creator of all the stars in the Milky Way—of which our sun is but one star, and a star which gave birth to the planets two thousand million years ago—unable to believe that such a Creator came and lived as a limited man for some thirty years on one of the less distinguished planets called Earth. Eternal agony for all poor disbelievers. And yet—and yet Cardinal Newman believed it and insisted passionately on it, and poor F. D. Maurice, a famous parson, was deprived of his fellowships in Divinity and History because he argued against so monstrous an idea. Quintus, I walk through the wilderness of this world—that's Bunyan—in a state of chronic bewilderment at what intelligent people can believe—or make themselves believe. It pleases me enormously that you at your age, dear Quintus, are experiencing the same bewilderment.'

'Yes, but ...' Conal stammered. ... 'Yes, but, supposing in spite of all, it *is* true. Canon Patrice says it's impossible for us to question anything God has said. And, as you say, terrifically clever people have believed it. Thousands of them.'

'Well, Quintus——'

'Quentin——'

'Who? What?'

'My name is Quentin, not Quintus.'

'No, no. It's Quintus, surely?'

Conal shook his head. 'Quentin.'

'Sure?'

Conal nodded.

'Well, I suppose you know best.... Well, Quentin, if it's all true—and if God *does* exist, I suppose it's conceivable that his outlook differs from mine—all I can say is that, as far as I am concerned, and as far as you are concerned, we should say to him, "The power is yours, sir, and we must accept whatever you choose to do with us, but not one penn'orth of love or worship do we give you because, with all our faults, we know we're better than you. We've no desire to torment the wickedest man for more than perhaps a decent hundred years or so, and no desire to torment any poor unbeliever for ten seconds. So do what you like with us— we'll take it if we have to—but don't for all eternity expect our love." That, my dear Conal Quintillian, is the attitude I would wish to commend to you or any other intelligent youngsters, if it's the last thing I do.'

7

God had spoken, the Rector had spoken, the Doctor had spoken, but the blended counsel of 'all these characters', as the Doctor called them, had but little assuaged the storm and stress in Conal's heart. The Doctor's contemptuous dispersal of all that Creed or Preacher had affirmed had taken some root in the logical regions of his head but it could not wholly undo the habitual beliefs of his short lifetime nor lay to a final sleep old loyalties in his heart. Leave out Lizetta and Marjorie, there was still his father, two continents away in Gondapore, who was a devout and regular churchgoer and, what was more, vehemently defended the missionaries in the Bombay Province, risking unpopularity with most of his fellow Anglo-Indians who liked their chaplains but tended to disparage all the Christian Missions as focuses of subversion and egalitarian ideas that could be troublesome to a ruling race. Never had Conal's father questioned Christianity before him; it was of course unlikely that he would have done so before Conal left India at eight years old; but once since then Father and Mother had come home and had taken him with them to church every Sunday. It did occur to him to write a long letter to his father about his troubles, but all his nature recoiled from the idea. It didn't seem natural to write to parents about the fires of Hell, and, besides, he was not without some shame for his trembling timidity. So, far from writing a letter to his father, he felt sure that he would never, never, not to the end of his days, make any mention of unbelief to his father if he thought it would hurt him. He would hide it from his parents, and go to church with them silently, for ever.

Sunday had been the occasion of the Rector's terrifying sermon, Monday had seen Conal's despairing visit to the Rectory, Tuesday his equally despairing visit to Dr Balder, and now on Wednesday he still did not know where he was or what more he could do in search of comfort. So he decided there was nothing to do but to live alone with bewilderment and secret terrors.

Four more days and a new and exciting affair thrust this despair aside. Sunday and the family—or at least Marjorie, Conal, and Lizetta—went to church as usual for Matins at eleven; and under the church porch, on the very threshold of the church, they were met by Mrs Wrenne-Chamberlin, a neighbour and friend. Mrs Wrenne-Chamberlin, a large lady and as large in will and dominance as in frame, was standing there with anything but Christian love on her handsome face; indignation rather, and a resolve to speak of it to all who passed her. It was indeed a handsome face with flashing brown eyes, imperial nose, and lips as ready for stern injunctions and objurgations as lips could be. The dominance in her face and features had been noted by Uncle Bertie the first time he cast a glance at her. 'Hmm...' was his comment, and 'Hmm ...' again ... followed by, 'What that old battle-cruiser says, *goes*.'

What she said to Lizetta now was, 'Have you seen what's happened in there? It's a perfect scandal. I'm going to speak to Sir Harman about it, and I hope you'll support me. It's he who's landed us with this new Rector. And we surely have some right to say what we'll put up with. I'm sure we've not got to take just what's given us. I thought at the Induction that I was going to like this Canon Patrice, but after last Sunday's sermon—and now! I didn't care at all for what he said about smuggling new forms of faith and practice into our church. What we've had for all my time has been good enough for me. Anyhow, I'm not putting up with this without a fight. I don't know how many are ready to swallow it, but if there are many, there's going to be a split in our church.'

'Why, what's happened?' asked Lizetta. 'What's the trouble?' Obviously she had not been the least troubled by last Sunday's sermon with its hearty condemnation of unbelievers.

'Trouble?' echoed Mrs Wrenne-Chamberlin. 'Just go in and see. I don't know how people dare to do such things.'

They hastened in with a high curiosity and at first observed nothing unusual because there was a large congregation taking their places and so obscuring chancel and sanctuary. But under Lizetta's leadership they found seats in the second pew from the front (because of the remarkable and universal fact that, however large an audience in hall or church, few will immodestly put themselves in front rows). Seated in front they saw what had ignited the fires of Mrs Wrenne-Chamberlin's wrath. The altar in the sanctuary was bare. It had been denuded of brass cross, brass candlesticks, dorsal and riddel curtains, and liturgically coloured frontal that had always screened its table-legs. There was now nothing on it but the 'fair white linen cloth' prescribed by the Prayer Book and a bowl holding a bunch of flowers. For the reredos, instead of the dorsal curtain, the old arched panel with the Decalogue and the two smaller panels with Creed and Pater-noster were back in place below the east window. They must have been resurrected from some muniment room among the vestries.

'My goodness me!' Lizetta whispered to Marjorie; and then, 'Surely he has no right to do that?'

An excited woman behind Lizetta, whom she'd met only at shop counters in Wedgery, touched her on the shoulder and asked of her turning face, 'What do you think of that?'

A silly question, Conal thought, because a detailed answer would be impossible in this religious silence.

Lizetta could give her nothing but a bewildered lift of eyebrows and shoulders. For her part the woman added, with palpable pleasure, 'There'll be trouble. Trouble, mark me words.'

All through the service there were other alterations. First there was no processional cross to lead the choir from their vestry. The church's fine processional cross, hitherto affixed to the eastern end of the choir stalls, was gone from sight. Behind the choir the Rector came in without stole or scarf, wearing only his academic hood. Neither Rector nor choir turned to the east while reciting the Creed. Coming from his stall to the pulpit for the sermon, the Rector did not bow to the altar before leaving it but sauntered across it as casually as if it had been the sideboard in his dining-room.

But the sermon which he now preached was as unexpected as that of last Sunday, and very different; so different that its effect on Conal was almost a total opposite of that produced by last Sunday's solemn and shattering dissertation on the Four Last Things, Death, Judgment, Heaven and Hell. Extraordinary: here was the same voice—a beautiful instrument perfectly managed—but speaking words that achieved so different a result that it always remained a small factor in Conal's thoughts, a factor in full conflict with its predecessor. And here in it, strangely too, came the name 'Athanasius' but an Athanasius in a new robe, not black and terrifying but bright, inspiring, a shining hero.

The sermon began with no allusions to the changes he had introduced; it was as if, in his view, these had been so necessary that they required neither explanation nor apology. Almost all he did was to tell a story. But he told it as only a skilled orator could, extracting from it every value and power it possessed, often not without humour, not without histrionic pauses, and most notably not without smiles of affection for his audience. Soon the audience was so captured that it had forgotten about that naked table in the sanctuary and about any ceremonies it had been denied. As for Conal, these ceremonial and ritual alterations meant nothing; he had little apprehension of what was High, what Low, and what Broad in the Church.

Canon Patrice had begun with no text but had waited, as usual, for all to be comfortably seated and for silence to fill the church; then straightway opened his story. 'One day in the dawn of the fourth century there was playing beneath the Egyptian skies of Alexandria a small boy. He was playing at Baptisms. One after another he gathered his friends together and—let us hope it did not sound so profane to God as it may do to us—proceeded to baptise them in the name of the Father and of the Son and of the Holy Ghost.'

Conal's eyes were now fixed upon the pulpit; and so were everyone else's; none, whatever their age, were above being alerted by this 'Once upon a time'. The preacher knew that he had won them, so allowed himself the dramatic pause, and continued, 'The small boy's interest in matters ecclesiastical became later a distinct vocation so that when he was about sixteen he attracted the notice of the old Bishop of Alexandria, Alexander, who took him into his household, made him his secretary, and determined that he, like the child Samuel, should be "lent to the Lord". The boy's name was Athanasius, and we are told that he was small of stature but "of a countenance radiant like an angel's". This may be hagiology, of course; I just give you what we've been told. Now, working in a church in Alexandria, was a parish priest called Arius. Note the name well: Arius. He was a tall person with a melancholy face and something sinister perhaps in his manner, but with a voice of great sweetness. One writer tells us that he had attracted seven hundred ladies to his way of thinking. "Seven hundred virgins" is the way the great Gibbon puts it.'

At this a low titter rippled through the church, and Canon Patrice accepted it with an accompanying smile; which surprised some because he now stood in his pulpit before them as an extremely 'Low Churchman', and they imagined that all puritans of this type, unlike 'High Churchmen', could be shocked by laughter in church.

His smiled abandoned, he went on, 'I suppose few people in the year 313 A.D. could have foretold that the small youth in Alexander's household and the tall priest were going to fight for the possession of the whole Christian Church. But so it was: the fuse was lit, the train fired, and the explosion created by the old Bishop Alexander himself. He issued a Charge to his clergy in which he insisted on Our Lord's absolute equality with the Father. And Arius, the tall priest, startled the world by accusing the old bishop of heresy and giving his own version of the relation of the Son to the Father. The doctrine that Arius promulgated, known for ever after as Arianism, was plausible: it taught that Christ was not co-eternal and co-equal with the Father, but the first and greatest of his creatures, created, if you will, before all Time and invested with the attributes of Godhead. It was symbolised by the sentence, *There was once a time when Christ was not.*

'Arius, having thrown down his challenge and published his faith, showed himself a master of publicity and propaganda. He invented all sorts of catch-phrases and rhymes for circulating among the people, till at last the boys in the market place, the labourers in the fields and the sailors on the quays of Alexandria were singing and bandying light rhymes about the Holy Trinity.

'Instantly the penetrating intellect of young Athanasius in Alexander's court saw that Christianity was at stake. He saw that this subordination of Christ to the Father could make him, not God, but a vulgar heathen demi-god, and if Christ was not of the same essence—or *substance*, as the word became known—but only of like essence, then he was little more than ourselves who are created in the likeness of God and have seeds of the divine within us. And his Church would die. Focusing on this vital point, he decided that some word proclaiming Christ's identity of essence with the Father must become the battle-cry of those who would fight Arius.

'Urged on by this fervid youngster, who was now a deacon, old Alexander flung back Arianism at its author as a pernicious heresy. Warfare was declared, and the Church split like a mirror.'

Split—Conal recalled Mrs Wrenne-Chamberlin's words 'There's going to be a split in our church' and, liking drama or melodrama, foresaw vaguely a local fight in Wedgery which would be like a little picture of the great battle in Christendom sixteen hundred years before. His interest, well alive already, quickened yet more.

The Rector's next words produced, if not laughter, a plenitude of brooding smiles over the faces of his audience. 'The Emperor, Constantine, sent a charming letter to both Alexander and Arius, a letter exactly typical of most Governments yesterday, today, and forever, since their attitudes must usually be weighted in favour of expediency rather than truth. He exhorted them to peace and mutual toleration. But this was only like a jug of water thrown into a house on fire, so Constantine, the man who had made his Empire officially Christian, decided on a new thing. There should be a great council of all the bishops in the world. Away went his messengers over Europe, Africa, Asia Minor—even Roman Britain—summoning these rulers of Christendom to the Emperor's palace at Nicaea, till, as one ancient chronicler says—"the highways were covered with bishops galloping".'

Understanding like any good orator that an introduction of rhymed verse into an address will always, if well spoken, grip an audience and deepen their silence, he quoted:

> 'He named a trysting day
> And bade his messengers ride forth,
> East and west and south and north,
> To summon his array.'

The words worked their spell and he continued, 'You can still see on the shores of the Ascanian Lake a few broken pillars which mark the palace of Constantine at Nicaea; and to its great hall, in the year 325, came the bishops of the world. It was a fine scene.

The seats of the bishops were along the sides of the apartment, and a golden chair was placed for the Emperor. Among the bishops were many scarred old confessors, victims of the late persecutions, and many of younger blood who had only seen the winters of persecution made glorious by this summer sun of Constantine. But most arresting of all young persons there was the youth of puny stature with the face of animated beauty; Bishop Alexander's young deacon, Athanasius.'

By now Conal was wholly identified with this brilliant and courageous youth, aspiring to be exactly like him (except for the puny stature) and to be doing battle for great truths. This was very muddling, because there still lay deep within him, and now momentarily remembered, the terror which could be allayed only by disbelieving all that the radiant young deacon preached.

But this muddle was overlaid and postponed by the vivid picture which the Rector was now painting. 'A signal announced the coming of the Emperor. He entered and all the bishops rose and gazed with a thrill at this entrance of the Augustus into a Christian synod. The tall commanding figure, the purple robe and the diadem (so we are told) were less impressive than the downcast look, the blush of diffidence, and the standing position which he maintained till his fathers-in-God motioned to him to be seated.

'Then the momentous debate began. I will not trouble you with details. Enough to say that the storm threw up one great word around which thereafter the controversy beat: *Homoousion.*' The preacher repeated the great word. '*Homoousion. Homo* is the Greek for "same" and *ousia* for "essence" or "being"; so the word means "of the same essence" or, as we are familiar with it in the Nicene Creed, "of one substance". Young Athanasius saw that it was the only word that could close the door on Arius for ever. Arius would probably have accepted *Homoi-ousion*, "of like substance", but the bishops, largely inspired by the impetuous young deacon, stood out for "of one substance". There was only a difference of one Greek letter between these two words, and this the smallest letter in the alphabet, the *iota* "i"—which gave Gibbon the chance for some characteristic satire when he wrote that the universal Church went to battle and split in two over a diphthong. But greatness is never to be measured by size. Athanasius saw deeper than Edward Gibbon. He saw that with that *iota* Christ stood or fell. If *Homoousion* was beaten by *Homoi-ousion*, then Christianity in a few years would be nothing more than a legend. Finally the Council of Nicaea inserted *Homoousion* into the Creed, and we say it day after day; we have said it this morning and the world will go on saying it till the Church need be no more.

'But Arius and his followers were not defeated. They proceeded now by secret diplomacy and backstairs intrigue to overthrow their conquerors and, most of all, they beat up towards the man they most feared, Athanasius. He, though still only thirty years old, was now Bishop of Alexandria and primate of all Egypt, in succession to his old patron, Alexander. Alexander had died with the ominous words on his lips: "Athanasius, thou shalt not escape."'

Here a pause that the congregation might wonder what menace these death-bed words implied.

'Well, Athanasius' enemies manufactured a case against him, accusing him of murdering a man called Arsenius; but Athanasius contrived to produce the man Arsenius in court, alive and well, which rather upset the prosecution.' This elicited a general but properly muted laugh, and the preacher accepted it with a pleased smile, and hastened on.

'The young bishop left his enemies in scorn and, after his direct fashion, took ship straight for Constantinople to lay his innocence before Constantine. We read that he stopped the Emperor in the middle of the road as he was riding into his capital. The Emperor was startled. Who was this small man who dared to stand in his path? When told it was Athanasius, poor Constantine who, as I have hinted, only wanted peace at any price, looked at him as much as to say, "Art thou he that troubleth Israel?" and tried to pass him in silence. But Athanasius was never a man you could brush past easily. The Emperor consented to accord him a trial, but, perhaps thinking that such a firebrand would be best out of the way, condemned him to exile.

'By such methods Arius and the Arians began to carry all before them, and at last Arius convinced the Emperor of his orthodoxy, and Constantine ordered another Alexander, the venerable Bishop of Constantinople, to receive him into communion in his church on the Golden Horn. But Alexander, old veteran of the wars, declared that he was a guardian of the Faith proclaimed at Nicaea, and that he would not admit the inventor of heresy through his doors. Jubilant friends of Arius declared they would bring him into the church by force, and sadly the old prelate turned away. "He bade farewell", says one old writer, "and took refuge in God." He advanced to his chancel, flung himself down on the pavement and prayed, "If Arius be brought to Communion tomorrow, let thy servant depart." Such was the prayer of Alexander on the vigil of his Communion Service, and that same evening, when Arius, flushed with triumph, was walking and conversing with his friends, he suddenly stopped short, withdrew from his companion and dropped dead.

'So runs the old story.'

Artist that he was, Canon Patrice fiddled with the notes on his lectern and laid one note aside, as if suggesting that he left it to his people to determine whether they believed this story or not. He did however mention, because he could not resist it, the comment of his sly favourite Gibbon that 'the strange circumstances of his death might excite a suspicion that the orthodox saints had contributed, more efficaciously than by their prayers, to deliver the church from the most formidable of her enemies'.

This offered, and eliciting the smiles, he again hurried on, 'I wish I had time to tell you how Athanasius, because of his loyalty to the *Homoousion*, suffered exile after exile, always returning in triumph while the whole of Alexandria streamed out like another Nile—I am quoting a picturesque chronicler—to meet him. One picture I will give you.

'Arianism had covered the world like a sea, save for one rock, the ageing little figure of Athanasius, Bishop of Alexandria, supported by his faithful Alexandrians. Constantius, a successor of Constantine, was resolved to drive the intransigent Athanasius from his stronghold. And one night Athanasius is keeping a solemn vigil in the church of St Thomas, and his faithful are with him. About midnight there is an uproar without and five thousand soldiers attack the church. At once Athanasius ascends his throne and orders the deacon to read the hundred-and-seventh psalm: "O give thanks unto the Lord for he is gracious and his mercy endureth for ever". There is no doubt that he put himself in the place of honour that the soldiers might take him and spare his flock. The doors burst open, the soldiers rushed in, the people fled, calling on Athanasius to fly with them. "I do not stir," he said, "till you are all away safely"; and he was finally dragged away by his monks. It is always believed that the soldiers chose to be strangely blind.

'So Athanasius fled to the desert of Upper Egypt, the Thebaid, taking with him his flag, the *Homoousion*. He was unbeaten and unbowed, and from this lair in the desert he directed such of the Church as were still true by letters of instruction and encouragement. He was known as "The Invisible Patriarch", and for six years he lay hid, but powerful. Thus was given to all nations and languages the famous phrase, "*Athanasius contra mundum*, Athanasius against the world."'

(Let all ecclesiastical terrors stand aside and be forgotten awhile for Conal's heart was now crowded with a surging aspiration to be just such another as Athanasius, fighting for a truth which the world rejected and returning to—well, somewhere—with all his followers who loved him streaming out to welcome him. He was only a beginner in Latin but always the mere sounds of the old language rolled and resounded in his mind; and these words, splendid in English, 'Athanasius against the world', in their Latin —at any rate this morning as Canon Patrice spoke them— '*Athanasius contra mundum*'—were a trumpet call to arms: '*Conal Quentin contra mundum*' sounded well.)

And there was another phrase—or sentence—from the Canon which pierced to Conal's heart. 'It's an old adage,' he was saying, 'that the darkest hour precedes the dawn; and that was very much what happened here. Constantius died to be succeeded by Julian the Apostate who sought to re-establish the old paganism. At once the Church, always at her best when the world is deserting her, the Enemy at her gates, and she fighting for her life, now chose to forget her differences, close her ranks and stand ready. Arianism which had only flourished with the support of the mighty began gradually to yield ground to the more lifegiving faith of Athanasius. In times of trouble men want Christ to be God.'

Doubtless this sentence struck home in many a heart hearing it, but it found no more wistful response than in Conal's who was now recalling all his troubles. So strange that the voice which had plunged him into despair should now be filling him with excitement, comfort, and happy dreams. 'If I could go back and believe in this Christianity of Athanasius, in spite of old Balder, I should be in no danger of eternal punishment.' But soon this comfort lost its completeness. Conal, brought up as he had been by churchgoing parents and within a churchgoing foster family, must believe in altruism as an idea and even if his practice of it up to now had been somewhat limited and unremarkable, it was not non-existent. It quickly showed him that while he was 'believing' properly and so escaping the fires of hell, they would still be there for all those poor persons who simply couldn't believe; and he didn't feel happy with this. The only solution, it seemed, would be to believe in Christianity but *not* in Hell-fire. But was this possible? Would it be allowed?

To this question he had no answer. Nothing to do but go on listening to what the Canon was saying. 'Athanasius returned to Alexandria for the triumph of his life. The whole tumultuous city, men, women, and children, flocked out to greet him, singing hymns and psalms and the *Te Deum*.' (Conal, listening, was picturing just such a triumph for himself, though he was modest enough to leave out the psalms and the *Te Deum*.) 'At the great Council of Constantinople, years later, after the death of Julian and the failure of his gallant attempt to restore the old gods, the *Homoousion* was finally ratified.'

Finally ratified. This could have been the end, but the Canon did not turn away to repeat the usual ascription after a sermon; he just stood looking at his congregation. A few people wondered. But in fact this was no more than an orator's desire to frame within a silence some closing words yet to come. The artifice succeeded probably with all in the church, it certainly succeeded with Conal, for these final words were to echo within him for ever after; even more than '*Athanasius contra mundum*'.

'"Of one substance". Cold hard words,' said the Canon, 'dry bones; not the words to stir a man's soul? Well, I don't know.... Once a poet stood in a church and looked up at a faded and torn piece of cloth hanging from a dry and bleached old pole, high up in the chancel. And in his heart he thought:

A moth-eaten rag on a worm-eaten pole—
It doesn't look likely to stir a man's soul,
But it's the deeds that were done 'neath that moth-eaten rag,
When the pole was a staff and the rag was a flag.'

That was all; but it left a flag flying (alongside opposing flags) in one young listener's heart.

8

Meantime Mrs Wrenne-Chamberlin was on the march. Or perhaps we can adapt the Canon's quotation and say, 'She'd made her messengers ride forth, East and west and south and north, To summon her array.' This would have its aptness because she had also 'named a trysting day'. From Sir Harman Drood, patron of the living who, in her words, had 'with typical but unpardonable indifference foisted an extreme Low Churchman upon a parish accustomed to higher things', she had secured the promise of a 'parish meeting' in Drood Place itself on a Friday less than twenty days after the appearance of the Ten Commandments behind the altar. More surely than any of her messengers she had fared forth, east, west, south and north, within the parish and beyond its fringes, like a wandering breeze raising its little dust-storms everywhere. It was she who arrived one morning on the doorstep of Slings, in tailor-made tweeds and a straw hat as large as an open parasol. Lizetta took her into the living-room where Conal and Marjorie sat playing draughts, and before Lizetta could send them away Mrs Wrenne-Chamberlin was in full spate.

'I know you are only here for holidays but you are householders here and have a full right to speak your minds. I shall want both you and your husband to be present on Friday because we've got to show ourselves in large numbers. It's amazing how——'

'I'm afraid my husband——' Lizetta began—but without further success.

'It's amazing how many people say they don't mind, one way or the other, what the Rector gets up to, and they may turn up to oppose any protest. They say they like the Canon and his sermons—incidentally he's no canon but only a prebendary—' this left all three of her listeners in the dark—'but that isn't the point. As a person I quite like him too and have no doubt that he's a good and holy man. For all I know, he's a saint. I thought that was a wonderful sermon he preached on Ahasuerus—or Athanasius, was it? Yes, Athanasius fighting the world, but it made me suspect that the Canon intends to do some fighting of the world, and two can play at that game. These are not feudal times when the Lord of the Manor has the sole right to say what sort of rector we shall have. The days of feudalism have gone by, but no one seems to have told this to Sir Harman. *He's* satisfied with Canon Patrice, and imagines he's done his job quite well by providing us with a canon who's considered a fine preacher. But it's the principle, the principle, Mrs, Mrs . . .'

'Mrs Sheridan,' Lizetta supplied.

'Yes, Mrs Sheridan. The principle of the thing, and if we're to assert our rights we've got to make a good showing on Friday. You and your husband——'

'I'm afraid my husband——'

'The Bishop's going to be there. He's a great friend of Sir Harman's. Believe it or not, Sir Harman is surprised by the trouble in the village and doesn't know how to deal with it, so he's asked the Bishop, who's a frequent visitor to Drood Place, to come and talk to the people, and the Bishop's coming'll attract a lot of people, so it's tremendously important that those of us who want our services to be as they've always been, not all that High but at least——'

In point of fact, the Canon's predecessor *had* been all that High but, being also a high-born gentleman like his new patron, he had arranged a most gentlemanly compromise between the High and the Low in Wedgery for his services in All Hallows.

'I will certainly come, Mrs Wrenne-Chambers,' Lizetta managed to intrude into the cascade, but it was a cascade which so overwhelmed her that she got the lady's name wrong, 'but I don't think my husband'll be able to manage it. Not on Friday.' Thus she suggested that at three on a Friday afternoon Uncle Bertie would be deep in business instead of enjoying his pipe, his paper, and an intermittent doze in a garden chair, after resolving to 'have nothing to do with a crowd of cackling women'. Before this morning's invasion by Mrs Wrenne-Chamberlin he had heard in the Brotherhood bars of her campaign, and had returned to Slings calling her, with a slight mixture of metaphors, a game old bird but God save him from all such domineering, dictatorial, bossy and cocky old cows.

This attribution of bossiness the lady justified now for she insisted, 'No, oh no. You must *make* him come. We must have a good showing of the men if Sir Harman and the Bishop are to be impressed.'

It was here that Conal, who'd been listening with an interest far above Marjorie's, spoke. 'Couldn't *I* come instead Lizetta?' Several motives were behind this seemingly considerate offer. Along with the delightful prospect of a public row there was some hope in him that the meeting might touch on the problems that so troubled him; there was a driving desire to see and enter Drood Place, the ancestral home of the famous Droods whose murals hung about the chancel walls; and some readiness to look upon the Bishop again. A bishop was a bishop, and as natural an attraction as a celebrated lead, actor or actress, in a theatre. 'I'd love to come,' he said.

'*You?*' This was a sneer from Marjorie.

'But you're only a child,' Lizetta reminded him. She hadn't dared remind him, before so formidable a Christian as Mrs Wrenne-Chamberlin, that it was only the other day he'd been announcing his disbelief in religion—or, more probably, she had forgotten all about this.

Mrs Wrenne-Chamberlin smiled genially at his offer, but her smile said the same as Lizetta.

'But I'm going to be confirmed next year,' he submitted to them both, he too forgetting, in his desire to see Drood Place and the religious row, all about his current apostasy. What he did remember was the qualification required from those desiring to be confirmed. 'Daddy must think I've arrived at years of discretion, if he wants me confirmed.'

Mrs Wrenne-Chamberlin laughed loud at this, while Lizetta, disapproving, told him to keep quiet and not be silly; to which he objected, 'But it must be so, or he couldn't think I'm fit to be confirmed. That's what the Prayer Book says.' And to Marjorie, who had grumbled, 'Goo' gracious, 'joo ever hear anyone like him?' he recommended, 'You shut up. Just because you aren't at years of discretion, it doesn't follow that I'm not.'

Mrs Wrenne-Chamberlin laughed gaily again, while Marjorie

snorted, 'Don't talk such stuff. You're only six months older than me'; and Conal found what he thought adequate replies, 'Yes, but you can learn a lot in six months. Besides you're only a girl.'

This last remark, in the presence of Mrs Wrenne-Chamberlin and Lizetta, didn't seem to him tactless, partly because he'd forgotten that they'd once been little girls, but far more because he couldn't imagine these two formidable ladies in any such character.

It was all true about his father. The Collector and his wife were of a High Church persuasion, remarkably so for India, and they had suggested to the Sheridans that at twelve years old Conal could well be confirmed and enjoy the advantage of attending Communion. They would like, they had even said, that before he entered the age of puberty he should be made ready to receive the grace of the Blessed Sacrament. All of which sounded very High to Lizetta.

By this time Mrs Wrenne-Chamberlin had decided that even if Conal was only a schoolboy he would add something to the mass of her supporters and his age might be overlooked in the crowd. So she said, 'Of course he can come. He has every right to come.' Which prompted Marjorie to demand 'And may I come too? I'm longing to see that gorgeous bishop again. I thought he was absolutely divine.'

'Yes, he is rather exceptionally good-looking,' Mrs Wrenne-Chamberlin allowed. 'He's said to be the handsomest bishop on the bench. And the best dressed.'

'Nobody *could* be handsomer,' Marjorie argued. 'Oh, I *must* come.'

'But you won't be confirmed for ages,' Conal pointed out to her, glad of this opportunity to put her in her place.

And Mrs Wrenne-Chamberlin agreed at first with this discrimination. 'Yes, I think we must limit attendance to the confirmed, or those about to be confirmed—unless, of course, your father is very busy and there'll be no one to look after you. Would you like to bring her, Mrs Sheridan?'

Marjorie urged her mother, 'Oh yes, Ma.'

'Well, her father'll certainly be occupied,' Lizetta suggested, while visualising him asleep on his hammock chair with the newspaper or a book on his knees.

'Then bring her along, of course, child though she is. After all, Our Lord did say, "Of such is the Kingdom of Heaven".'

That Marjorie should be typical of the Kingdom of Heaven Conal found about as difficult to believe as so many other things in the Bible. He could only imagine that this lady was 'trying to be funny'. As, in fact, she was.

'So that's settled,' she pronounced. 'You'll all come.'

'Oh, hurray!' said Marjorie. 'I shall see my beloved Bishop again.'

9

To approach Drood Place you passed between tall urn-capped
piers and wrought-iron gates flung wide. Twelve feet up the drive
a lodge, cased in eighteenth-century white stucco, watched the
gates. The drive was a broad avenue of ancient chestnuts, more
than a hundred yards long and providing, since it was as straight
and unbending as justice itself, a vista at its far end of the great
park but no sign of the great house. You had to turn a sharp
elbow at its end to come upon the mansion's south-western
front. Thus it was an odd fact that Conal and Marjorie, though
they had been coming on holiday visits to Wedgery for years, had
never seen the splendid façade of Drood Place. Lizetta had seen
it only once, on the occasion of a Conservative Garden Party.
Conal as they turned the corner at the avenue's end thought
it the grandest house he had seen since gazing at Buckingham
Palace, the King's home, from the Mall.

'A little sister of Buckingham Palace' he called it, and thought
the remark clever.

Like the lodge by the gates it was now rendered in white stucco
of the eighteenth century; three storeys high, it had a pillared
and pedimented portico reaching above the first two storeys. The
windows within this great portico were tall and graceful: he was
not to know till later that they were 'golden section' windows.
The windows above this floor and pediment were perfect squares.
They were windows of rooms beneath a great roof of Horsham
slates which, as ever in this downland country exposed to strong
southerly winds from the sea, was quilted with lichens and mosses
of orange, golden and mimosa hues.

'Quite a nice little bungalow,' said Conal, and again thought
that his wit was in fair condition this afternoon.

Marjorie's wonder and excitation were limited to 'Gosh!'

The whole of this majestic front had a terrace before it, over
which it gazed at the park, the first half of which was tennis and

croquet lawns stretching to a ha-ha or sunken fence, beyond which it became a heaving parkland timbered with lonely elms and planes and cedars, till it rose to become a dense woodland forming a dark green arc against the sky.

Beyond the mansion itself you could see coach-house and coachman's lodge, stabling for many horses, brewery and laundry —the whole array surmounted by a clock-tower with a weather-vane. Three o'clock was the hour of the meeting, and the clock struck three as they approached. Fortunately it was three minutes fast.

It was a thrill to enter through the high door behind the stout pillars of the portico. They entered a huge square hall which, apart from one small table, was furnished only with deep oblong pictures of knightly Droods and noble dames in costumes dating from Tudor times.

A footman in what looked like semi-evening dress, swaying his white gloves among the visitors, pointed towards a door and said, 'Please go into the Parlour, madam. All the ladies and gentlemen are in the Parlour.'

The Parlour proved to be a room as large as the Great Entrance Hall, and that it should be called 'The Parlour' was a surprise to Conal who had always heard from Lizetta that only the 'common people' called their chief sitting-room a parlour. Here was no small sitting-room but a vast chamber with tall windows looking out through their brocaded curtains at terrace, park, and distant wood. There were over a hundred people in the room, many sitting on an army of white-and-gold chairs, while a minority stood against the walls between elegant pieces of antique furniture: console cabinets, Gesso chests, hanging pier-glasses and a wide Georgian sideboard with a crowned urn at each end. Round the ceiling ran a decorative frieze in white and gold. Parlour! State Room of Drood Place, or the White and Gold Ballroom, would have seemed a better name.

So warm and wide had the preliminary propaganda been that there were many faces among this audience that one would never have expected to see at a religious meeting. Probably persons who had come mainly to see a show; most of them males, and even grinning males.

There could be no dais on the polished wood floor, and Sir

Harman sat behind a small pedestal table. The Bishop sat on his right hand. The Bishop may, or may not, have been, in Mrs Wrenne-Chamberlin's words, 'The handsomest bishop on the bench' but he fitted well in this handsome chamber, with his episcopal gaiters and apron, his jewelled ring, his golden chain and pectoral cross, and the strong, crimped silver hair crowning all. He was a man of excellent height and figure and so finely tailored that unkindly persons suggested he was too conscious (for a bishop) of his appearance and thought it well worth the finest tailoring, and his silver hair well worth the most careful dressing; but if this was a truth, it was the only weakness the many could find in him.

Conal had been instructed by Lizetta to stand against the wall among other males and leave the white-and-gold chairs to ladies. Marjorie chose to stand beside him so that she could see better.

When it seemed that all who would come were present, Sir Harman rose. Expensively dressed, and with his erect military carriage, he fitted in the room almost as well as the Bishop. His language too was of an expensive kind and matched well with the dignified ornaments around him.

'Ladies and gentlemen,' he began, 'it is, I think, most kind of you all to come here, and it shows a most praiseworthy interest in our parochial affairs. As you will all know, there has been some opposition in the parish against certain changes introduced by our new Rector—though, so far as I can understand, the opposition is by no means universal.'

It was soon clear to many, if not to Conal, that he was in some disarray about the whole business. Belonging himself to none of the competing parties in the Church, he regarded the tenets of all with an easy indifference. And with an equal benevolence. But it was not so with many others in the room. Religious differences bulked large in these first years of the century. He proceeded:

'Here perhaps I should say that Canon Patrice expressed his readiness to be here with us and to listen to any who were upset by any course he had felt compelled to pursue, but I submitted to him that, as chairman of our little causerie, I should be obliged to ask him to withdraw while we discussed any differences of opinion about his work among us—his devoted work, I am sure —and he decided that in these circumstances, there was perhaps little point in his attending. I am however in the happy position of having at my side our Bishop—may I say our well-loved Bishop (Applause)—who at his own suggestion offered to be with us. We shall be greatly helped, I know, by his pastoral advice. But before asking him to open our discussion, I would like to say, if you will allow me, a few words about my position as the so-called "lord of the manor" who has the serious duty of appointing the rector of our church—our so beautiful church.' He paused and looked through one of the tall windows as if he could see the stolid defiant fortress tower of All Hallows. 'It was not built by my ancestors—I wish I could claim it had been—it only came into the possession of my family after the destruction of the monasteries by Henry VIII—and what you feel about that, Bishop, I don't know, (Laughter) but it has been in our hands ever since the good—or bad—King Harry. (More laughter.) Thus we have owned for some four hundred years the advowson or right of presentation to the benefice, and I doubt if these Tudor ancestors of mine thought too badly of King Harry. Now, Bishop, may I ask you to guide us in the way we should go?'

The Bishop rose from behind the small table, revealing to all how tall he was—and, indeed, how well accoutred from head to foot. 'If you will stand, ladies and gentlemen,' he said, 'we will begin by prayer'; at which Sir Harman explained apologetically, 'Oh yes, I forgot that.'

All stood and slightly bent their heads, while the Bishop recited 'O God, forasmuch as without thee...' and other appropriate collects. Prayers over, he said with a close-lipped smile that projected over the room his sympathy and affection for all, 'Do be seated.'

All who could sat down and stared at him.

And he began, 'Let me say that I completely understand what has brought you all together today. Your new incumbent whom it fell to my lot to institute, and entrust with the care of souls, in your lovely church a few weeks ago is a man of deep convictions and considerable theological scholarship, and these have determined him to make some alterations in the adornments of your altar—or Holy Table, as he would call it—and in the nature of your services. Well, I am grateful to my old friend, Sir Harman, for having asked me to come here and speak to you; though it may surprise you to hear that there is hardly anything your bishop can do in the matter.' Here the tight-lipped smile broadened across his face. 'My position is simply one of highly dignified impotence. (Laughter.) And that goes for every bishop in our remarkable country. Nothing is more completely illogical and English, or more successful in its illogicality, than the position of your bishops when it's a matter of appointing a new incumbent. Your bishops are rather like your monarch, in that they reign and are greatly reverenced—at least I hope so—but do not rule and can hardly interfere with anything at all—overtly, at any rate, though they may sometimes get up to something covertly. We bishops have perhaps a shade more power than our monarchs in that we can dismiss a minister in an extreme case of heresy. His Majesty the King, God bless him, can't do this with his Prime Minister or any other of his ministers though I daresay there've been occasions when he very much wished he could. (Laughter again.) Someone has said that the best of men may have overcome the "ape and tiger in Man", but that there is another animal in him who is not so easily dismissed: the donkey. How far this interesting creature survives within His Majesty's ministers today (Loud and appreciative laughter) it is not for me to say. Or how far he is represented on the episcopal bench.' By now he had his audience continually laughing. 'But let me try to show you, if I may, how this apparently absurd business of private patronage to a living—if you will forgive me, Harman—and the apparently absurd limitation of episcopal authority in such goings-on, has really worked to the advantage of the Church that we all love. It has meant that our parish priests have been men limited to no one pattern but have been men of all types and schools of thought. And comprehension of many types, I hope I may suggest to you, is one of the glories of the Church of England. (Dutiful applause.) Did you know that more than half the parish priests in England have been appointed to their benefices by this system of private patronage, though with the passing of the centuries the patrons may have changed into institutions or colleges, or cathedral chapters or the Crown itself—or even, here and there, a bishop? But at first this system of patronage was almost everywhere associated with the land. The churches would be built on their estates by the squires and lords of the manor, such as

Sir Harman here, and the right of patronage would be a form of property which the owner could bequeath to a son or a nephew or perhaps—in a death-bed hope of salvation—to some monastery, which has today become a cathedral chapter.'

Here there was a moment's hesitation while, like the Chairman, he turned and looked towards a window with its view of the park, which the sun was now brilliantly floodlighting. The people waited in silence, till he should be with them again.

'So, ladies and gentlemen, what about your new Rector, Canon Stephen Patrice? Some of you may not know that his predecessor, your rector for over thirty years, was a much Higher churchman than his practice showed. Being a man of great consideration, and knowing that there were members of all parties in his congregation, he contented himself with what he always liked to call a gentlemanly compromise. He merely—by a gradual process, I gather, and like the subtle fellow he was—put curtains round your altar and a cross and candles on it. And there he stayed his hand. Well, Stephen—Canon Patrice—is emphatically a gentleman of the opposite—I was almost going to say "faction"—of the opposite point of view; and, believe me, there's nothing *official* your bishop can do about it—even if he wanted to. There is such a thing as the "parson's freehold", which means that, once he's been instituted, he's in final and absolute possession of his living, and nothing but a very unusual and expensive business of legal process can deprive him of it; and this only, as I have told you, for extreme heresy or extreme misconduct. There is certainly something to be said for this "parson's freehold"—if only that it preserves him from dictatorial oppression by his bishop. (Laughter.) So all I can do as an impotent bishop—but I'll do it for you— is to point to the example of his predecessor and urge him to attempt—from his opposite side of the ecclesiastical fence—a similar gentlemanly compromise that will be acceptable to you all. Further than that, well—' he shrugged—'when I hear from Harman—Sir Harman—that Stephen's first sermon was an enthusiastic recital of the Thirty-nine Articles I cannot, you will agree, question his Anglican orthodoxy; and as for the only other question, his moral fitness, let me assure you, dear people—I am glad he is not present to hear me now—let me assure you that he is a man of the deepest spirituality, and I would even dare to say, in his absence, a man of profound and undeviating saintliness. So there it is: you now have a pastor of great goodness among you, and I, as your Father-in-God, can only ask you to accept him as such, not without some gratitude and hope.'

Applause, formal rather than fervid, was accorded these closing words. It was followed by an embarrassing silence, no one presuming to be the first to speak. Not even Mrs Wrenne-Chamberlin, fount and origin of this assembly, rose to speak, or spoke from her chair. Perhaps the Bishop had disarmed her by his mention of a compromise. Sir Harman, as president, said without rising, 'Now let's hear from anyone wishing to speak'; but apparently for the present, no one wished to do so.

'We shall be glad to hear from anyone,' Sir Harman tried again.

Silence. People looked all round the room for someone to break the silence. No one.

So the Bishop, also without rising, attempted to ease the discomfort by something approaching a jest. He said, 'I feel sure I can persuade Canon Patrice to make some concessions but I don't see how I can ask him to remove the Tables of the Law.'

Alas, this produced not a ripple of merriment anywhere, so he went on, 'He has a very good precedent for placing the Tables of the Law in a holy place. Moses, after receiving them on Mount Sinai, placed them in the Ark of the Covenant with the Mercy Seat above them.'

This was no more successful in producing smiles or eliciting a speech.

The Chairman appealed again, 'Now then, come along, someone.'

Four or five seconds of silence, and then, suddenly, the last person whom Mrs Wrenne-Chamberlin would have wished to speak rose from the midst of the audience. She had overdone her propaganda in the village and raised—not as Uncle Bertie put it later, the devil—but Jake Horrabin. The 'village atheist', their late rector used to call Jake, some analogy lurking in his mind with the 'village idiot'. After all, had not the psalmist proposed that it is only a fool who says in his heart, There is no God. Jake was the son of two devout peasants; and so sternly devout had they been in his childhood that by the age of seventeen he was a delighted, proud and obsessional atheist; so devout an atheist that for ever after he was arguing in homes, in streets, in the bars of the Brotherhood, and even on festal occasions from a rostrum on Wedgery Green to an audience of five or six people. His happy and excited atheism had possessed him like a devil for forty years, and he was now a middle-aged man with a grey beard like that of His Majesty King George V, though the face above the beard was more worn by his excess of disputation. Indeed he prided himself not only on his fluent atheism but on this limited likeness to the King. Seldom had such an opportunity been offered him than by Mrs Wrenne-Chamberlin's activity in the creation of this fine audience. Why, here was the chance to expound God's non-existence to a mighty prince of the Church, and to explain to a local magistrate, Sir Harman, who might convict on a charge of blasphemy, where he would be wrong—or, to state it in his own language, 'tell him where he got off'. Also to appeal to the intelligence of a hundred and more fellow-villagers. Besides, there lay stowed and bursting within his head all the arguments he'd used a thousand, ten thousand times.

He rose. 'Since no one else seems inclined to speak, Mr Bishop, I should like to express certain views about what you're pleased to call the Tables of the Law. In my view——'

It being likely that he was the only atheist who had troubled to come to this religious meeting; likely also that he was the only person in the village, apart from Dr Balder, who was gravely exercised, one way or the other, about the existence of the Deity; and furthermore he being a figure of fun in Wedgery, his opening met with amused cries of 'Oh, sit down, Jake,' and 'Come off it, Jake' and 'Shut your gob, old boy,' or 'Put a sock in it, Jakems.'

But nobody in the forty years of delighted argument had succeeded in putting a sock between the jaws of Jake Horrabin. And certainly no one in this room this afternoon, certainly not Sir Harman in the Chair, knew his Bible as well as Jake Horrabin did—because he so delighted in attacking it. He knew it even better than the Lord Bishop who had long since resolved its difficulties for himself so that they now lay less than word-perfect in heart and memory. Not so with Jake; he was word-perfect.

Unheeding all protests, confident in his ammunition, he forged on with his 'views'—even as a feminine voice, presumably from some woman who had suffered more than once from his rhetoric, bewailed, 'Oh, *no! Please*'—'In my view,' he announced, 'the best thing Moses did was to cast down the so-called Tables of the Law and smash them beneath the mount, Exodus thirty-two. Lor' bless me—' an inappropriate invocation in this context—'how can any sane man believe that, according to the Bible, these ten laws were written "by the finger of God"? Who, please, can accept a furious and vengeful God who is prepared to visit the sins of the fathers upon innocent children for generation after generation? You may be able to; I can't. All said and done, what are these laws but the dictates of a primitive, aggressive, and even murderous tribe, wandering in a desert and ready to put to sword or flame anybody who disagreed with them? I may say also that I often wonder how the lady who has organised this meeting and who—if I may be allowed to say so—is nobody's mild plaything—is willing, in the last of the so-called laws, to be accounted as a piece of property somewhere between her husband's house and his servants, along with his ox and his ass——'

Sir Harman raised a warning hand, ready to declare these allusions to Moses and Mrs Wrenne-Chamberlin irrelevant, and to stop the orator, but this was something not easily done.

'One moment, Mr—Sir—Drood, let me say something else—' the speaker had now some spittle on his ardent lips—'you have only to go on to the very next chapter of Exodus, after these there ten commandments, to read another law which declares that if a slave does not want to be emancipated his master shall bring him to the door and bore a hole in his ear and nail him to the doorpost as a symbol that he is a slave for ever. If that's your idea of a God we ought to worship, it ain't—it isn't mine. The ear, you see, was regarded as the organ of hearing and therefore of obedience. What do you think of that, eh?'

The Bishop, looking distressed, leant forward as if to rise and speak, but the 'village atheist' now raised *his* hand, to silence a Lord Bishop. 'What do you say to that? We are to be bound for ever, are we, by these laws of a callous and ruffianly race——'

This was too much for the Chairman. It lifted him out of his chair. 'Really, sir, I cannot allow these wholly irrelevant remarks to proceed. We are not assembled here to discuss the existence of God; we are a gathering of Christian people committed to our faith in Him——'

'Hear, hears' came from several parts of the room, and murmurs of 'Chuck it, Jake; we all know what you think'; or 'Go and get lost,' or simply 'Turn the tap off, Jake, old boy,' an appeal which was supported by a muttered enthusiasm somewhere, 'Lord, yes! The bath's overflowed already.'

'All right, sir,' said Jake, heeding none of these mutters, though someone in a far corner of the room had suggested, 'Tell him to try a lozenge.' 'Just a minute, sir. There's one more thing I *must* say.' He was determined, before obeying the Chair, to blazon forth his most passionate and least answerable argument, because he could confirm it from beginning to end with scriptural quotations. 'Don't tell me this is all Old Testament stuff. I always want to ask an assembly of people committed as our good chairman has said, to a belief in the God preached by one, Jesus of Nazareth, these questions: What do I read in his so-called Sermon on the Mount, Matthew Five, twenty-nine, thirty? Simply that if any man offends his whole body shall be cast into hell. Mark endorses him, Mark Nine, forty-eight, adding the charming words that in this hell the worm dieth not and the fire is never quenched. Luke bears it all out for us, Luke Thirteen, forty-nine, fifty, where Jesus assures us that there was not a hope in this hell of tormenting flames for poor Dives—not even when he is showing the first signs of some love for his brothers and a desire to save them from his torments——'

'Really, sir,' the Chairman began again, but Jake, well away, presented the palm of his hand to Sir Harman, as if it were his, Jakes', business to extinguish an interrupter and require him to be seated. 'In Matthew Thirteen, sir, we are told by Christ that at the end of the world, the angels shall come forth and sever the wicked from the just, casting them into a furnace of fire where there shall be weeping and gnashing of teeth. In this Last Judgment parable he promises that he will personally say to the wicked "Depart from me, ye cursed"—*cursed*, look you—"into the everlasting fire prepared for the devil and his angels". Born sick but get well, or burn everlastingly! This, if you please, from a God of Love. It don't make no sense to me.'

However well this tremendous diatribe was justified by Holy Writ, most of the audience were laughing at Jake and getting fun out of his famous and fanatical atheism; but not Conal. Some perhaps were little worried by the wrath of God, confident that it waited for others rather than for them; but Conal was gradually sinking deeper and deeper beneath the weight of words. This impassioned speaker was quickening into horrid life again, with every chapter and verse at his command, all the unallayed terror which Conal had been trying, and at times managing, to forget. He found himself wishing, wishing, the man would stop, stop, stop. Every word of his was pressing, pressing, on a wound.

But the tormentor hurried on, lest the Chairman should seek to suppress him; he kept his eyes on the people and well turned from Sir Harman. He believed in never seeing what he didn't want to see. 'It's not only Christ's first disciples who assure us that this vengeful and torturing God is the one we are bidden under pain of hell to believe in. Paul in Two Thessalonians, One, seven, eight, tells us that "The Lord Jesus shall be revealed from Heaven with his mighty angels taking vengeance on them that know not God and obey not the gospel of Christ." He harps on it again in Romans Twelve. "Vengeance is mine, I will repay, saith the Lord." How's that for vindictiveness, and not returning evil for evil? Or what about St Peter, Acts Four, the so-called Vicar of Christ, and therefore, in your view, the Representative of the Deity, sentencing to immediate death poor Ananias and poor Sapphira for lying a little about their contribution to the collection? Christian and forgiving, would you say? And finally (A voice: 'Thank God') in the Bible's last words—I will not keep you much longer ('Hear, hear' and 'Hurray') though I could give you much more —in almost the very last words of the Book of Revelation— *revelation*, note you—we read, "I saw the dead, small and great, stand before the Lord and the books were opened ... and whosoever was not found written in the book of life was cast into the lake of fire". Such is your God. Worship and love him if you can. I, thank God, can't and won't. I don't see how any sane——'

But enough. Sir Harman was on his feet, saying, '*Will* you sit down, sir. If you refuse to obey me, I am sure there are those among us, who, at my request, will remove you from the room.'

'Yes, sir. Yes, sir,' came from willing volunteers.

But their services were not required. Jake, not liking to be spoken to in this fashion, committed his final offence by saying to the Chairman, and in the presence of a bishop, 'That's all right, cock. I'll say no more. I've said all I wanted to say.' And, turning towards the people, he concluded with a grin, 'God bless you all, folks, if he exists to do so,' and sat down cheerfully, waiting to hear what comments might result from his few observations. His smile was at once so self-satisfied and so friendly that it seemed to be saying, 'A hearty goodwill to all my listeners.'

After a glance at the Chairman, the Bishop rose to speak. 'Sir Harman has rightly ruled that everything we've heard from our good friend, Mr ... Mr——?'

'Horrabin,' some voices supplied. 'Jake Horrabin.'

'Our good friend, Mr Jake Horrabin, is totally irrelevant to the question before us, but I hope he will allow me to say that there has been nothing said today on God's wrath to which I could not give you the answer. Perhaps your good rector will allow me so to do one day. Meanwhile how is this? From Leviticus, a book whose origins are lost in antiquity: "You shall not pervert justice either by favouring the poor or by subservience to the great. You shall not seek revenge or cherish anger towards your kinfolk. You shall love your neighbour as a man like yourself. *I am the Lord.*"'

The Bishop knew how to use his voice. These last four words belled out like a proclamation from on high.

A whisper in Conal's ear from Marjorie, 'Isn't he divine? Don't you think he's *too* beautiful?' while applause from Mrs Wrenne-Chamberlin's supporters was greeting the Bishop's words, and Conal's heart, for a minute, had risen out of its pit of despair—though certainly not to its brink, nor to any sunlight above.

But one of the Low Church ladies was not disposed to let the Bishop's words pass without amendment. Poor Mrs Wrenne-Chamberlin by her restless and widespread activities had raised an Opposition larger and more articulate than a Party Support for her campaign. This new speaker was a lank woman in late middle-life with more power in her sharp features than her long, frail body suggested. And it looked to be an unsparing power. Here probably was a woman as formidable in her stringy thin-ness as Mrs Wrenne-Chamberlin in her imposing amplitude.

'I think, my lord, with great respect, that what I shall have to say is relevant to the discussion. Naturally, as an earnest Christian, I have no sympathy with, but only disgust at, all the blasphemous words we've been compelled to hear from Mr ... Mr——'

'Jake Horrabin,' the well-informed—and proudly informed—provided again.

'—from Mr Jakes. I wonder the Law allows such blasphemies——'

But here the Bishop, half-rising, interrupted in gentle tones: 'Everybody is allowed to speak his mind in this country, and the Church is not afraid of any attacks. In twenty centuries they have not prevailed against her.'

'Rubbish!' The voice was Jake's. 'They've prevailed with all sensible people.'

'But, my lord,' the stringy lady persisted, 'I've always understood that blasphemy is a misdemeanour at common law and punishable by fine or imprisonment——'

Sir Harman was on his feet. 'Perhaps as a magistrate, Miss Merriweather, I can clarify the position——' which he proceeded to do in most magisterial terms. 'As the Law stands, Miss Merriweather, no prosecution could be sustained for calmly discussing, or even calling in question, the truth of Christianity. The offence of blasphemy consists in attacking it by ribaldry, profanity, or indecency and not in endeavouring by legitimate argument to prove its falsity.'

'There you are, lady!' said Jake triumphantly. 'So sit down.'

But no more than Jake was this stringy but formidable lady to be easily interrupted. By bishop or anyone else. 'Well, if what we've heard from Mr Jakes was not ribald and profane and indecent, I haven't got ears in my head.'

Unwittingly many looked at her ears as if to reassure themselves that these members were in position.

'I can only accept your ruling, Mr Chairman,' she continued. Obviously here was a spinster lady who knew all about proper behaviour in committee. Indeed the late Rector, in lively and private moments, used to say of her that she was one of his parishioners who could look back on a lifetime of committees. 'The question before us, as I understand it—is whether the Decalogue and Creed are to be given a prominent position above our Holy Table—are they not our Christian Faith and Practice? Well, I feel most strongly, after all, what Mr Jakes has said in such abominable but apparently not blasphemous language, that someone among us should affirm that we, as earnest Christians, give our full and fearless support to the doctrine of eternal punishment which he derides. I will not listen to anyone disputing that it is an unavoidable part of our faith proclaimed again and again—as indeed Mr Jakes has shown—in the Bible and by Our Lord himself. I've no use for those who think they can pick and choose what they will accept from his plain words. Too many people want to listen only to his comfortable sayings and to have nothing to do with those that are terrible in their sternness. As the Bishop will know, the word for hell, as invariably used by Our Lord and his disciples, is Gehenna, which in New Testament days meant the final punishment for the wicked in the next world, the punishment being by fire, and the fire eternal. Of course we do not know if the fire is to be understood literally or figuratively——'

The Chairman intervened with a smile, 'We've just had one long diatribe. Need we now have a sermon?'

But Miss Merriweather needed to go on. 'Or figuratively. The symbolic way in which fire is often spoken of, and the expression "where the worm dieth not and the fire is not quenched"—in which "worm" and "fire" can scarcely both be literal—allows us to have an open mind on this solemn question. But in any case some fierce and most terrible agony is meant. Some Jews at a later date regarded Gehenna as a temporary place of punishment for some and eternal for others. But there is no trace of such an opinion in the Palestine of Our Lord and his Apostles. Thus it is certain that no argument for a temporary purgatory—or, still less, for an ultimate universal salvation—can be deduced from any words spoken by Our Lord or written by his Apostles——'

'Good Christ!' came Jake's mutter, not without more aptness, perhaps, than he intended; while the Chairman pleaded with something like a sigh, 'Miss Merriweather, are you going on for long?'

'No, no,' she promised, to soothe him, 'but I just want to say this. Let there be no doubt about the terrible character of a permanent alienation from God. And God has made it abundantly clear that he will take "No" for an answer and allow the consequences to follow. The language of the New Testament is forcible enough but I suggest there is no more powerful aid to the realisation of the appalling alternative before us than the extent of Our Saviour's sufferings to ransom us from these consequences. The depth of our redemption can only be estimated by an appreciation of the price paid. Christ's passion draws us with a two-fold cord of love and fear—fear of that inevitable doom which cost so much to avert and love to him who so willingly paid this price. The Cross is the only valid yardstick wherewith to measure the hatefulness of sin and the horror of its consequences. There it stands for us to accept and be saved, or reject and be damned.'

A good peroration and Miss Merriweather resumed her seat.

Sir Harman, shrugging his shoulders helplessly, suggested, 'Now perhaps somebody will deal with the question before us.'

No one seemed eager to do this. Jake's tirade and Miss Merriweather's powerful sermon had shattered the meeting. They had, so to say, laid the meeting flat. Only Mrs Wrenne-Chamberlin, fount and origin of the assembly, felt bound to say something. And all she could think of to say was, 'I suggest we can accept gracefully the Bishop's assurance that he will put the views of us all before Canon Patrice and attempt to achieve some sort of compromise that will be satisfactory to all.'

And, if it will be believed, no one else, in spite of repeated appeals by the Chairman for someone to contribute some views, spoke at all. Mrs Wrenne-Chamberlin's meeting for which she had laboured so diligently had discussed nothing but the existence of God and the certainty of everlasting punishment for impenitent sinners or persistent unbelievers.

It was remarkable when all rose to go that no one's face had paled in the least at the prospect of his or her possible damnation. Probably, as has been suggested above, this was because they conceived that the terrible pains described by the Merriweather prophetess would be directed towards others than themselves. One person, however, had been stretched and twisted on the rack of words and was now suffering the aftermath of an hour on that instrument of torture, as he went from the room with Lizetta and Marjorie.

'God will take No for an answer and allow the consequences to follow.'

10

That was Friday evening. And throughout the evening, and during much of the early night in his bed, Conal moved and had his being, haunted and possessed by the questions that so frightened him. Almost everything said at the meeting had underlined and enlarged his fears. It seemed there was no doubt about the 'truths' which a Christian and a churchgoer was ordered to believe. How on earth did Lizetta and Marge and possibly Uncle Bertie live so comfortably with such beliefs? Didn't they ever consider that one day they must die, and perhaps then...? His head shook on the pillow: certainly his present fears didn't trouble any of them for one minute of the day, and if he took *his* trouble to them, Lizetta and Marge would only snub him and hardly listen; while Uncle Bertie would only laugh and make merry. To whom could he turn for comfort? Not the Rector. The Rector had already declared, like that Miss Merriweather, that the Bible words were plain and not to be questioned. You had this life only in which to decide if you would be happy for ever or suffer for ever. For ever. In all Wedgery there was no one to whom he could turn, unless—unless it was old Dr Balder.

By this time, having no father to consult, Conal was feeling something like a filial affection for this kind, teasing, flattering old Doctor who had called him 'the best listener in the world'. Would it be an insufferable impertinence for him to ring the Doctor's bell again and ask to come in with his endless perplexities? Would the Doctor think him a 'frightful nuisance'? Somehow he thought not. Somehow he thought the Doctor, perceiving who it was on his threshold, would welcome him with merry eyes and say, 'Come in, Connor Quintilian, or whatever your name is. Come in at once.' And he would take him into his museum-like room, make him sit down and take a chair opposite him, ready to hear all. But Conal couldn't bring himself to do this. His mind was so astonishingly muddled now that along with his fears there lay a desire to be a kind of Athanasius fighting the world for some truth or other, and the only possible truth to fight for was the Christianity in which he'd been brought up—so would it be possible to fight for all of it, *except* the one unbearable doctrine? But he knew what the Doctor would say to this—he could almost hear him—the Doctor pulverising all that Athanasius had preached and tossing its dust to the archaeological winds. It was possible, of course, that by dispersing Athanasius, and laughing loud at Miss Merriweather, the Rector, Lizetta and all unquestioning Christians everywhere, the Doctor would lift from him the burden of belief with its terrors. What to do? Conal hesitated. He tarried and tarried through three days, walking alone, or playing with Marjorie, or bathing with the family, and wearing his private, invisible cloud around him most of the time.

But the hesitation couldn't go on for ever, and on the Tuesday morning, after further hours of hesitation, he set off for the Doctor's stucco-fronted house, 'The Last Lap'.

It was nearly noon, and it surprised him to see, standing before the house, whose door was open, a tall young policeman, a white van like an ambulance, and a long handsome car with a uniformed chauffeur. It was a fashion at this time for schoolboys to distinguish and name cars, and he knew at once that here was a Rolls-Royce cabriolet. All this was exciting, and he drew near the open door to peep through it. Three men were standing and talking at the door of the Doctor's room. While he was wondering what to do next, the young policeman spoke. A fresh-faced youngster from his native village, East Dean behind Beachy Head, he spoke in broad South Saxon. 'Did 'ee want anything, sonny?'

'I was coming to call on Doctor Balder.'

'Ye'll have to call pretty loud now, sonny, I tell 'ee that.'

'Why, why?' Fear began to swell in Conal's heart.

'Because he ain't in this world any longer. The lady what does for 'um found 'um this marnin' layin' dead on a sofa. Properly dressed and all, an' dead as you can get 'em. And bin layin' there a couple o' days, peaceful like.'

'*Dead?*' In his shock Conal could only repeat the word.

'Surelye. It's a hem of a biz'ness in there nah.' The policeman turned his glance to the open house-door. 'He was all'us an unaccountable quirty o'ald bird—didn't seem to have no gurt friends anywhere about—but I don't reckon nobody thought he'd a'gone and done this.'

'Why? What do you mean?'

'Mean? Mean 'e done umself in. 'E was layin' there dead by his o'an hand.'

'I don't believe it. I don't believe it.' Conal could only say this to keep intolerable news an arm's length away. The loss of something that had been for a few brief days an affection almost filial, sprang tears to his eyes, but for seconds only; he managed to hold them back behind the eyes—or nearly behind them. 'I—I—I don't believe it.'

'Do'ant 'ee now? Well, I'll tell 'ee——'

'If he died, he died naturally.'

' "Naturally" be hemmed! I'll tell 'ee summat.' Doubtless it was improper for this young policeman to tell anyone his 'summat', but he had a fine feeling for the drama of the business in the house and was eager to share it with another. Safe enough to share it with a schoolboy in a school cap who wouldn't recognise such talk as a misdemeanour or report it as such. 'You do'ant believe it, you say. Well, I reckon the o'ald man knew what 'e be'an done. There's a gurt long letter propped up on his mantelpiece. Propped up against a gurt yeller urn that looks like a cemet'ry thing.'

'Oh, no ... no....' This was a cry from a child who was being battered again and again. But he still managed to stifle tears before a fellow male.

Of this struggle the young policeman perceived nothing. 'That letter's a crowner's matter, for sartain sure. The Crowner's officer's bin in there. Sarge fetched 'um at once. When they done wid the o'ald gem'man, that there van's to take 'um to the mortuary. That big car belongs to some unaccountable famous doctor, I'm to'ald. One of the most famous in the country.'

'Perhaps he was a friend,' said Conal, trying to speak through the baffled tears. 'Dr Balder was a doctor.'

'Mebbe, but 'ee's no' from these parts. 'E's a furriner from West Kent or somewhere. Reckon 'e makes an unaccountable big summa money. That there car's left a tedious big ho'al in his pocket.' Young like Conal he had the same pleasure in identifying cars. 'That there's a Rolls-Royce, that be. A Rolls-Royce cabriolet. Danged if it be'ant! And you do'ant get that for a tanner.'

The South Sussex Coroner, Mr Grimswade Bantham, conducted his Inquest on the Wednesday morning, only twenty-five hours after Dr Balder had been found dead. He conducted it in the Doctor's long sitting-room so like a museum, amid all the antiques in their show-cases or on the walls or on the overmantel—axe-heads and arrows of palaeolithic men; implements and weapons of the Bronze Age or Iron Age men who came after them. And the yellow funerary urn of yesterday, in its place of honour.

Chairs, presumably from bedrooms and kitchen, had been added to the two easy chairs and the long Chesterfield sofa on which the Doctor had died. The Coroner, a small, unremarkable, middle-aged man, in disappointingly commonplace civilian clothes, sat at a small Sheraton table, so small that it rocked as he wrote. There were less than thirty people in the room, but even so, some had to stand. Two standing were pressmen, one from the *South Sussex Times*, the other from the *Sussex Daily News*. One of the audience who had secured a chair was Lizetta. Lizetta never missed anything of excitement in Wedgery, and she had been at the door of the Doctor's house before the Coroner arrived and before it was opened to the public. She alone represented Slings. Uncle Bertie was at his office in town, and she had kept quiet about the Inquest—and about her excited interest in it—before Conal and Marjorie. An inquest, with morbid evidence perhaps, was no theatre for children. For herself it had all the attraction of a play.

The Coroner's officer called the first witness. 'Mrs Christine Dryburgh, please.'

Since this was no Coroner's Court, furnished with dais, witness box, press table and jury box, the Coroner said pleasantly, 'Perhaps you will just come and stand a little closer to me. Then we shall all hear.'

'Yes, sir. I see, sir.'

Lizetta watched the buxom woman of sixty or so go and stand near the Coroner's table. 'You are Mrs Christine Dryburgh?'

'Yes, sir. I——'

But the Coroner continued, 'And it was you who found the doctor lying——'

'Thet's right, sir. I come and did for him four days a week, Monday, Tuesday, Thursday and Saturday. Of a morning.' Like many active women Mrs Dryburgh was loquacious and repetitive. 'That was how I come to come in yesterday morning and find him layin' there unconscious like. He never bin ill all the time I done for him so I didn't know who his doctor was, and I runs round to the nearest doctor and tells him. Mr Balder didn't seem to have many friends, so I dunno what else I could'a done, like. The doctor come and finds him dead and goes and telephones the police.'

The Coroner wrote it all down on sheets before him, the tiny table rocking as he wrote. Then he spoke. 'Mrs Dryburgh, you have said that he had few friends so I conclude you must have seen as much of him as anyone else. Will you tell us what, in your view, was his state of mind when you last saw him. Did he——'

She interrupted. 'That'd'a bin the Monday, like?'

'Yes, yes ... but did he seem in any way depressed? Depressed, like?' The 'like' was catching.

'Oh, no, sir. He always seemed to be what you might call merry and laughin'. He always had a joke for me when I come and another when I was goin'. Always full o' fun, as you might say. With me, anyhow.'

'When you came yesterday did you see the syringe on the table by his side?'

'The what, sir?'

'Oh, well, never mind. We'll ask the doctor about that. Did he ever—at any time—in your hearing—say anything about taking his own life?'

'Lordy, no, sir.' So great her assurance, she was probably unconscious of her frivolous expletive. 'And I can't believe he done so. Not for the life of me, I can't.'

'Did you observe a letter or document propped up against a marble urn on the mantelpiece?'

'No, sir, I never see that. I wouldn't hardly notice it because the room was so full of straw'nary things.'

Here the Coroner asked a question which seemed less prompted by his official duty than by his curiosity. 'Did you by any chance know what the urn contained?'

'No, sir. I don't think it contained nothing. I thought it was just one of them things all over the room, about a million years old, most of 'em.'

'I see. Oh, well, thank you, Mrs Dryburgh.'

The next witness was the doctor whom Mrs Dryburgh had summoned, a young man, Dr William Kendle, new to Wedgery, having succeeded to the practice of an old doctor retired. His was a clean young face with a full fair moustache and beard, both worn, Lizetta suspected, to lessen his youthful appearance before patients who would have doubts about a doctor who looked young. He gave evidence of having found on the little table by the sofa's side—which was actually the table on which the Coroner was now writing—two empty phials, a syringe, and a tablespoon in which were a few drops of clear fluid. The syringe had not been dismantled, and the phials were labelled, 'Morphine Sulphate' and 'Morphine Hydrochloride'. The liquid in the spoon was morphine. He had no doubt that death was due to morphine poisoning.

The Coroner: 'Doctor, you will know that under *The Poisons and Pharmacy Act, 1908* no shop for the retailing, dispensing or compounding of poisons can sell such a drug as morphine to any customer without a prescription from someone fully qualified. Thus no layman can obtain morphine at will. Would you say that Dr Balder in his professional character, as a qualified doctor practising but seldom, would have had any difficulty in obtaining this morphia?'

'None whatever, sir. And in view of the fact that I found in a desk drawer two further phials each of which contained half-grain morphia tablets, I can feel no doubt, personally, that the cause of death was morphine poisoning, self-injected.'

'Thank you, Dr Kendle.'

Dr Kendle was followed by Police-Sergeant Harry Gowers, a

familiar figure to Lizetta and all Wedgery because he came from a small semi-detached red-brick villa in Greenways Road, than which nothing could have looked less like a police station. Instead of names such as 'Homecroft' or 'Dove's Nest' or 'Love's Nest' it bore on its narrow garden gate the fine words 'South Sussex Constabulary' and along its garden railing official notices about Wanted Persons, Precautions against Petty Thieves, Information about a murder eight months old, details about a Great Career in the Police, and notice of a forthcoming Police Dance.

Sergeant Gowers had little to do but testify to his summons by Mrs Dryburgh, endorse all that the previous witness had said about the scene in the room, and explain, perhaps a little proudly, on Dr Kendle's pronouncement of death, his instant report to the Coroner's Office.

He did however, answering the Coroner, add that his view of the deceased was no different from Mrs Dryburgh's. 'He seemed as lively as could be and ever ready with a joke for anyone he met. He was particularly liable to make jokes about me as a police officer, telling me I didn't half know what was going on in Wedgery.'

'Thank you, Sergeant. We needn't detain you.' The Coroner addressed the audience. 'As to Dr Kendle's statement that the morphine was self-injected, we will now have evidence from Dr Balder's solicitor who rightly, as you will see, has in his possession the letter or document found against the marble urn.'

At a glance from the Coroner, his officer called, 'Mr Algernon Eric Graves, please'; and a grey-haired, clean-shaven, hawkish-featured man in wing-collar, black bow-tie and severely dark suit, looking very much a lawyer fresh from his office, stepped up to the Coroner's table. Of a certainty all in the room were now eager to know what the document had contained, but none more than Lizetta. Her interest forced her to lean forward in her chair as if to catch every movement of the lawyer's lips and miss nothing. She was aware of no other emotion than curiosity and interest in a drama; why should she feel pity for Dr Balder who had stirred in her nothing but ridicule or distaste and, thank goodness, had nothing to do with herself or her family?

The formal question from the Coroner: 'You are Mr Algernon Graves, of Graves and Weldon, Solicitors, 8 Ferne Buildings,

Eastbourne, and you acted for the deceased?'

'Yes, sir.'

'And you have the letter—or document—that was found on the mantelshelf and addressed to you?'

'Yes, sir, and my partners and I desire to thank you for your immediate conveyance of it to us.'

'Please read it.'

'It's long.'

'Never mind. It's all relevant, I think, to the question before us.'

The solicitor, putting on his glasses, unfolded a set of foolscap sheets. Before reading from them he said, looking over the spectacles at the audience, 'This is an odd mixture of a personal letter and a final will and testament. It is written with a strange merriment, if I may so put it, considering the circumstances, but at the same time, even if it is all rather irregular, it fulfils all the legal requirements of a will, signed in the joint presence of two witnesses.' Here he pushed the spectacles higher on his nose, cleared his throat, dropped his gaze to the sheets and read.

'Dear Algy, this letter will amount to the will of myself Julius Balder, M.D., F.R.C.P., F.R.A.S. and a whole lot more of the alphabet. Some days ago an exceedingly frank friend of mine told me over a lunch table that I was beginning to look as yellow as the yolk of an egg, and though I was feeling as fit as a fiddle I am but human and went to my doctor, Sam Blaker, who, damn him, sent me to the Brighton General Hospital where they opened me up, sewed me up again, and when I came round from the anaesthetics, told me they'd discovered cancer of the pancreas. Well, I may have forgotten most of the medicine I once knew, but I knew enough to know that this was inoperable and that I probably had less than a year to live—maybe only months or weeks. So I said to them, 'Oh hell', and came home to weigh up the matter. Knowing the truth, I began to feel, after the fashion of foolish mortals, an ever-increasing pain, or it could be they bungled the operation—I've no great faith in doctors—and today I decided to exercise my natural right as a free human being to die when I, rather than anyone else, think best. I see no sense in waiting in expanding pain for an assured but could-be lagging and tardy end. Some instructions about my interment or the disposition of my ashes may be necessary, so I am writing this letter to you, dear Algy—not without thanking you for much help in the past. Since I am an infidel, believing nothing in the Bible except the excellent words, 'Dust thou art and to dust shalt thou return' I take it upon myself who am but dust and ashes to express a wish that, if it is legitimate my ashes and those of my good friend and companion Marion Fitzraven (which can be found on my mantelpiece) should be scattered to the winds on a summit of our Downs, but——'

The quiet in the room was total as he turned a leaf over, and then rearranged the sheaf of foolscap pages; his words were holding captive the eyes and ears of all.

'—but if this is not allowed—and I haven't troubled to find out—I would like them to be buried side by side and in one grave, but whether in consecrated or unconsecrated ground I, for my part, care not. Still, we are all sentimentalists to the end, and if it is permissible to lay the ashes of a hoary old unbeliever in the churchyard here I would ask for ours to be laid together, because like most women she had some sort of faith and would occasionally attend services in the church. And if the minister would want to say a service over us I offer no objection. It can do me no harm. I desire to thank my immediate neighbours, Mr and Mrs Timothy Upperton, for having come in to witness (as I understand is required) my signing of this my will, especially as there is not a half-penny in it for them. A life-long friend and associate very dear to me, with whom I have discussed for many an hour this right to die, and who is in complete agreement with me, will certainly accept the task of overseeing my obsequies. He is——'

but here the solicitor looked up from his papers and said, 'There is no need for me to mention the name; we are in touch with him,' and resumed his reading.

'He is a man of substance and needs no legacy, though I wish him to take a hundred pounds as my thank-you. Subjoined is a list of a few gifts, either in money or goods, that I would like given to some other friends, especially my faithful Abigail, Mrs Dryburgh. The residue of my capital estate, after the Revenue men have done their worst—alas, I can see no way of outwitting the Excise—will be but small, a few thousands all told, but I should wish it to be given to the little homunculus who goes by the name of Conal Quentin Someone and lives during his school holidays at Slings in Wedgery.'

Lizetta, whose thoughts had been anywhere but in this room, suddenly sat upright and stared. Gaped. But the solicitor's voice went on indifferently.

'During the continuing infancy of the homunculus I imagine that the money would have to be held in trust by his father, who, so he tells me, lives in India, and according to the boy's fervid descriptions is a most excellent man. To this excellent man I express a desire that he will devote the money to the boy's Higher Education, for which he seemed to me a most worthwhile recipient. What more? If I am buried with my friend in the churchyard I would wish her name to be on the stone, but let there be no mention of mine. What is over, is over. There will be no purpose served in remembering me. Did I believe in a God I would wish to thank him for a long, usually happy, and always interesting life. If I am wrong in my disbelief—but I don't think I am—here is my thank-you. That is all, and in witness thereof—I give you your tedious jargon, dear Algy—I have herewith set my hand.'

The solicitor raised his eyes from his sheets, and a sad little smile widened his thin lips. 'There is no more, sir, except his signature, those of his witnesses, and a farther but, for him, strangely inappropriate conclusion: "Yours ever, Julius".'

Lizetta's surprise, as she heard of the old man's bequest to Conal, was more than amazement; it amounted almost to a shock. Her condition was an amalgam of bewilderment, excited pleasure, and a very small grievance. Her affection for Conal may have been slight and her irritabilities many, but behind all irritabilities there was a generous heart, so that the excited pleasure was uppermost and largest. with a huge desire to rush home and tell Conal. Compared with this happy thrill the grievance was tiny. It was no more than a transient jealousy because the money had been entrusted to a parent far away instead of to her husband and her, and because Conal had referred so enthusiastically to his father. She had perception enough to detect in this a comparison between his father in India and his guardians in England. Dreams were rushing through her mind: till one minute ago it had been understood that, after leaving his prep school, Conal would go to his public school but not, without a scholarship, to Oxford. Now it was assured that he could go on to the university. Only a few minutes, and she could hurry home to delight and excite the boy with this splendid news.

But the Coroner, without rising from his chair, had begun to speak.

'There is but one question before me, and it is: how did this man come by his death? The medical evidence proves beyond doubt that he died from a lethal injection of morphine, but is there anything to suggest an element of accident or mischance? I accept the letter—or the will—to which we have just listened as conclusive evidence that the poison was self-administered, so it remains for me to decide whether this was a case of *Felo de se*— that is to say a deliberate self-killing by a person of sane mind, which is a felony in the eyes of the Law, or whether I can find that there was enough disturbance in the deceased's mind that would mitigate this harsh verdict and enable him, as he seems to have wished, to be buried in consecrated ground. There can hardly be any question that he was an eccentric recluse, but also that, until a very recent date, he was a ripe scholar of vigorous intellect. I do however think that the eccentricity is emphasised by the extraordinary levity of his letter to Mr Gowers and, moreover, that there are traces in it, faint perhaps, but such as we can charitably consider evidence of some senile confusion. There is some blundering about the name of the boy, Conal, and some absurdity in the words, "Yours ever", coming from one who is about to die and had no belief in a Hereafter. These are very little things, but I have decided that they will justify me in bringing in a verdict that he killed himself while the balance of his mind was temporarily disturbed.'

This was the end. The Coroner's officer called, 'All rise, please,' and all rose in respect for the Coroner as he gathered up his papers, rose, and disappeared from the room. Then all made their way out of the house, but none so eagerly as Lizetta. There were only a few hundred yards between The Last Lap and Slings, but in all her life Lizetta had never enjoyed a more happy and excited walk. It was wonderful to be bringing a sensation to her home and a magnificent promise to Conal.

11

A good-hearted Coroner may have strained the evidence to accede to the wish of a dying man that his ashes might lie with those of his friend in a churchyard, but in this mercy he had reckoned without Canon Patrice. The Canon, on hearing of the verdict, declared at once, though regretfully, that his principles, and, as he saw it, his duty, forbade him to bury an aggressive infidel, and suicide too, in his church's consecrated ground. So different a man was he from his gay and often irreverent predecessor who was reported to have said, after reading about a Burial Bill in the Lower House of Convocation which would open the country churchyards to deceased Nonconformists, 'There's nothing that would give me greater pleasure than to read the Burial Service over all the dissenters in Wedgery.'

Lizetta knew nothing of theology, but with the generous side of her nature, was indignant at first when she heard of the Rector's decision. 'I had no love for old Dr Balder; I thought him an awful old man, but surely now that he's dead and the Coroner has pronounced him slightly insane—which he certainly wasn't—he ought to be able to lie with his lady love—whoever or whatever she may have been.'

Marjorie, who reproduced all her mother's sentimentalities and superstitions, agreed vehemently, and called Canon Patrice a 'horrible old man', but Conal, though he was the only one who had loved the dead Doctor, found himself agreeing with Uncle Bertie's words, 'Once you're dead does it matter a damn where your ashes lie? So far as I'm concerned, you can put me on the compost heap.'

But the question of Dr Balder's ashes did matter a few damns to Sir Harman, who was beginning to wonder whether the 'godly and learned man' he'd presented to the Bishop for the Cure of Souls in Wedgery, however famous a preacher he might be, and however distinguished as a 'canon', was not perhaps, in his godliness and learning, a shade too legalistic and uncompromising. This was the second cloud of trouble he'd brought down upon his patron's head in his first few weeks. As Mrs Wrenne-Chamberlin had suggested, Sir Harman, Lord of the Manor, had carried into the twentieth century a view of his patronage that was still somewhat feudal. In other words he held Canon Patrice to be more or less a vassal holding churchyard and glebe on the condition of giving acceptable service to his lord. A magistrate and no small legalist himself, he doubted if it was within the competence of his Rector—and vassal—to upset and defy a decision of the Coroner who was the voice of His Majesty the King, sole owner (in theory) of all land in the country with Sir Harman merely his tenant-in-chief. Now, once again, he'd have to call in the help of their Father-in-God, the Bishop—and here Sir Harman, not lightly muddled, began to wonder whether technically the Rector owed his fealty to the Lord of the Manor or to the Lord Bishop of the diocese. No haste was needed in this general quandary, because the urned ashes could wait on a shelf in the crematorium; but fortunately the Bishop, frequent visitor at Drood Place, showed himself quite glad to come on a visit to the Droods a few days later and speak with Canon Patrice and any others interested.

Now it happened that, on the day after his arrival, Sir Harman and Lady Drood were giving a garden party for the councillors of the Rural District Council of which Sir Harman was chairman for this year. In Wedgery's feudal climate there was every reason why he should be the permanent chairman of the Parish Council since the parish had its origin in the old Saxon 'vill', approximately the manor surrounding the church; but in Wedgery's democratic climate (which was there too) his chairmanship of the R.D.C. was temporary and he had a mind to celebrate this temporary office with a garden party in his great park. So the Bishop sat down to dinner with twelve other guests, most of whom were Cambridge friends of Isidora Drood, daughter of the house, or undergraduate friends of Adrian, her younger brother. These were there for a week-end house party. In such company with sixteen at table the Bishop was seated on Lady Drood's right with Sir Harman in the far distance of an immensely long table; and he made a joke, not for the first time, with his hostess, 'Angela dear, how can I discuss parochial affairs with Harman if he's sitting in what's almost another parish?'

'You can't, Bishop, and that's splendid, because you can now enjoy a little freedom from episcopal burdens.'

'Well then, Angela, what you can do, while my main business waits, is to tell me who is this small boy to whom that merry old miscreant, Balder, has left all his money.'

'I really don't know,' she answered. 'I've never seen him. I think I met his mother once—no, not his mother, a kind of foster mother who looks after him while he's at school in England. His real parents are in India where his father is a magistrate of some sort. He only comes here during his school holidays. He must have been a clever little boy to collect a small fortune for himself during a week or two away from school.'

'I've seen him, I've seen him,' cried Isidora triumphantly. She was sitting on the other side of the Bishop, at her earnest insistence, because, like Marjorie at Slings, she at Drood Place was possessed, inspired, overwhelmed by adoration of the Bishop—so much so that Adrian, her brother, trying to be clever, suggested that her name ought to be changed to Isanadora. But hers, at twenty, was the fine flowering of Marjorie's raw small plant. It breathed a young woman's vast admiration for his fine appearance ('the best-looking and best-dressed bishop on the bench') and an intelligent girl's profound appreciation for all his qualities, mental, spiritual, and social. 'I've seen him. They come to church when they're here. He looks quite a nice little boy. Pleasantly wistful. Actually they were all at that disgustingly silly meeting of Mrs Wrenne-Chamberlin's when nobody had anything to say except the atheists and Miss Merriweather who consigned them and most of us to the flames. And the astonishing thing is that he's only met old Dr Balder about four times, so they tell me, twice at Easter, and twice this holiday.'

'An odd child,' said the Bishop, 'who can woo the love of a rather misanthropic old gentleman in four meetings.'

'Yes, but then the Doctor was a bit mad. I tell you what, Ma, couldn't we invite them all to the garden party tomorrow? There's a daughter who's younger than he. Would it seem rude to invite them so late? We'd have to have them all, I suppose.'

The Bishop said, 'I think you should certainly invite *him* since he's the talk of the town. Four small encounters, you say—one on the Downs, one in the old sinner's home, another on Wedgery Beacon—was it?—and one in the church, of all places—and the outcome: a small fortune. I wish I knew how it was done.'

'Yes, and the remarkable infant, eleven or twelve years old, paid a strictly spiritual call on the new Rector only a day or two after his Induction, and before the poor man was half settled in his Rectory.'

'A boy who should go far,' suggested the Bishop. 'I wonder what'll happen to him.'

'Can't imagine,' said Isidora, shaking her head. 'Because he looks such an ordinary little boy.'

'So perhaps did Cardinal Wolsey and Cromwell and Cranmer, at eleven or twelve, Isidora dear.'

'Well, we simply must have him at the party, even at the price of having all the others. Couldn't we say, Ma, that the Bishop has expressed a desire to meet him—or, rather to meet them all? You have, haven't you, Bishop?'

'I'll allow you to say I have, Isidora.'

'But Izzy,' her mother objected; 'do remember it'll be only three—no four—days after his benefactor's death.'

The girl's hands slapped down on the table, as if she was suddenly alight with a wonderful idea. 'But that'll be the perfect alibi for not having invited them earlier. After all, there's all this how-d'ye-do about the Ten Commandments, and we could say——'

'An alibi, Isidora,' the Bishop interrupted, never able to tolerate the ignorant use of this word, 'is not the same thing as an excuse. An alibi is only a proof that you were in some other place—*alibi* being the Latin for "elsewhere"—than that in which the crime was committed. And you were all sitting here on the spot. In Wedgery.'

'Oh, what does it matter what we call it, Bishop? You all know what I mean. It's a perfect reason for my going to them tomorrow morning and saying that they're all to come to the garden party because His Lordship the Bishop has issued a summons to that effect. After all, he does want to talk to people about the Ten Commandments. Is that all right, Ma? Because I want to get to know him, just as the Bishop does. And dammit—sorry, Bishop, but that's what Daddy says fifty times a day and he's damning like blazes now over all this business—there's plenty of room in the park for all of them. We can easily lose those who have no great interest for us.'

'What a way for a hostess to talk,' Lady Drood reproached her.

'No, but is it all right, Ma, to go and invite them?'

'Of course it is, darling. And, however you sound now, I'm sure you'll do it with perfect tact.'

'Oh *yes*, I'll use the tack all right.'

'I wager she will,' said the Bishop.

So Lizetta, answering a bell, saw on the threshold of Slings a tall, fair girl whom she did not recognise as the daughter of Drood Place. She looked at her with some confusion, brows knitting. Guessing her as in her first twenties, she found herself thinking how charming and attractive a fresh-skinned girl of that age could be. Especially if, as Lizetta deduced from the girl's first words, she was 'obviously a lady'.

'Oh, Mrs Sheridan,' Isidora had begun, 'I don't suppose you remember it, but we have met once at one of Daddy's garden parties. At Drood Place. I'm Isidora Drood. I was just helping Daddy and Mummy to receive the guests, and we shook hands. It was last year, and look, we've got a garden party this afternoon —it *was* meant only for all the old Rural District Councillors of whom Daddy is chairman, but the Bishop has turned up— turned up last night—and he so wants to meet you all. I think it's to do with all this business about the Rector's alterations and so on.' This excuse was an inspiration which had returned to her on the doorstep, and she cheerfully used it. 'We want you all to come, especially the children—it won't be all funny old councillors —there are a lot of Adrian's friends and mine who are week-ending with us. I'm sorry about this awful short notice but you see the Bish only arrived last night and it's really in a sense his invitation. He particularly longs to meet—to meet as many of his parishioners as possible. So please come. Please do.'

Here this cataract of friendly if insecure words came to an abrupt stop, as if its source had failed, and the spring was dry.

But the charm had succeeded. Lizetta was delighted that the Bishop should want to see her especially—her it must be since

Bertie was no churchgoer and two young children could be of no account.

'I'm sure we shall be delighted to come. You mean the children too?'

'Oh, yes, the children certainly. I think they'll enjoy it. There's all the park to play in, and there'll be an ice-cream tea. And a band.'

'A band? A brass band?' asked Lizetta in surprise.

'Oh dear no! Only Chris Petty's chamber orchestra on the terrace. I've told him to keep it as jolly as possible. I don't think old rural councillors want Beethoven's string quartets, do you? They'd much rather have *The Merry Widow* or something from *The Mikado*. I'm sure I should. And anyhow they'll all be talking at the same time and not listening.'

Lizetta agreed that rural district councillors wouldn't be interested in Beethoven's string quartets, though she had no notion what they were.

It was at this point that Conal peeped round the door of the living-room to learn who had arrived and was talking at such length. Isidora perceived his face and, ever willing to play the ignoramus when a social occasion demanded it, she exclaimed, 'Oh, is that your little son? I think I've often seen him in church.'

'No, he's Conal Gillie. He's living with us,' and Lizetta in her turn began to talk at length about India and Mr and Mrs Gillie and prep schools in England, while Isidora struggled to say and at last succeeded in saying, 'Oh do let me meet him, may I?'

'Conal,' Lizetta called, and 'Conal' again, for he had retreated hastily behind the living-room door on realising that his peeping face had been observed. 'Conal, come and meet Miss Drood. She inviting us to a wonderful party today at Drood Place. Where's Marjorie?' she asked, assuming that Marjorie would be as interesting, if not more interesting, than Conal, a stranger from India.

'I don't know,' said Conal, coming forward shyly. 'She disappeared.'

Hardly had he spoken before a loud and crude noise from upstairs of vehemently flushing water told everybody where Marjorie was. A door clicked upstairs, shutting away the sound of water filling a cistern, and Lizetta called, 'Marjorie, come and meet Miss Drood. She's inviting——' but Isidora, to ease the general embarrassment at these liquid resonances, asked, using the top of her charm, 'Oh, not "Miss Drood". It sounds so dreary. Could I be Isidora to the children?'

She had put out her hand, and Conal took it awkwardly. Still holding his hand, she said, 'We so want you to come to the party. Actually it was the Bishop who wanted you.' And then Isidora, a liar uninhibited when she considered that truth was of less importance than the pleasure of someone she was addressing, went on, 'He noticed you in church at the Rector's Induction and again at that silly meeting the other day.'

'I'd ... I'd love to come,' Conal stammered, 'but I shan't have to talk to the Bishop, shall I?'

'Oh, yes; and you'll love him. We all love him. He's wonderful with children. I've adored him ever since he confirmed me nearly ten years ago.'

Then it was Marjorie's turn for the Drood charm to be sprinkled over her like asperges at Mass. Isidora even declared that the Bishop had especially noticed *her* at the Induction and the meeting. Which had nothing to do with truth.

When Isidora was gone, and the hall door closed, Marjorie said with a skip of joy, 'Oh, lovely, lovely; I'll take my autograph album and get the Bishop to sign it. The Bishop's signature and possibly Sir Harman Drood's, though he doesn't interest me so much, but he's quite famous in his way—and certainly not that odious old Canon Patrice's—or perhaps I'll ask him because he may be a bishop one day.'

There was a craze among schoolchildren at this time, especially among girls, to get their friends and, better still, famous persons to sign their autograph albums after writing some quotation or motto or message of goodwill. Marjorie was an easy victim to this craze, fearing but praying always that the contribution offered would not be 'Be good, sweet maid' because it suggested that she was not and could never hope to be clever. Canon Patrice's hearty predecessor had willingly complied with her request and, thinking

her when she was ten years old a pretty little creature, had
written, to her delight:

> Forgive and forget is a proverb of old.
> I have learned but one half of it yet.
> The theft of my heart I shall freely forgive,
> But the thief I shall never forget.

It amazed Conal that anyone could feel and write like this
about Marge. *Marge.*

Marjorie's own contribution to her schoolfellows' albums was
nothing like so breezy as this. There was not a little of the pos-
euse in Marjorie, and, posing as a devout Christian believer
like her mother, she decided that a couplet of some piety would
be best suited to her and wrote in all the girls' albums, unworried
by any incongruity with the frivolous contributions on previous pages and thinking it fine:

> Contemplate when the sun goes down thy death
>   with deep reflection;
> And when again it rising shines thy
>   resurrection—Marjorie Jacky Sheridan

Some of the parents of the girls, to whom this irreproachable
admonition had been addressed, when they read it so neatly
penned, were less than pleased with it.

Both Marjorie and Lizetta were resolved to go to the party in
their best frocks and hats; in which resolution they were dwelling
at an opposite pole from Conal, who was disturbed almost to the
point of sickness by Lizetta's insistence that he must wear his
Eton suit and straw hat with its school ribbon. Etons during a
holiday! No one else would be wearing Etons and he'd be stared
at and laughed at. But it was so dressed that he went with Lizetta
and Marjorie between the piered gates and up the long, broad
chestnut avenue of Drood Place to park and terrace and mansion.
On the croquet lawns, divested of hoops and nets, they saw a

motley aggregation of 'councillors with their ladies', strolling in groups or chatting in groups together. To a male eye, and especially to one not yet twelve years old, it seemed that, while the ladies' dresses were bewildering in their variety, they nevertheless all looked much the same, with their large picture-hats flowered or feathered, their gowns tight-waisted and reaching to the ground, and the parasols of many open (for the sun had emerged to join the party). Every parasol was different, and yet each seemed a sister of all the rest. The men, on the other hand, seemed of every shape, size, and dress: some in straw hats and light suits, some in bowlers and dark suits, and several of the older ones in top hats and frock coats. The young week-end guests were all hatless and in simple holiday kit, some even in their tennis flannels. Nowhere, as Conal had foreseen, was there a boy in a black Eton jacket and starched collar. Why had some women no sense in these matters? The little seed of shame which he'd brought up the avenue sprouted above ground into something like pain—a shameful little bloom which he'd have to wear throughout the afternoon, walking among hundreds of people. And among some children too, worst of all.

Easily the most noticeable figure on the lawns was the Bishop, made conspicuous by his height and by his princely attire—frock coat, apron, gaiters, gold pectoral cross—the whole array crowned or capped—since as a house-party guest he too was hatless—by the crimped silver hair. As the most lordly person present he was encircled by a listening, chattering flock of people, mainly women.

The orchestra played on the long white terrace. It consisted of a string quartet backed and strengthened by an upright piano brought out on to the terrace from Lady Drood's sitting-room, known in Drood Place as 'The Boudoir'. Probably at Isidora's request, proffered with the best of her charm, head to one side and lips one persuasive smile, they were playing, not Beethoven quartets, but airs from the Gilbert and Sullivan operas and were at present engaged with 'Twenty Love-sick Maidens We'.

Conal observed Isidora in the distance. On the far side of the tennis lawns there was a succession of long rectangular flower-beds, each crowded with flowers of every colour and size—dahlias, roses, tiger-lilies, gladioli, marigolds, asters, violas, phlox—and

Isidora was leading along them a company of doubtless gushing admirers. She was quick, however, to see Lizetta and the children and she deserted her company and hurried towards them that they might feel welcomed and at ease. The Eton suit with its deep white collar had made Conal conspicuous (like the Bishop) but, while thinking this dress misplaced, she did not know that Conal was walking about in it, ashamed and in pain and wishing he were out of everybody's sight. Perhaps unclothed and in bed and with darkness around him.

'So glad to see you all,' she exclaimed, gathering all three into her glance. 'So nice of you to come. I hope there are people here whom you know.' It was clear that she had dressed for the party as studiously and eagerly as any of the councillors' ladies, though as daughter of the house was wearing no hat and carrying no parasol. What her present party dress might be was beyond male definition, old or young, and left Conal in confusion; but he had some impression of a long, pale-grey gown, with a network of lace above her breast, a sash emphasising her waist, and a skirt which stretched a long way down to her feet (for she was tall) and got narrower and narrower till it almost touched the ground. (Lizetta explained later that it was an 'afternoon gown of souple satin grenadine', whatever that might mean.) 'I'll get Daddy and Mummy as soon as I can,' Isidora was saying. 'They both long to meet you. And of course there's the Bishop who so longed to meet you all.' She said 'all' but her eye fell on Conal as she said it. 'I'll capture him for you as soon as he's got rid of all those encumbrances around him. You see, he's terrifically popular; most people adore him—at least all the girls do, including me. I can't keep away from him and must be a ghastly bore sometimes. Adrian, my brother, who's one of those people for ever trying to be funny, if he sees me with the Bishop, doesn't call me Isidora but says "Oh hell, there's the Bish and Hisadora again. Can't someone drag her away and give him a break——" '

Lizetta tried to insert a few proper words of gratitude and a protest, 'We really mustn't keep you', but Isidora, hardly hearing her, hurried on, 'And let's see: the Rector is here somewhere. Oh, yes, there he is, under the pergola, with heaps of people. You know Canon Patrice, don't you? There's a frightful row going on now about his putting the Ten Commandments over the altar. It's all rather fun. Which side are you on? I think I'm all for the curtains and the candles. They've always been there since I was born. Poor Daddy thought he was doing the parish a service when he appointed Canon Patrice, hearing that he was a great preacher and a prebendary, whatever that is, but now he doesn't know whether he's on his head or his heels. He likes Canon Patrice and so do I—he's a dear—but we were all a bit shaken, even Daddy, by getting the Thirty-nine Articles as his first sermon. Poor Daddy. He hasn't known much about High Church and Low Church, but he knows all about it now ... a shade too much, he says ... poor lamb.'

'I've never met this new vicar,' Lizetta contrived to intrude at this stage; and her remark gave Conal his chance to speak, correcting her: 'Rector'; and to boast, 'I have. I've had quite long talks with him in the church and in his rectory.'

'When was this?' asked Lizetta, pretending amazement, and Conal supposed that no one knew anything about his visit to the Rectory; but happily, before he could explain, Isidora said, 'Come along, all. I think the Bishop's free. Or I can liberate him. People shouldn't monopolise him so.'

It was not easy, she found, to liberate the Bishop, so she touched Conal's shoulder and said to him alone, 'Come to Canon Patrice since he's an old friend of yours. An audience with him will be easier than one with His Lordship the Bish.'

It was indeed easy enough, because the Rector no sooner saw Conal than he turned his face from his group of disciples and said, 'Aha! Here's a real friend of mine. My very first visitor. He set an example to all of you by coming to call on me almost before I was properly housed in the Rectory. And this in spite of the fact that he's only a parishioner of mine during his school holidays.' As he looked down upon Conal there was affection in his eyes, even though he failed to recall his young visitor's name. 'Colin, wasn't it?' he asked.

'No, sir, Conal.' And Isidora enlarged upon this. 'Conal Quentin Gillie. Of Slings, Wedgery High Street.'

'Conal, of course. And with Slings for your holiday cottage. Conal: an Irishman, clearly. I always think I must be an Irishman too, with a name like Patrice. I'd much rather it was a corruption of Patrick than have anything to do with Patricians.

Who'd want to be a patrician if he could be an Irishman? Well, Conal, how much longer have we got you with us? When do you go back to school?'

'Not till mid-September.'

'Good: a long time yet. You'll have time to come and see me again.' He seemed to remember that this boy had brought some trouble with him. 'I remember we had a fine theological discussion. Our Conal, Isidora, is a gentleman of strong opinions.'

For a moment Conal, though grateful for this affectionate greeting, found himself thinking that a question of life or death for ever and ever was hardly a subject to be dealt with so lightly. This moment of doubting disapproval, however, was tempered by the gentle words that followed. 'Don't forget, Conal, that I'm here to discuss anything with you at any time.'

Isidora was again impressed by this academic and theological relationship between an Eton-clad schoolboy and a canon of the Church but, after hearing a few more exchanges between them, she said, 'We mustn't monopolise the Rector,' and drew Conal away from among the Canon's appendages and led him to a bench at the pergola's end beneath the last of its festooned and creeping roses. 'Did you really,' she asked as they sat side by side, 'call upon him immediately he arrived?'

'Yes, but it was about four days after.'

'After what?'

'After his Induction and Institution.' He was proud of these weighty words because he was feeling shy and humble and embarrassed among these rich and stately people with their palaces and parks and patronages, so he added, 'His Institution by your father, or rather his Presentation,' to add to the display.

'And you had a learned theological discussion with him?' Isidora was now looking down upon Conal at her side almost as if he really were some infant prodigy. She was remembering that there'd been infant prodigies among pianists and chess-players and mathematicians and wondering if there'd ever been an infant prodigy among theologians.

'No; it was only that I wanted to ask him some questions about that first sermon of his.'

'First sermon? Oh, the Thirty-nine Articles thing. Oh, yes I was there. I always have to be there, under Daddy's orders. But

I've no memory at all of what he said—except that it was uncommonly boring.'

So this rich and radiant girl from a Stately Home had been troubled not at all by the prospect of perishing everlastingly if she didn't keep the Catholic Faith whole and undefiled. None of it had seemed important enough to stay in her memory. But then, he remembered, neither had Lizetta or Marge appeared to have been troubled for ten seconds by these hideous possibilities. Was he the only person whose head and heart were raked by them? Thinking this, he felt he'd like to question Dr Balder about this universal indifference—but the Doctor was no more. And the Doctor was a sinner in the eyes of this kindly Rector—a sinner unworthy of burial in consecrated ground and condemned, presumably, to dwell for ever in torment with the Devil and his angels.

'What was the sermon really about?' asked Isidora with the brightest of smiles.

'A lot of it was about hell.'

'Oh, dear! Was it? And you went and argued it out with him? Do tell me all that he said, and all that you said.'

As she sought this from him, she rested a hand on his knee, and there was the same affection in her eyes as that in the Rector's, so Conal was encouraged to pour forth to her all that had been racking his mind for days and days. Could she really believe in this, that, and the other: in all the awful things Jake Horrabin had quoted and Miss Merriweather had vehemently affirmed at that meeting in her father's parlour, and in all that the Rector clearly believed. He told her about going to Dr Balder's house in search of an answer and learning that he was dead. 'Can *you* believe it all?' he requested. 'I can't make it out. It doesn't make sense to me.'

'I don't think I've ever given it a thought,' she said. 'But go on.'

He poured out more of it in a spate because whenever he stopped she encouraged him to go on. He spoke of the Doctor's astounding bequest, and that it surely couldn't mean that he was an out-and-out sinner, and that it would enable him to go to Oxford, which didn't altogether please him because it would mean he'd have to stay longer in England instead of going back to India, and which he could never have done without the Doctor's gift because he hadn't the brains.

'*That's* something I don't believe,' said Isidora.

It was as she said this flattering thing, gazing down upon him, that he became aware of an increasing interest and affection lodged here at his side. And in the same instant a curious thing happened. Conal was on the brink of twelve years old, and this was the first time in all these years he'd looked at anybody with a new kind of pleasure in beauty. He was now conscious of this pleasure in admiration but as yet quite unaware of its sexual content. It was just a sharp and surprising pleasure, and rather exciting. And he knew that it was transmuting the love which he'd felt for the flattering old doctor into a love for this beautiful and flattering girl. He was loving her looks and he'd loved the Doctor's brains, and ready and eager to find an intellectual haven with her.

They had not finished their colloquy when they saw that all the guests were trooping from the gardens on to the terrace and into the house, the orchestra accompanying their procession with an especial vigour.

'That's Tea,' said Isidora with some enthusiasm, thinking this would interest her companion perhaps more than theology. She picked up his hand as if thinking him, at this moment, younger than he was. Quickly she recovered from this misapprehension, and dropped the hand rather than chafe his pride. So it was only side by side that they went into the house, and she led him through the great hall and past the Grand Staircase into the Picture Gallery, where an elaborate tea awaited the guests.

The Picture Gallery was a long and lofty room, 'a western wing', she expounded to Conal, 'added about 1760 by the Adam brothers'—none of which conveyed much to her listener. The high ceiling arching above this majestic room was an elongated dome (if one can talk of such a thing). This dome was divided by plaster ornamentations into panels, each containing frescoes, now faded, of classical or legendary fables. Chandeliers of cut glass and ormolu hung from among them. The tall windows, looking out upon terrace and park, and open to the August warmth, let in the music of the orchestra.

A great oval table, brilliant with much of the Drood silver

plate, stood at the room's far end. From this well-stocked table footmen in pearl-grey tail-coats and black bulging knee-breeches, together with maids in decorative caps and ornate bibbed aprons reaching to the carpet, carried trays of offerings among the crowded guests. In general command of the battle, like Admiral Lord Nelson on the deck of the *Victory*, the butler stood by the table; a little man in mere civvies (so to say), he compared poorly with his uniformed footmen and even with his natty maids.

Once again the Bishop was the most conspicuous figure in the multitude (apart from the footmen); was he not, like them, arrayed in picturesque uniform? He was encircled, as usual, by a fringe of talkers, but Isidora could easily have brought Conal to his notice, had she not decided that a boy of his age would be more interested in the sugared cakes and other *bonne-bouches* on the table than in episcopal questionnaires. So she led him to the butler (no less) and said, 'Parkerson, for pity's sake look after my very great friend, Mr Conal, and see that he's properly fed.'

The butler with a faint bow and a faint smile, as of one who appreciated a humorous situation, said, 'Most certainly, Miss Isidora. You leave him to me.'

And Conal was soon proving that Isidora had been right in thinking that he would, for some time, be concentrating his interest on the fare before him. And she, not wishing a hostess's presence to hamper his activity with the cream cakes, went off to play a hostess's part among other guests. Thus it came about that the encounter between Bishop and Dr Balder's young heir was not achieved on this day and had still to be contrived.

12

Bishop and priest sat on the terrace in the warm August evening. They sat where, a few hours earlier, the orchestra had been playing outside the Boudoir to the people on the lawns. Eight o'clock, and the sun was setting. It sank behind the westerly woods on their low hill and, leaving a golden glow in the sky, with ribbons of crimson above it, turned the woodland into one dark silhouette.

'Well, it's time we got these vexatious matters settled, Steve,' said the Bishop to Canon Patrice. 'We've had the last of the sun.'

He was enjoying one of Sir Harman's long cigars and, no puritan, had a second cognac on the little round table before them. Not so the austere canon, who was indulging in neither of these luxuries. He had not even allowed himself a cigarette. Evangelical and puritan, he neither drank nor smoked. There was only a second cup of coffee before him which was getting cold in the evening air.

The little table stood near the terrace's brink, and they could look over the carpet of perfect turf which sloped steeply down to the lawns. 'Did you ever see mown grass with a pile so perfect?' asked the Bishop, diluting the troublesome subjects which sat between them. 'Show me another country that can produce it. There isn't one. It's all dried up by this time. The price we pay for it is our climate, and it's a price worth paying.'

But the Canon, more interested in the troublesome subjects than grass, responded only, 'I hope I shall be able to do everything your lordship commands.'

'His lordship will command nothing, my dear Steve. He may counsel plenty. No more. There are two vexations, aren't there? Let's take them in chronological order. First, some of your people are upset by your removal of the riddel posts and the curtains around the alt—the holy table—and the substitution of the Decalogue as a kind of reredos——'

'That's where it always used to be, my lord.'

'Quite. Quite. So I believe. So I know. But then there is the removal of the candlesticks and the liturgically coloured frontal from the holy table?'

The Canon nodded agreement.

'Well, Steve, you may think these are small refurnishings but you will know that strictly—according to the letter of the law—no alteration or addition to a church or to anything in it can lawfully be made without a Faculty.'

'As you say, Bishop, that's the exact letter of the Law, but who feels it necessary to——'

The Bishop interrupted. 'Certainly. Certainly. You may think that these alterations are so small that they come under the principle of *de minimis non curat lex*. But, dear Steve, there are those of your people who don't consider them *minima* at all.'

'My lord, if you wish it, I will replace the candlesticks in case any visiting minister might wish to use them, though I should never light them myself. Every compromise your lordship suggests I shall try to accept. A pair of brass candlesticks are no great matter, but the Decalogue I cannot remove—no, no! It is the Decalogue by which we live. Rather than do that I would seek a Faculty.'

'With the consent of your wardens and vestry?'

'Sir Harman would hardly obstruct me and he would carry most of the others with him. He goes back to the days when the Decalogue had always been there. As far as I can learn, my predecessor didn't trouble about a Faculty at all when he substituted curtain and candles and all the rest.' He allowed himself his usual small jest. 'Faithful to the traditions of his parish, he just smuggled them in.'

The Bishop, desiring amicable terms, responded in the same tone. 'Knowing him, Steve, I can well believe it.' He carried on with the jest, *allegro ma non troppo*. 'In the language of that Gillie boy's late lamented old Dr Balder—to whom we'll have to come in a minute—he managed to outwit the Excise.'

Canon Patrice abandoned the jest. 'As a matter of fact, Sir Harman doesn't really understand what all the fuss is about.'

'I can perceive he doesn't,' grinned the Bishop. 'And I feel no small compassion for him. But now he only wants to please everybody. Which is going to be difficult. How about your replacing the riddels and the dorsal and putting the Decalogue above them? That would see to that, wouldn't it?'

'I dislike riddels and dorsal immensely but I—yes, I would do this for his sake and yours.'

'Splendid, Steve. But then there's the question—which has upset many—of your taking the north end of the ... the altar when you're celebrating the Blessed Sacrament, the—er—the Lord's Supper ... instead of the now almost universal "eastward position".'

'My lord, at my ordination as priest I vowed on my knees to minister the sacraments as this Realm has received the same. And the rubric in our Prayer Book is perfectly plain: "The Priest: standing at the north side of the Table shall say the Lord's Prayer...."'

The Bishop's smile broadened. 'I know it does. Who doesn't know it? But, Steve, you also vowed to "reverently obey your Ordinary and other chief Ministers set over you" and "to follow with a glad mind their godly admonitions and submit yourself to their godly judgments". "With a glad mind!"'

Canon Patrice did not return the smile; his head shook sadly. 'This I shall always strive to do; but I should be very loth to go back to the eastward position. For me, there is doctrinal significance here. The eastward-facing position with its back to the people suggests a priest offering a sacrifice.'

'I understand your attitude perfectly, Steve.'

At this the Canon, as one who has taken a trick, proceeded quickly, triumphantly, 'It was only a few years ago that Archbishop Benson——'

'Yes, in 1890,' said the Bishop, who saw what was coming.

'—that Archbishop Benson pronounced the eastward position as "permissible". Only "permissible". Not legal. Actually, in my view, by suffering this, he reversed a decision of the Privy Council and countenanced disobedience of the Law.'

The Bishop grimaced. The grimace, which was first cousin to a smile, suggested the unspoken words, 'Damn the Privy Council'. But he only went on. 'Don't imagine I'm going to trouble you as to where you stand for the celebration of the Euch—of the Lord's Supper. Indeed I am in no position to do so. The "north side" rubric is certainly there. But may I remind you, Steve—' here the grimace which had been half a smile became a wholly teasing smile—'that there are other rubrics, and things in the Prayer Book Calendar, about which I feel sure you wouldn't approve— such as "Fasts" before every red-letter holy day. But let us pass on to the other matter: the burial in your churchyard of that rather pleasant but avowed old heathen, Dr Balder. You and your vestry have control of your closed churchyard, and of who can be there and what can be placed there. At the same time it's certain the good lady, since she was a churchgoer, has an in-alienable right for her ashes to be buried there——'

The Canon nodded. 'Of course. No question about it.'

'—but it is another matter whether this decisive old heathen's ashes can be placed by her side. Steve, do you not feel that you could allow this since he hinted at a desire for it?'

'No.'

It was refusal absolute. He softened it by adding, 'No, my lord,' but it remained so absolute that the Bishop was for a moment halted—and halting. 'But ... Steve ... the Coroner did go out of his way to grant the old scoundrel his wish by declaring the balance of his mind disturbed.'

'Yes, and there's not a person who doesn't know that this verdict was a lie. It was an evasion of Truth. And indeed of the Law. No man was ever less insane. I stand by the Truth. And the Law.'

The Bishop meditated on this for some time, smoking the last of his cigar, while the dark deepened around them, and a star or two became visible in a clear sky above the dark and distant wood. At last he spoke. 'Steve ... the Church has its need of rules and laws and formularies, but can anyone doubt that God is larger than them all?'

'Maybe, but that's not for us to act upon blindly. We must stand by the Law and the rules—or where shall we get? And the Church's Law is obvious. Not only has every parishioner the right of burial in my churchyard but—of great interest to a seaward parish like mine—so has every human body cast ashore by tidal waters. But Christian burial, in the very first rubric of our Burial Service, is forbidden to all who die unbaptised or excommunicate or are known to have laid violent hands upon themselves—which is undoubtedly the case with this man, Balder. While I am incumbent here, no deliberate suicide will be laid by me in my church-yard. The decision rests with me.'

The Bishop paused. He stubbed out the last of his cigar. He sipped the last of the cognac. 'You have spoken your truth. I will now speak mine. It is this. I think my God's acre is larger than yours, Steve. Let us go in. It is getting cold, and I'm strangely tired tonight.'

Rarely a morning but Lizetta sent Conal or Marjorie on what she always called an 'errand'; an errand to grocer, greengrocer, dairy or post-office—or to two or three or more of these. It was usually Conal whom she sent on an 'errand', and he suspected that this was because he was not her child but a stranger on her hands who might well be made use of—for there was little that Conal didn't perceive. The suspicion was true in part; but in part only; he was older and stronger than Marjorie and a male; and Lizetta was inclined to believe that anyone masculine, even if under twelve, would receive more prompt and honest attention than a little girl. And she still thought of Marjorie, so recently her infant, as about five years younger than she was.

The Monday after the Drood House garden party there was an errand for Conal to 'Ashley Bros, Universal Stores'—a single-windowed shop in the High Street—for tea, jam, vinegar, and salad oil. When he came out of this universal stores with his purchases clumsily carried as four separate items in brown paper, and turned homeward to Slings, he heard a voice calling him, 'Conal. Conal.'

Turning and nearly dropping the salad oil, he saw Isidora on the brick footpath ten yards behind him. Her tall, slim figure was all in white, from the large white-feathered, white-lined hat to the hem of her white dress and her lace-trimmed white sunshade. Elaborate and expensive attire for eleven o'clock on a Monday morning.

Conal waited for her. She came up to him, and after smiling and asking the superfluous question, 'Doing the shopping?' and getting the superfluous answer, 'Yes', she said, 'The very person I wanted to see! Don't drop those things. May I walk along with you? I'm going to luncheon and a big afternoon affair at the Bakewells', and I don't want to in the least. They live at Winfield House just beyond your Slings. Know them?'

'No.'

'Well, you haven't missed much.'

'Lizetta may know them.'

'Lizetta? ... Oh yes, your temporary mama. You and I—and them of course—never got to the Bish after all, and he so wanted to see you—to see you all. But you all got away somehow, but tell ... tell "Marjorie", is it? ... that I'll get the Bishop to write in her album before I've done with him. Well, a whole lot of things have happened since Saturday. The Bishop's more or less solved everything. Everything about what the Rector gets up to at the altar, and everything about whether your ... your friend, old Dr Balder, can be buried in the churchyard, and all that sort of thing. I must say that Canon Patrice has behaved very decently too. I'm getting quite fond of him. Everybody's trying to please everybody else, so far as they can, and certainly Daddy's trying to, bless his darling heart.'

'Oh, do tell me what's happened,' Conal begged, holding his parcels tighter.

'Of course I will—but do hold those things carefully; I'm sure one of them's going any minute. Are any of them bottles or jars? They look like it.'

'Yes, all except the tea.'

'The Lord look down upon us and protect us. Don't let me hurry you. Well now, the Bishop, you see, wanted the old Coroner's verdict to be accepted so that the naughty old man could be buried alongside his old girl. He said he would willingly have performed the ceremony himself, but it wouldn't do for a bishop to publicly overrule—now I've split one of my infinitives which he wouldn't approve of at all—to overrule publicly one of his clergy and, as it were, snub him, so would the Canon allow him to send another parson who'd have no objection to doing what the Rector felt he couldn't possibly do. Canon Patrice said that would be perfectly all right with him; he would be content to have made his stand for what he held to be the Church's Law. And the Bishop said that this was the great glory of the Church of England, that it could be comprehensive enough to contain parsons who believed precisely opposite things, and so were able to come to each other's assistance in the friendliest way on difficult occasions like this. He said how glorious it was that the Articles—which we had in that sermon, good God—were all deliberately phrased so that they were capable of being read either as an affirmation or a negation—or both —or even something else—of any doctrine that cropped up. This suits Daddy down to the ground—and you'll agree that toleration and comprehension can hardly go farther than this. The Church, you see, is pluriform.' Isidora had lately heard this attractive word from the Bishop, and was proud to use it.

'Is whati-form?'

'Pluriform. Composed of almost every form of Christian you can imagine—and I'll say it certainly is, if you compare our old rector with the Patrice—though I like the Patrice. Daddy wants everybody to be happy and stop quarrelling and like the parson he's provided for them. So another parson, who believes the opposite from Canon Patrice, is coming from Eastbourne tomorrow afternoon to perform the ceremony, and nobody much need be there to know what's going on. No one much *is* there, as a rule, when ashes are dispersed or put in the earth or something. Any service will have been read at the crematorium—and the churchyard business'll all be over in five minutes.'

'Tomorrow afternoon did you say the parson from Eastbourne was coming?'

'Yes, about three o'clock, but I don't think you should tell your parents or anyone. The Rector wants it done quietly, because, of course, he doesn't really agree with it.'

'Oh, I shan't tell them. Lizetta fully agrees now with Canon Patrice that an unbeliever, who tried to make me one too, shouldn't be buried in consecrated ground. She gets quite hot about it.'

'Does she? Well, I don't think I agree with her. The poor old boy, wicked or not, obviously rather wanted his ashes to lie with his lady's, and she, I'm sure, would want both to be buried in a churchyard and to have him with her. I suppose I take after Daddy; I just want everybody to be happy.'

*   *   *

Canon Patrice's far more liberal predecessor, arguing that if God could create a cosmos out of nothing he could without too much difficulty recreate the bodies of his faithful from their ashes, had formed in his churchyard a little 'Garden of Remembrance' for those who would wish their ashes to be laid here. This railed 'garden' was a square of untidy grass beneath the east end of the church, where the headstones and table tombs were few. The whole churchyard was encircled by a flint-and-stone wall, four feet high, that looked to be of the same age as the great church's walls, which were of local flints with greensand quoins. Because the little 'garden' was so recent it was some way from the church and close to the encircling wall. Thick clumps and shawls of ivy draped the wall at every point, with this year's shoots sprouting above them, so it was easy for a child to watch, unnoticed, over the wall and between the shoots, any interment in the 'garden'. Also the church stood in the centre of the 'Wyn', as the village green was called, after the ancient meadow from which it was formed, and there were public seats against the wall, so the Rector was not unaccustomed to, or interested in, faces watching a funeral from over the wall.

Conal had noticed this garden once or twice because Lizetta had an interest in tombs, especially in recent ones, and would often walk round the churchyard after a service, and he had heard her animadvert warmly against this new and unChristian method of burial.

So Conal knew where to be, at three o'clock on the Tuesday afternoon. Ever secretive and shy, he had stolen away from Slings at about half-past two and wandered to the churchyard wall, where he found a good place to look between the ivies at the 'garden'. He had arrived too soon and could only wait and wait. Time crept along; no one approached from the church; a few people passed carelessly behind him; and he wondered if anything was really going to happen. At last the big clock in the church's battlemented tower struck three, and still nothing happened. He looked at the trees within the churchyard: limes and ashes and beeches, and one great yew so dark and solemn that it seemed to be rebuking the facile and branching levity of all the others. He looked at the trees without the churchyard—mostly beeches slanted away from the rough, salted sea-winds. He listened to the birds overhead: doves crooning, larks still singing aloft though it was August now, and rooks cackling and croaking. Still no one. 'About three o'clock,' Isidora had said, so he remained there, sometimes fingering the ivy or the stone wall. The clock struck the first quarter, and he was still there, tired enough at times to lean against the wall.

He looked at the church's east window there before him. It had three lights, and he knew well, from staring at them when kneeling in the church without any prayers, that they pictured the three great Sussex saints, St Wilfrid, St Dunstan, and St Richard—Wilfrid the greatest name of all, because he'd converted the South Saxons when no one else could do this, because they were men not easily 'druv'; and Dunstan who'd tweaked the Devil's nose with red-hot tongs so that he had leapt with one leap out of this unfriendly Sussex into Kent—to the spiritual welfare of Sussex, no doubt, but to the material welfare of Kent because he'd bathed his suffering nose in the waters of Tunbridge Wells, and so endowed them with their extraordinary healing quality. Conal, from his view-point outside the church, was now tracing the leaden slips that shaped the mitred pictures of Wilfrid and Dunstan.

But at last, suddenly, surprisingly, four people were approaching from some church door: a tall and very young priest in surplice and violet stole; a handsome old gentleman with rich white side-whiskers and moustaches, presumably the old friend whom Dr Balder had asked to preside over his obsequies; a man in a grey suit and a cloth-cap, carrying an urn, presumably an official from the Crematorium, and Canon Patrice. The Rector was in his ordinary black suit, unrobed, and acting only as courteous host and guide to his visiting priest. It might be his duty to pronounce the committal over an urn that held the ashes of some unknown churchgoer, but to avoid doubling the committals it seemed he had been content to leave all to his young visitor. Conal was not untouched when he saw that the handsome old gentleman with the white whiskers was carrying the yellow urn he'd last seen on the Doctor's mantelpiece. He had to brush his eyes.

The four men entered the untidy little garden, and for the first time Conal observed a small hole or pit, not two feet square, in the long uncut grasses. They stood about it, more or less facing Conal but unaware that there was a mourner on the far side of the ivy and the wall.

The tall young priest looked very young indeed. He could not have been priested before he was twenty-four and must therefore be about twenty-six or twenty-seven, but with his smooth, rounded cheeks he could have passed for twenty-one. Like Sir Harman, Conal had known little about High Church and Low Church but knew plenty about them now; even so he did not yet recognise that in the two priests before him, one in surplice and violet stole and the other in his week-day suit, he was looking at polar opposites in the Church. He began to perceive this dimly as the ceremony proceeded.

At a sign from the young priest the old gentleman laid his yellow urn in the pit, and the priest, scattering a handful of earth upon it, said the words of committal. 'Forasmuch as it hath pleased Almighty God of his great mercy to take unto himself the soul of our dead sister here departed, we therefore commit her body to the ground; earth to earth, ashes to ashes, dust to dust, in the sure and certain hope of the resurrection to eternal life...' as he said the words he was making a sign of the cross over the grave. It was this sign of the cross that began to open Conal's eyes.

Now, taking the other urn from the Crematorium official, he stooped and laid it himself by the side of the first urn in the grave. It looked to Conal as though he was troubling to see that the sides of the two urns touched. This done, he made a small sign of the cross on his breast, and Conal now decided that he must be 'enormously High Church' in a way that Lizetta would certainly denounce.

But what words of committal could he now say over the ashes of a vowed and vehement old heathen like Dr Balder? Conal strained ears to hear and eyes to see. He caught the words because they were spoken in a voice young and clear and fearless —and they stabbed into his heart. Tossing earth on to the urn, the priest said, 'We commit the body of our dear brother here departed to the ground, earth to earth, ashes to ashes, dust to dust; his soul we commit to the uncovenanted mercies of God who knoweth all, and whose property is always to have mercy, not weighing our merits but pardoning our offences...' and he made the sign of the cross over this urn as over the other.

Now the same sign on his own breast, and he was speaking words that none could understand except, probably, Canon Patrice, a scholar. But Conal had enough prep-school Latin to recognise the tongue, and not without some uncomprehending pleasure in its beautiful organ-notes; though he was remembering at the same time how Lizetta would bewail, with shock and opprobrium, that nowadays some young priests liked to say prayers in Latin so as to feel a little closer to the innumerable congregations of Rome. The actual words were, *'Omnipotens, sempiterne Deus, qui semper promptior es ad exaudiendum, quam nos ad orandum ... effunde super nos abundantiam misericordiae tuae...'* and maybe Canon Patrice identified them as part of the Collect for the Twelfth Sunday after Trinity: 'Almighty and everlasting God, who art always more ready to hear than we to pray ... pour down upon us the abundance of thy mercy....'

Canon Patrice stood hearing them with no expression on his face, either of approval or disapproval. The handsome old gentleman and the Crematorium official stood there, wondering, perhaps, but quietly and reverently withdrawn from all understanding. Conal loved the sound of them.

Yet another sign of the cross over Dr Balder's ashes and one on his breast, as the young priest, remembering, no doubt, his Theological College days not so far in the past, ended this little ceremony with the last words of Compline, the service which closes the day. *'Benedicat et custodiat nos omnipotens et misericors Dominus....'*

Whereafter all four turned away and went back into the church. Now no one was in sight anywhere; no gravedigger or sexton came to fill up the little grave, so after waiting a little longer and still seeing no one who was likely to watch him or rebuke him, Conal made his way into the churchyard and into the garden, where he stood looking down upon the two urns lying side by side and touching.

Feeling an affection for the tall, young, nameless priest who'd been willing to discharge the old Doctor's wish, Conal came out

of the churchyard on to the Wyn, and strayed homeward, thinking he'd quite like to be a parson in robes, saying prayers in
Latin, making a small sign of the cross on his breast whenever
suitable, and being enormously High Church in a way that would
shock Lizetta. A strange fancy to bring away from the open grave
and last sight of a briefly known but well-liked old mentor who'd
flourished his Unbelief like a victorious banner.

13

Now it was the Bishop and Isidora sitting at a table on the terrace in a warm August evening. The Bishop was again sipping a cognac, and there was no question of Isidora limiting herself to coffee; she was enjoying a large glass of her father's noblest port. August had worn on, the sun was down behind the great woodland, its gold and crimson afterglow, though brilliant, was low in the sky, and the first of the twilight was already around them. This session would have to be short. It was the evening after the interment of Dr Balder's ashes, and they were speaking with admiration of Canon Patrice's readiness to welcome into his churchyard a priest whose ecclesiastical complexion was the opposite of his own; a topic which brought them to further talk of the boy who had won the heart of a learned old blasphemer, and the residue of his estate, in four brief meetings.

'I was sorry I missed him at the party,' said the Bishop. 'I'd have liked to have a look at him. After all, he's the "talk of the town".'

'But will he really ever get all that money?' asked Isidora. 'Or does the Coroner's "unsound mind" invalidate that will?'

'I really don't know any law,' said the Bishop, 'but I daresay somebody could contest the will. But where's anyone in sight to contest it? The old boy had no children, no relatives, no descendants even, as far as we know. No, the child'll get the money all right.'

'We couldn't get near you at the party. You were surrounded—naturally—by devoted admirers all the time.'

'Flattery, Isidora, will get you nowhere.'

'And meanwhile the Sheridan lot slipped away.' She gave no heed to this talk of flattery.

'Oh yes, and there's the little girl who wants her autograph album signed. I must do this for her. But, Isidora, she wants some poetry written in it as well as a signature. What in Heaven's name am I to write? You must help me. Give me something intelligent to write, so long as it isn't "Be good, sweet maid".'

Isidora ransacked her mind for something in the least suitable, but only one poem danced in her mind, a lingering relic from her schooldays. Tentatively she suggested it. 'What about:

> Shall I compare thee to a summer's day?
> Thou art more lovely and more temperate:
> Rough winds do shake the darling buds of May,
> And summer's lease has all too short a date.'

'Why, that's perfect,' the Bishop exclaimed. 'It fits perfectly with their Easter and Summer holidays in my diocese. Dear me, what should I do without Isidora?'

'Flattery will get you nowhere, Bishop.'

'Don't be impertinent, girl. And it's not flattery. It's just the simple truth. You know that you tell me exactly what to do, and I go and do it.'

'Well, it's flattery for her, and she'll be dazed with happiness. She'll be showing it all over her school... But I think it's a bit too flattering. She's rather an over-pious little person—or pretends to be, so as to please her mother. Couldn't you give her something frivolous? I feel it would do her all the good in the world to know that a bishop can be really frivolous—not holy all the time.'

'You're probably very right. Well, give me something really flippant. Something far from a right reverend.'

'Me? Oh, I can't think of anything. You'll have to think of it. Or invent it.'

'Invent? Oh, no. Good gracious, no. I can't invent anything. At least, not in rhyme.'

'Oh, yes. You can do anything, if you put your mind to it.'

His head shook; after a time his lips moved as if he were shaping syllables to himself; his fingers beat rhythms on a knee; and at last he said, after closing his eyes in thought and opening them again, 'Listen. Look. How would this do?—

> They call it my See that I see from the Downs;
> Those hamlets and pastures and dozens of towns,
> But Wedgery hence-forr'ard All Hallowed shall be
> Since here you required an inscription from me.'

'But Bishop! That's perfect! That's *it*. Oh, she *will* be pleased.'

'Good. Let her be happy. And now what about the boy?'

Isidora recounted to him all that Conal had poured out to her—here in this very garden—about his secret terrors after the Rector's sermons and after Jake Horrabin's and Lucy Merriweather's Biblical quotations. 'They left him distracted——'

'Oh, *no*!' the Bishop pleaded, in a burst of loving sympathy.

'Yes; and he decided that the only way he could escape from these terrors was into the happy infidelity of his new friend, Dr Balder.'

'Oh, but we can't have that.' The Bishop shook his head. 'We must save him from that. You say he's a nice child?'

'Well, I don't know. He rather charmed me because he was unhappy, and obviously aching for someone to listen to him. As I've told you, he seems quite an ordinary little boy.'

'I wonder.'

'He seemed to me a child rather lost and distracted. I don't think he's happy, living away from his parents in India. He adores his father, the magistrate or something in Poona or somewhere. I doubt if the woman who looks after him now, the Lizetta woman, is of much use to him. He'll get no sense out of her. I thought her good-hearted enough and ready to be kind to him, but not over-bright and therefore likelier to snub him than to help him. And there's no help in her husband who's a happy-go-lucky accountant more *au fait* with stocks and shares than with religion; whereas his father in India is apparently the keenest of churchmen.'

'I'd like to hear about the Church in India.... An odd little boy.... Must be, since he went and carried all his troubles to Stephen Patrice the very first day after he'd arrived at the Rectory. Before anyone else in the whole of Wedgery. To discuss eschatology with him. Because that's what it amounted to.'

'Yes, I began to wonder if he was rather an infant prodigy.'

'No; I don't think so: no prodigy; just an odd child, fairly bright, who's starting—at nearly twelve, you said?—starting on his perilous climb out of childhood. All he needs is to share his anxieties with some acceptable adult. Someone whom he can trust and who'll say, "But I can have my doubts too".' The Bishop looked away from Isidora towards the great wood in the distance where there was no golden afterglow any more but only the first grey dusk in which a star could be seen. 'No shielding him from his difficulties. No denying them. Just sharing them with him. Sharing them....'

Because the Bishop was so distracted and far away, Isidora did not speak. Talking, it seemed, only to himself, the Bishop repeated, 'Never shielding ... sharing ... sharing....'

Then he returned to her. 'Who really understands the mind of a child? A child of twelve? I'm sure they can suffer now and then like a lost soul. I said at the meeting that I could have given answers to all that the admirable Mr Horrabin and Miss Merriweather said, if it had been the least bit relevant to the business in hand. I'd like to give them to this boy. I'll come especially to do so.' He smiled at Isidora. 'Always glad of an excuse—not to say, in your vile and ignorant language, an "alibi"—to come to Drood Place and see Isidora. Now listen: I appoint you my episcopal legate to go and arrange an audience between me and this child. You say he loves the Downs and wanders about on them?'

'Yes, because they remind him of his Western Ghats in India. And of climbs with his father.'

'Well, tell him that I know precious little about the Downs and want to learn all that he knows about them. And that I would like to hear about India, so please will he let me go for a long climb with him on the Downs?'

'Oh, Bishop, that'll be wonderful of you.'

'Not at all. If he's sick and in some sort of emotional prison, it's my business to visit him. And it's your business to arrange it all between us.'

'Oh, I think this is terrific. You mean you'll give up a whole afternoon to a worried schoolboy?'

'Surely.'

'But not to you. Not you. To a mere child. And you with a great diocese to look after?'

' "Who shall say which is greatest, Isidora? Who shall say which is least?" ' asked the Bishop, quoting less than accurately a poem lately published. And with a lift of his eyebrows and a questioning smile, as of one who must obey orders, he completed the quotation in his own way. ' "That is my Master's business, said Eddi, Wilfrid's priest." '

To Isidora, easily moved, this seemed a quotation so beautiful in its aptness that for a moment the tears in her throat inhibited speech. And the Bishop, perceiving this, said with the same smile, 'Like Eddi, what am I but one of Wilfrid's latter-day priests?'

'Oh, when will you do it? When can you do it?' Isidora was impatient to be off and away on this mission of mercy.

The Bishop produced a diary from somewhere inside his frock coat. 'Hmm ... nothing possible this week. Nor ... next week. Monday? Monday after that would be possible. What about Monday week?'

'Oh, I'll go and tell him tomorrow morning, as ever was. Tell him he's got to escort you over the Downs and teach you everything he knows. He may be nervous of so important a charge, but if I know him at all, he'll be thrilled as well.'

'All right,' said the Bishop. 'You have your episcopal instructions. Go and do your duty. Your apostolic duty.'

So, next morning when, after breakfast, the Bishop had been driven home in his Wilton-Rover cabriolet, waved away by Isidora, she hurried to Slings, carrying this invitation like a happy burden.

The door of Slings was opened so quickly by Lizetta that Isidora suspected that Mrs Sheridan, like herself, was rendered instantly curious and hopeful by any ring on a hall door-bell. She saw surprise and wonder in Lizetta's eyes at the sight of the girl from Drood Place again on her threshold.

'Oh, Mrs Sheridan,' Isidora began. 'I've come with a rather extraordinary invitation. From the Bishop.' Tactfully she said, 'You remember he wanted to see you *all* last Saturday but we never got round to it. Now he——' but here her tact went further. Conceiving that any mother, however nice, might feel some jealousy if, instead of her daughter, it was an unrelated child in the house who was receiving a special invitation, she said, 'He's asked me to ask you for your daughter's album because he knows she wanted him to write in it. And he's told me what he proposes to write for her. It's rather lovely. I simply don't know how he thinks of these things so quickly.'

'Oh, she *will* be pleased. Marjorie, Marjorie,' Lizetta called. 'Come here. Bring your album. The Bishop wants to write in it.'

'Yes,' Isidora pursued. 'He especially asked me to bring it so that he could do what your daughter wanted.' And she seized upon this happy interlude, while Marjorie was bringing the book, to introduce the mention of Conal. 'And there's an invitation for Conal too. I was telling him how Conal loved the Downs and knew so much about them, and, if you'll believe it, he wants Conal to go for a long walk with him over the tops and tell him all he knows. He says that it's appalling how little he, though he's their bishop, so to speak, knows about them.' Instinct told her to stop here and not speak of the Bishop's other desire: to hear much about Conal's parents in India. Nor was it the moment to dwell on the Bishop's longing to recover the boy for a Faith that had once been his, and was his parents' still, and which it was the task of a bishop to establish in the hearts of his people.

'Go for a walk with the Bishop on the Downs? How wonderful!' There was no jealousy in Mrs Sheridan's voice, but only pleasure, now that Marjorie was at her side and almost dancing with delight, the album waiting in her hand. 'When would this be?'

'Some time away, I'm afraid, but I told the Bishop that Conal had several weeks of holiday before him. He suggested next Monday week. In the afternoon. He could sign Marjorie's book then.'

'You'd better see Conal,' said Mrs Sheridan. 'He's in the garden somewhere.'

'I'll fetch him. I'll fetch him,' cried Marjorie, also devoid of jealousy, since Conal's visit would carry her album to the Bishop. Marjorie retreated into the back parts and returned with Conal.

There was no shyness in Conal's face at the sight of Isidora; only delight and affection, after his long and fascinating theological discussion with her in her garden under her pergola and her roses. He was able to say, 'Hallo' quite naturally, as to a friend.

Isidora told him all, and at first, though flattered, he demurred, 'But I shall be terrified. And I shan't know what to say.'

Isidora wouldn't accept either of these. 'Oh, no you won't; and oh, yes, you will. There's no one like the Bishop for putting anyone at ease. He'll ask the questions, and you'll provide the answers.'

'But all I know about the Downs came from Dr Balder and he was an atheist.'

Isidora laughed. 'I don't think Theism or Atheism has much to do with the history of the Downs.'

But Conal took a different view, and, feeling so free and easy and fond with her, he explained, 'Oh yes, it does. Because he didn't believe that God created them.'

'You mean he thought they created themselves?'

'I suppose he meant something like that.' And very ridiculous this statement sounded.

'Well, I'm sure that in itself will interest the Bishop hugely. Poor old Downs.'

'And he called them only quite modern stuff.'

'He called them *what*?'

'Modern stuff compared with other parts of the earth's crust.'

'In fact, he didn't take them very seriously?'

'No, not very.'

'Don't talk all that nonsense, Conal. To Miss Drood.' This Lizetta. And to Miss Drood she apologised, 'He talks all this awful nonsense that he got from that old man, Balder. I wonder he dares say it to you.'

'It's not nonsense,' Conal insisted. 'It's just the truth.' And he was glad to be able to unhorse Lizetta with some really big words, while he himself shone before Isidora. 'Their chalks belong to the Cretaceous period and that's about two thousand million years later than the Eozoic.'

'The Eo—*what*?' begged Isidora.

'—zoic.'

And Isidora was now wondering again if here was an infant prodigy—this time in zoology, while Conal continued, 'He said they'd been built under the sea and in due course they'd all be washed back into the sea. Probably.'

'Conal, *will* you stop it?' Lizetta demanded. 'I've no patience with you. This stuff and nonsense. I pray God he won't talk to the Bishop like that.'

'He's only showing off,' said Marjorie.

'Well, I don't know what Miss Drood will think of us.'

'She thinks,' said Isidora, 'that Conal and the Bishop are going to have a wonderful time. The Bishop, I know, will have a lot of answers for you, Conal, as well as you for him. And you needn't think he won't be pleased to hear about Dr Balder. In spite of everything, he had a lot of admiration for the old man. Next Monday week, please, Conal. In the afternoon.'

'But what do I do? Where do I meet the Bishop?'

'Come to us and collect him. Then lead him all over the Downs telling him all you know.'

'Oh, dear,' said Conal with a wondering sigh. But within the sigh, and along with the nervousness, there was gratification, and something like a zest for the occasion. 'What do I call him? "My lord"?'

'Lord, no! He'd soon stop you saying that. "Bishop", perhaps.'

'Oh, I couldn't call him that.'

'Well, don't call him anything. Just talk. You'll be happy with him. Wait and see.'

'What if it rains?'

'It's not going to rain. I won't let it rain. If it does, I'll let you know what to do.'

'Oh, I hope it doesn't,' Conal heard himself saying, and knew then that his pride was greater than his fears.

So far from raining, the day could not have been kinder. The sun at noon was flooding all the downland summits and the coombs between. And the old south-west wind instead of being rude, lay asleep, leaving the sun to spread its pleasure and encouragement along every hollow and hill. The whole wide valley of the Grayling lay burnished and smiling under this lively sun.

Conal, through the last dozen days, had imagined the Bishop awaiting him for this walk in a frock coat, apron and gaiters and even in a high silk hat beribboned. Instead when he arrived in the great Entrance Hall of Drood Place, heart beating irregularly, the Bishop emerged from the Parlour in a grey lounge suit, perfectly tailored, as always, but plainly his holiday wear. The only evidence of episcopal rank was the purple stock between waistcoat and clerical collar and a glimpse of the thin gold which held out of sight his pectoral cross. And, of course, when you noticed it, the great episcopal ring on his finger. Even so, Conal was getting perceptive enough to think the Bishop, with his height and silver hair, one of the most distinguished figures he'd ever seen. And this made him all the more nervous.

Perceiving the nervousness, the Bishop set about putting him at ease with a lively welcome. 'My guide and counsellor! It's extremely good of you to give up so much of your time to a greenhorn like me. I'm told there's little you don't know about our Downs, and I want you to show me everything and tell me everything. For a bishop it's really reprehensible how little I know about this part of my diocese.'

Conal felt he must say something modest so, still nervous, he stuttered, 'I didn't know anything much till Dr Balder told me everything.'

'Well, there was nothing much he didn't know,' laughed the Bishop, 'so please transfer to me all that he told you.' He picked a coarse ash walking-stick from an umbrella-stand near the door; and that was all. Evidently he was going to wear no hat, and Conal, in his prep-school cap, was left wondering what sort of hat a bishop wore when he wasn't in full episcopal uniform.

Now Isidora emerged from the Parlour, and her appearance was a relief to the shy Conal. She smiled upon them both as if to bless their journey together. 'Have a wonderful time,' she said. 'Look after the Bishop, Conal. I commit him entirely to your charge.' And to the Bishop she said, 'Goodbye, Bishop, I'm leaving you in good hands.'

It was only a few hundred yards from the great piered gates of Drood Place to the churchyard wall, and from here to the first slope of 'The Hill'. So bishop and boy were soon done with this gentle incline and breasting the steep, the Bishop asking questions when his breath allowed this, Conal answering them proudly, and the Bishop detecting from these answers, as Dr Balder had done, seeds of vision and youthful poetical imagination. Desiring to display the great learning which had been assigned to him, Conal was quoting Dr Balder abundantly. By the time they were on the ridge of Wedgery Beacon he said learnedly, 'This part used to be known as Wedgery Band,' and on the summit, flattered by the Bishop's interest and now almost wholly at ease, he indicated the earthworks of the Roman camp and the traces of the sunken pathway down which the legionaries would descend invisibly to harry the poor Britons in the great Anderida forest below. He looked towards the Sussex Weald below them, stretching to the North Downs in the sun-flushed, hazy distance, a vast patchwork pattern of woodlands and pastures, ploughlands and hamlets and spires, and expounded, 'Sylva Anderida the Romans called it, and Andreasweald the Saxons after them, who followed the old Britons and Romans. Worth Forest and St Leonard's Forest and Ashdown Forest are still there, remains of old Sylva Anderida'; and the Bishop, listening, forebore to mention that almost everything now within their view, from the marches of Hampshire to those of Kent, the whole chequerboard of green pastures and dull-gold harvest fields with woods and townships spaced about them, was the see over which he presided.

There were some things, however, which he was truly learning from Conal, as vicar and voice of the late Dr Balder. There were the lychets or narrow shelves along the sides of the hill's escarpment; long overgrown and broken remains of artificial terraces cultivated by prehistoric men. There was his talk of the dewponds on downland summits, great tarns never empty, summer or winter, however dried up other ponds might be, because on these bleak heights the nightly dews kept them filled.

The Bishop let him talk on and on, because it was only slowly that he could work his way to the real business of this summer afternoon. When they sat down for a time on the Beacon's undoubted summit, he began, 'Now tell me something about India. Your father's a real Burra Sahib there, isn't he? "Burra Sahib" is about the only word I know of your Anglo-Indian language.'

'He's a Burra Sahib now, but it's only since I left India that he became Collector.'

'Well, tell me all about him. And his District. I'd like to know a lot about that.'

Ever ready to talk about Gondapore and the Ghats and his father, Conal was soon pouring forth (feeling now as free and happily easy with the Bishop as he had with Isidora) a nostalgic description of his native city Poona on its high plateau and the Western Ghats running parallel with the sea, but throwing out spurs on to the Deccan tableland which carried Gondapore as its chief city and military station. He told the Bishop how his father would take him up on to the Ghats to show him mountain views and forest scenery. 'I think that's why I love climbing the Downs, though they're almost the opposite of our Ghats.'

'Why "opposite"?'

'Because they're so bare and empty of trees. And, of course, the Downs are only about eight hundred feet at their highest—

we're sitting at eight hundred feet now—but Gondapore itself stands at about two thousand feet high and the Ghats are often three thousand feet and more.'

As they talked together the gulls were wheeling and screaming over their heads; a curlew cried its name, skimming inland, which meant that the tide must be high under the cliffs; and a wheatear dropped to ground near them, hopping from patch to patch till it found a place where it could stand easy and flirt its tail.

This led Conal—proud again to air knowledge acquired from the omniscient Balder—to inform the Bishop in case he didn't know (which he didn't) that the wheatears packed on the Downs for their immigration south; and then into talk about the brilliant birds on the Ghats and the Deccan which his father used to identify for him : birds from the Himalayas and the Malayas; the orange-breasted eaglets, green parrots and exquisite little plum-headed parrakeets—to all of which the Bishop listened faithfully, and indeed with some interest, though it was not the main business of the afternoon.

'Your father is a keen churchman, isn't he?'

'Oh, yes. He and Mummy go regularly either to the church in the civic station or to a chapel of the missionaries.'

'Missionaries! But I've always thought that most of your magistrates in India wish to heaven the missionaries had stayed at home. And left the Indians in peace.'

'Not Daddy. He likes them. He's all for them. He's an awful lot interested in Indian religion.'

'Tell me how.'

'I don't rightly understand. He just says the Christians can learn a lot from the Indians.'

'And I suspect he's very right. Extraordinary how near the Brahmans are to Christianity—' and the Bishop echoed the very words of Dr Balder—'with their Trinity of Brahma, Vishnu and Seva and their avatars or incarnations of Vishnu.'

All this about India, thought the Bishop, but nothing so far about a child's escape from terror by way of Unbelief. He beat his ash stick upon the ground before his feet and raked it along the thyme and clover, stirring an aromatic fragrance, while a chalk-hill butterfly flittered before them, its wings almost as grey-blue as the summer sky above them. Then deliberately he said, 'But their ideas of Reincarnation which they share with the Buddhists and—come to that—with Pythagoras and Plato hardly tally with the Christian doctrine of Heaven and Hell.'

Instantly he knew that he was where he wanted to be. His words had plunged his companion into some dark silent deep. The door he wanted open stood ajar.

Conal did not speak, and the Bishop guessed that he was wondering if he dare open his troubles to a bishop, tall and great and important—and 'old', with white hair. The Bishop waited, gazing down at the boundless theatre of the Weald beneath them. It was just possible to discern the herds on their pastures and the newly harvested wheat standing in shocks on their golden stubble. He poked the ferrule of his ash stick into the soft turf, as he decided that, unlike Isidora's 'Lizetta woman', his first task was to heighten a child's sense of his own dignity and worth. And, Conal remaining silent, he began gaily, 'Didn't someone tell me, or am I imagining it, that you were thinking of becoming an unbeliever?' (Even a bishop could act a semi-lie if the cause was good enough.) 'Where can I have heard this? Of course this Reincarnation business is one way of dodging the awful difficulty of Hell and everlasting punishment.'

Then Conal spoke. As with Isidora under the pergola he poured out the whole packet of his troubles, kicking occasionally at the turf: all about Canon Patrice on the Athanasian Creed, and all about Jake Horrabin and Miss Merriweather and what the Rector had said to him in his study—and of course all that Dr Balder had said about rising above all these old superstitions and the terrors that went with them. He told him how Canon Patrice had said it was only possible for those who could plead 'Invincible Ignorance' to be saved, but however could he plead this, brought up as he had been by his parents in India and his foster parents in England?

Now the Bishop was free to say all that he longed to say. This magnificent outflow had opened every gate. 'Conal,' he said, 'you are at an age when all sorts of brightnesses are opening before you. Never mind Invincible Ignorance. Where I agree with everything Steve said to you is——'

'Steve?'

'Canon Stephen Patrice—I agree with every word he said about the Invisible Church being composed of the great and good who can't make themselves believe—though I think I should allow that it contains far, far more members than he would consider fit for it. The Visible Church may have all the formularies and Athanasian Creeds in the world but God is very much larger than any creed, and only he can see into a soul. Into every single soul. So the Invisible Church is just those whom God sees as his own.'

For Conal these words worked a small wonder. He felt an instant willingness to be a member of this Invisible Church. And with this willingness came a first sense, sudden, unexpected and happy, of release. Of freedom. While the Bishop was saying, 'My dear boy, don't worry about doubts. Don't strain after some faith in things that are still beyond your understanding. Faith without doubts wouldn't be faith; it'd be knowledge, and there's no great credit in that. Faith isn't an intolerant assertion that something is true under pain of death; it's trust … trust that something your whole soul loves is true. Just love and trust, Conal. That's all that's asked of you.'

The astonishing sense of release widened in Conal. It told him, or began to tell him, that despite Dr Balder, despite Lizetta, despite Canon Patrice at his sternest, there was that in him which hungered to be back in the old ways—in the ways of his father. No doubt this liberation on the summit of a down was due in large part to the great position in the world of the bishop who was talking to him; and even to the height and commanding appearance of this bishop, and to the view of his whole kingdom which stretched beneath them on the Sussex Weald as far as eye could see; for these things were like a demonstration of his position and power. Dr Balder had seemed a great and remarkable man, but here was a greater.

And the Bishop went on, almost as if he knew what was astir in the boy's mind. 'There's never been a great man without his doubts—or shall we call them "wonders"? Even St Paul, surely the most tremendous Christian who ever lived, could write about his wonderings and his doubts—doubts about himself and his understanding, that is. Doesn't he say "now we know only in part, but one day we shall know in full", and somewhere else only "I *think* I have the Spirit" and, most plainly of all, "How unsearchable are God's judgments, and his ways past finding out".'

So friendly and smiling was the Bishop's manner as he dilated on these great questions that Conal dared to ask him a question which one hour ago he couldn't have imagined himself uttering. 'But do *you*—do you have doubts?'

'Of course, my boy; of course I do—I did to start with, and I still do—doubts about my knowledge and my understanding of things that remain for ever mysterious—but never, never, about my longing to love and to trust in them all, and to help others to do so.' Unconsciously, as he said this, he cast a glance at the great outlay of his diocese with its woods and its fields and its churches spread far below. 'Conal, there was a bishop once—oh, fifteen hundred years ago—Augustine, and he said it all. He said that in all men there is a strange "yearning, hoping, longing, hungering and sighing" for something more than, on the face of it, this world offers; and I'm sure, fifteen hundred years later, that he was right: there is a hunger in all human souls, whether they allow it or not, for something wonderful on which they can stake their lives; and I'm also sure, after all that's been happening to you, that you are one of those who'll never be able to live in a world which offers nothing but emptiness. These immortal longings are in *you*. Shall we begin to walk back? You can tell me more about the Downs. I'm so grateful for all you've told me already.'

They had been seated, side by side within the lee of a small island of gorse, the only foliage on the Beacon's bare crown, Conal with his knees up and his hands clasped round them; the Bishop playing his stick among the many harebells and thistles and tiny tormentils at their feet. Now they rose to return down the hill together. And now, deliberately, the Bishop spoke no longer, for a while at any rate, of holy matters, but of secular things: of the exact heights of the various summits they could see before them; of the first appearance of these chalk downs not so far from his palace at Chichester; of the seven tall white cliffs with which they confronted the sea, the Seven Sisters, and of their magnificent close and climax in the haughty white face of Beachy Head, and of its successor now far out among the waves.

This encouraged Conal—now so easily talkative with his great and famous companion, so captured by this assurance that he was one with 'immortal longings', and so ready to be such a one—to submit in full all that Dr Balder had said about the Downs being no 'everlasting hills' but mere deposits of chalk laid millions and millions of years ago and likely to disappear after some more million years; washed away by water action into new seas.

The Bishop gave thought to this, as indeed it deserved, and they walked on in silence for a minute or two. When at length he spoke, he was back again, necessarily, in the realms of theology—but theology without tears, for children. 'Well, he may be right—I don't know; I am no geologist, and he was a very clever man—but if he is then one thought occurs to me.' He looked down at Conal's prep-school cap. 'If all these millions of years, these thousand ages, in God's sight are as an evening gone, then the Church's mere two thousand years are hardly anything, and I don't suppose she knows the total truth about many things yet. She's still very much in her prep-school stage.' An amused grimace at the prep-school cap. 'The Holy Spirit may be guiding the Church into all truth but he's only got poor foolish and fallible men to work with, and an appallingly slow and gradual process it is. Think of Drake sailing in his ship called *Jesus* to capture black men for the slave trade, and the whole of Christian England treating him as a hero; or of Innocent III, a Pope, and a great Pope in his way, ordering the massacre of the Albigenses because they were heretics; or of the massacring of the Huguenots on St Bartholomew's Day, gloried in by the Pope; or of the loathsome public executions at Tyburn when the hanged people were taken down and dismembered and disembowelled while still alive—why, it was only a few years ago that we realised that these things were wicked and revolting and wrong. Less than fifty years ago public executions were being watched by thousands and thought right. Do you realise, Conal, that it was only in my lifetime that we've learned that such performances are gross and horrible? Oh dear, oh dear, I suspect the Holy Spirit has a long way to lead us yet. There are a lot of vengeful Christians still ... but one day ... one day ...'

As he mused thus, the Horrabin and Merriweather figures in Conal's mind began, like full-bodied ghosts, to fade. They did not disappear; they faded.

And the Bishop sighed and shook his head. 'Men are difficult and stubborn material for the Spirit to work in, but he goes on—he goes on—and slowly wins.'

The sense of release, of illumination, an exciting sense, was almost completed, as the Bishop added, 'The Church hasn't yet the last word about many things, or even the last but one. The last word is God's. So only go on believing what you can, and loving what you believe. Trust your love and follow where it leads. It always leads to larger things. I know because I was young once like you and wondered and worried about everything, though—' here the flattering smile—'I'm sure I was a year or two older than you when the wonderings really began. Are you going on to a public school in due course?'

Extraordinary change of subject—or so it seemed.

'Yes.'

'When?'

'This time next year, I suppose.'

'And you'll have to pass an entrance examination?'

'Yes, worse luck.'

'Well, somebody told me—was it you or was it Isidora?—that you were worrying about Hell. Well, the Church has certainly always said that Hell exists; but what she has never said, because she is in no position to do so, is whether anyone has ever gone to Hell or what it is like. What she says is that a man would only qualify for Hell if he died with an absolutely free and deliberate and final decision to reject God and all he stands for. He would have to have rejected in this utterly final way the grace of God given him to choose good rather than evil. It sounds a pretty stiff entrance exam to qualify for Hell, and you'll never, never qualify for it, dear boy. You're not the sort.'

There was little more. The Bishop did say again, 'Only love the man who told us to forgive till seventy times seven, and who gave us the story of the prodigal son, and who called down forgiveness on his murderers—only love him, as you do, and as who could do anything else?' He added, 'The love is enough; strain no further; it will look after itself'; and then the talk drifted, or the Bishop on its bridge steered it, towards the ways of the British Raj in India, the churches of their chaplains, the chapels of the Anglican missionaries, and the ashrams of other faiths.

So they came to the bottom of the hill and the churchyard

wall where they parted, with the Bishop shaking Conal's hand, holding it in both of his and saying, 'Thank you again for all your information about the Downs. I think I know my Downs now. And about India too,' as if these two subjects had been the real business of their climb together. But Conal, as he shook hands, was thinking about the Bishop's talk of love and faith—into which he supposed the talk had wandered by accident—and before his hand was released he said, 'Thanks most frightfully.'

A last pat on the back, and the Bishop turned towards Drood Place. When a footman opened to him, Isidora, having heard his bell and come with a rush, was already in the great Entrance Hall to greet him. 'How did it go?' she asked. 'Please, how did it go?'

With a half-smile the Bishop answered, 'Not too badly, I think. We climbed to the top of the Beacon talking all the way, first about the Downs, then about India, and then, somehow or other, about God.'

'And you had a marvellous afternoon for it. I'm sure God must have arranged it for you both. Of course he did.'

'Yes, a pretty perfect day. I've never seen the Weald look more lovely or the Downs. We both enjoyed it all immensely. A bright lad. I have every hope for him. It was about half-way up that we left India and found our chatter adventuring on to holy ground. I think we got somewhere.'

Meanwhile Conal by the churchyard wall had remembered that he was only a few yards from the little grave where lay the ashes of Dr Balder. He walked round the wall to look for it. It was now filled up, with no stone over it as yet; only a card on a stick to identify it. Conal's first thought, looking at it, was that the old man's chosen disciple—and heir—had now forsaken him, won away from his teaching by what was, for him, Conal, a greater and more appealing voice; but then he wondered, Had he really deserted him? 'Be yourself,' he had said. 'Think for yourself. Lead your own life, and never mind that Lizetta woman.' And once had he not even said something about weighing with the utmost care anything a palaeolithic old archaeologist might tell him? 'Always decide for yourself. Be yourself.'

He returned to Slings, to be questioned in its tiny entrance hall for half an hour or so by Lizetta, who was as curious as Isidora to know what had happened. Marjorie came running out too, craving to know whether he'd got from the Bishop her autograph album—an object which everybody had forgotten in the midst of matters so holy and profound. Conal was more than ready to tell them both, in self-flattering mood and with an unworthy desire to triumph over both, that he hadn't withheld one word from the Bishop about his loss of faith in Christianity and about all old Dr Balder's arguments against it—while Lizetta stared at him in amazement and shock, bursting in with, 'D'you mean to say you talked to a bishop like that? I've never heard of such utter impudence—never anything like it. You at *your* age! Worrying him with all the stuff and nonsense talked by that terrible old man. You mean you——'

'Yes, I told him absolutely everything,' said the victor. 'And he was terrifically interested in it all.'

'Well, I can only hope he cured you of all that wicked unbelief. *You* to say you don't believe in this and that! You at eleven years old——'

'Nearly twelve,' the victor interrupted.

'And to a bishop. I'm just horrified. I feel you've put us all to shame. He'll tell that girl and everyone else at Drood Place.'

'And he may refuse to write in my autograph album,' Marjorie put in.

'Oh no,' Conal said by way of comfort. 'You don't understand at all——'

'*I* don't understand?' That a boy of eleven should speak to her thus left Lizetta speechless.

'No. He was quite obviously enormously interested. He said I'd told him absolutely everything he'd long wanted to know about the Downs. And he'll certainly write in Marge's——'

'Don't call her "Marge".'

'—in Marjorie's album. We were just like terrific friends when it was all over. I'd quite forgotten he was a bishop. And I'm sure he'll do anything I want. I've only got to ask Isidora——'

'Isidora?' Lizetta repeated the Christian name so familiarly used. 'And is she now one of your "terrific friends"?'

'Oh, yes. I love Isidora. Absolutely love her. It was she who told the Bishop I could tell him all about the Downs. But we didn't talk only about the Downs. He gave me heaps of answers to all that Dr Balder had said. And he said a lot of other wonderful things, coming down the hill; and I must say I tended to agree with them all.'

'*You! You* tended to agree with a bishop! Who would *you* be to disagree with him?'

A sentence which almost persuaded Conal to be a non-Christian again.

But the Bishop's voice had been too strong for any such lapse. It had proved stronger than Dr Balder's, and by uncountable degrees stronger than Lizetta's. The memory of that walk with the Bishop would be with him always, he thought. Just now he was feeling as if the Bishop's words had routed for ever those miseries of doubt and fear, and would for ever hold the field.

Tended to agree with a bishop! A shrug, as of despair, and Lizetta withdrew from argument, defeated.

PART THREE

Christa Seva Sangha

I

The ultimate issue of this odd little war under the Downs where the field of battle was the ripening mind of a schoolboy did not fulfil itself for a decade; but it began to appear on a May day in Oxford, when Conal, during his second year at New College, was sitting in its garden, loveliest beyond any man's rebuttal, be he Magdalen or Worcester or even Balliol, of all the incomparable gardens in that holy city.

On this afternoon in May a visitor was approaching the portal of New College: a man of early middle-age and less than middle height, with a high broad forehead and a long black beard below it; a parson but the beard was almost deep enough to curtain the clerical collar. New College Lane, whereby he approached the gateway, he knew well, and had often, as a Balliol man, devoted some of the specialised Balliol humour to it, for there is nowhere in Oxford a narrower and more twisted little chasm between forbidding mediaeval walls. It led to as humble a gateway as you could imagine, a modest doorway under a four-centred arch, with its doors sternly closed and a letter-box hanging on them, so that it seemed no more than the menial entrance of a porter's lodge. Its modesty was hardly lessened by some worn and weather-beaten statues in Gothic niches above: three in all, the Virgin, St Gabriel, and the College Founder, William of Wykeham, fittingly on his knees as if praying with apostolic fervour, but with some dubiety, perhaps, for the students who would pass into his college. What with the homeliness of the portal and the narrowness of the lane, this visitor, once of Balliol, thought, as often before, 'Ah, well, narrow is the way and strait is the gate that leadeth to life. And the road of humility is often the way to glory.' For he knew the glory he would see once he was through the shadows of that little gateway. Today, however, this admirable meditation was rather marred by the thought, 'But, hang it, the

Broad is the road which embraces Balliol, so what are we to deduce from that?'

He passed through the gateway and entered into the glory. Here in the first great quadrangle was the majesty of New College Chapel, with its buttresses and pinnacles and wide Decorated windows; beyond it the great dining-hall, and then the cloisters with their buttresses and trefoil apertures. Before leaving this for the surpassing glory of the garden he stopped to take out of a side-pocket a letter. 'Dear Father Jack, you are dead certain to spend a part of your furlough in Oxford—what Balliol man would fail to do this?—so please look up my boy at New College. He has heard all about you from me and will love to welcome anyone from India.' On this note, he, Father John Copley Winslow, had pencilled a memorandum after a telephone call, 'On lawn if sunny —about 2.30—in the north-east angle of the city wall.'

He passed through splendid gates and there across the spacious lawns, bounding the garden on three sides were the fortress walls of the mediaeval city, with their bastions and battlements, their parapet and counterscarp. Scattered over the lawns sat many undergraduates with learned books (he hoped) in their hands or on their knees—one with about eight books ringed on the grass around him, some open, some shut—for their days were getting all too near those subfusc hours in the Examination Schools. Yes, and there in an angle of the fortifications between north and east, sat—or rather 'lay'—for his deck-chair was arranged at its lowest level, a young man who looked up, perceived his visitor, waved, struggled awkwardly out of his collapsible couch, and came across the lawn to meet him.

So this was Conal, son of Henry Quentin Gillie of Gondapore, and as they walked towards each other, Father Jack thought, 'Yes, very much his father's son—though with hair as abundant as his old man's is getting scanty. But for a tall youth who must be pushing twenty it's a young face; he could pass for seventeen. A rather indrawn expression as of a young contemplative, but with merry eyes that could emerge easily from contemplation, and be merry again. A notably unhurrying slowness in his movement that suggests deliberation rather than dullness—one who finds thought easier than action. Here's one who'll never be an impulsive youth.'

A tentative and temporary portrait that might need plenty of retouching.

'Father Jack,' said the youth, greeting him. 'May I call you that? I had a long letter from Dad all about you and your wonderful new scheme. I'm longing to hear all about it. Got a chair waiting for you.'

'And you are Conal? Your parents loaded me, like Bunyan's Christian, with a whole burden, not of sins, but of messages for you, which I shall be quite glad to get rid of.'

As they walked together towards the angle in the city wall Father Jack saw alongside Conal's another hammock chair which had collapsed into a tormented wreck. Conal arranged the chairs while the Father studied the rioting herbaceous border, a forest of tall feathering grasses and large-leaved plants, with flowers of every colour and shape aglow amongst them, all crowded against the base of the old battlemented wall. 'Strange bed-fellows,' he thought. 'Plants and exquisite flowers, all symbols of peace and beauty and life, huddled against an old grey fortification that was ever ready for hate and warfare and death.'

They sat side by side with the great lawns before them. Mingled with the fragrance of the flowers and plants came the scent of grass lately mown and from far away the drifting rustic smell of gardeners' bonfires.

'Please,' said Conal, after they'd talked about his parents and Gondapore, 'tell me about this new idea of yours.'

'It's no more than a dream at present, and may stay so.'

'A dream of what?'

Of what? Father Jack was silent while he raked for words. 'It only came to me suddenly a little while ago; and now I can't think of anything else. An ashram that would show our western Christianity clothed in an Indian vesture so that any Hindu would know it for his own.'

'First,' said Conal, 'I've never known what exactly an ashram is. It might be a help to know.'

'Ashrams used to be the homes of Indian rishis, sages, where they gathered disciples around them to train them as "religious". Now an ashram's come to mean any kind of monastery or brotherhood of religious. A friary, if you like.'

Friary. The word flung Conal's mind right back to that unfor-

gettable talk with the Bishop on the Downs. They had been near-
ing the bottom of the hill, and the end of it all, when they saw a
Capuchin friar, in his brown habit, emerging from a visit to the
church at Wedgery. And the Bishop had said, half laughing but
not wholly laughing, 'A friar in his habit is more convincing than
a thousand sermons.'

The memory caused Conal to ask, 'You said something about
"an Indian vesture": what would your brotherhood's "habit" be?'

'Why, certainly "khaddar"—the white home-spun and home-
woven cloth of India which is almost compulsory wear for Indian
nationalists now. A long khaddar cassock with a saffron girdle,
I think—saffron being India's chosen colour for consecration of
any kind, Hindu, Baptist——'

'Yes, I knew that.'

'But the vesture would be more than mere robes.'

'How?'

'Well, Gillie....' The Father was not as yet on Christian name
terms, so Conal helped him. 'My name is Conal. Conal Quentin
Gillie,' he said, just as he had said it eight years before to Dr
Balder on the Downs.

'Well, Conal, after five years as a missionary in India my idea
is that there's a huge gulf to be bridged between our European
ways of life and the Hindu's ways, especially the poor Hindus,
the low castes and the outcastes. Look at me: as a missionary in
Ahmadnagar I've been living in a nice bungalow like your father
or any other sahib, wearing British dress and eating English
food, seated at a table and managing the grub with a knife and
fork, and then sleeping in a comfortable bed.' The Father, in love
with his idea, was now charged with words which were coming
forth in a gush. 'Not so the Indians. They may live in a poor hut of
wattle and mud, where they sit cross-legged on the floor eating poor
food with their fingers, and at night they probably unroll a mat
and sleep on the floor. All right—but for all humans everywhere
the finest means of fellowship is a meal together, and how, pray,
can this at present be possible between a British sahib and a poor
Indian? The Indian would be bewildered by the knife and fork
and by the food—the meat especially. And he'd know that the
sahib, at the back of his mind, was thinking of him as a mere
"native", of inferior race. My ashram would express the very

opposite of all this: unquestioned equality with all Indians of whatever caste. "East is east, and West is west, and never the twain shall meet", said your Sussex—*and* Indian poet, but in my ashram the twain will be one.'

Conal, listening, felt a surging enthusiasm for all that the Father was proposing. Just as he had when he listened to the Bishop on the Downs. It was like an exciting identification with Father Jack, as he spoke; a certainty that he was saying something that was true—and would ever be true for him, Conal. Not that he could think of himself as ever becoming one of Father Jack's 'friars'. He was seeing this as a wonderful life for some other man; but a devoted calling far out of *his* reach.

All these thoughts stayed him from speech, and Father Jack, touched by Conal's obvious interest, by his steady stare revealing remote, lonely thoughts, and by his puzzled eyes, hurried on. 'We'd not ask any Indian to dress or behave in ways that were uncouth to him. We'd be dressed to meet him. Confound it, Conal, Christianity at present seems to the Indian a western thing. But it was *not* a western thing; it was a flowering of an eternal eastern wisdom. All its greatest saints and teachers of its first centuries were eastern men. Christ must not seem to India like a western idol brought by a ruling race to its vassals; he was an oriental like themselves. There's something like a presence of Christ just waiting for us in the best of Hinduism——'

'That's what Dad often says,' Conal put in, and remembered, 'So did the Bishop.' And so did old Dr Balder, he thought.

But Father Jack flowed on, unheeding. 'Of course there are shocking idolatries among the simple Hindus, and the abomination of Caste among all. We've never been bold enough in the denunciation of Caste; the price has always seemed too great. But Caste is obviously a total denial of Christ; so much so that I'm thinking our motto might be "Christ for the outcastes" or "Christ for the untouchables". Just think what that would mean to some Indians.' Abruptly he followed this with a strange question. 'You heard of Amritsar? Last month?'

'Heard of it? *Heard* of it? Why, the country rang with it. And Dad wrote to me about it in horror.'

'If he wrote in horror, he was unlike the majority of the British in India. They're all swearing that Amritsar saved the British Raj.

It showed, once and for all, who was master.'

'He *is* unlike them,' Conal said proudly. 'He wrote saying that Amritsar, so far from saving India for the British, will in the end have lost it for them.'

'A great man, your father. One in hundreds.'

Conal, modestly leaving this, asked, 'Father, what exactly did happen at Amritsar?'

Father Jack's fingers drummed a tattoo on one knee while he considered his answer.

'Amritsar is the greatest city in the Punjab, a sacred city for the Sikhs, so anything that happened there must have a widespread influence for good or ill.' He halted for further thought. 'Well . . . no one can deny there were riots in the city and a danger of mob-rule. Europeans had been beaten to death in the streets, and an English woman missionary flung off her bicycle as she rode to her school, beaten mercilessly, and left half dead in a ditch. This raised more fury than anything else. Martial Law was proclaimed—so far, so good, and necessary, I'm sure—troops were brought into the city and the General-in-command marched them through the streets with their armoured cars, and announced at different places, with a beating of drums, that all large gatherings were forbidden and if this order was disobeyed his troops would not hesitate to fire. But the people only jeered, never believing that British troops, or Indian troops, their blood brothers, would fire on unarmed civilians—and it was April 13th last, in the afternoon that they assembled defiantly for a protest meeting in the Jallianwala Bagh. The General heard of this defiance and immediately marched his troops to the Bagh, where he saw a crowd of many hundreds.'

Father Jack paused and flung helpless hands to either side of him, as if he could hardly bring himself to describe what happened.

'Go on,' said Conal.

'Well, as you know, Bagh means "Garden" but the Jallianwala Bagh is no garden; it's just a great square of sunburnt earth with houses all round it so that there are only a few lanes of escape. Nonetheless, without a word, the General ordered his troops to open fire, and they poured round after round into the throng. When it was all over, the "park" was strewn with nearly four hundred dead and over a thousand lying wounded.'

Conal stared open-mouthed, his breathing quickened, his heart swelling and sinking. Then he managed to say, 'And, dear God, the people over here have been praising the general to the skies, and the papers getting up a huge subscription for him.... Fifteen hundred dead and wounded...'

'Yes,' continued the Father, 'but that wasn't all, perhaps it wasn't the worst. I suppose you could argue that the General had warned he'd fire—but there was the "Crawling Order".' Here the Father's head shook and shook. 'The Crawling Order was the worst.'

'Crawling Order?'

'Yes, the General issued an order that all Indians who walked along the lane where the English woman had been assaulted must crawl along it on all fours.'

'All fours?' An incredulous frown from Conal.

'Yes, and if they didn't crawl they were to be publicly whipped ... whipped.'

'God and hell!' An eruption of amazement and horror.

'And the Governor of the Punjab applauded everything the General had done; and the General himself is still proud of it.'

'No, no, no, no!' gasped Conal in breathless repudiation.

'But even so. And what in my view is the most terrible fact of all is that the General is the kindliest and friendliest person in his private life, and so's the Governor. But what matter fifteen hundred Indians lying dead or wounded or dying on the Jallianwala mud, if that's the only way you can establish who's master? What's wrong in making them crawl like beasts if that's the only way to *learn* them?' Again the Father's head shook despairingly. 'As with so many of our most benevolent sahibs, only let the cry go up "None of our women are safe" and kindliness flies out of the window.'

Both were silent after this. Till Father Jack, in his enthusiasm, returned to his ashram. 'I'd been trifling with my fancy for an Anglo-Indian ashram before Amritsar. Amritsar rooted it for ever. I see it as an answer to Amritsar. It's the opposite of Amritsar. An ashram where British and Indians live side by side, unconscious of race or colour, master or servant, Brahman or untouchable. You know, Conal, what the Indian, somewhere in the depths of his soul, truly reverences, is not the pomp and power of the

191

Raj or of his princes, but the very opposite, renunciation and self-giving, the sadhu and the faqir. Then again, Conal, what more wonderful in India than a community of English sharing with Indian brothers our Lord's poverty in a land of everlasting want? Is it, or is it not, an answer to Amritsar? Conal, soon after Amritsar I was talking to a ripe Indian scholar who'd been converted to Christianity, and I was trying to justify the good things the British had achieved in India——'

'My father would be with you there,' Conal murmured.

'Yes—I know—and I suggested to this old Indian that, with all its faults, the British Raj had striven to maintain standards of incorruption and integrity and duty to India which were probably unsurpassed in all the annals of despotism. And do you know what his answer was?'

Conal stayed silent, gazing and waiting to hear the answer.

'I shall never forget it. I think it built my ashram for me. He just raised the spectre of St Paul and stood him before me. There's much poetry in great Indians. He said simply, "Yes, you've given hundreds of your sons to us, and they have removed mountains; you have given your goods to feed our poor; you have given your bodies to be burned by our Indian sun; now give us love."'

2

Three hours Father Jack and Conal spent together under the city wall, but at last the Father had to hurry off to Chadlington Road for an encounter with one of the most famous of Balliol's sons, old Arthur Anthony MacDonell, Boden Professor of Sanskrit, Keeper of the Indian Institute, Master of the American Oriental Society, and occupant of a dozen other distinguished chairs. He was the author of a Sanskrit Dictionary, a study of Vedic Mythology and a translation of the Brihaddevata. It would be a discussion with a great scholar very different from one with a second-year undergraduate in his college garden.

In fact the book which Conal had been reading before Father Jack's appearance was no scholarly work, like the books of other undergraduates in the garden; he was less concerned than they with his Schools, and the book was a detective story, an excellent thriller, into whose suspense and mystery he had been diving deep. Now, the Father gone, he began to read it where he'd left off—but he dropped it to his knees again. Exciting though it had been, the Father's romantic story and high argument had flung a tighter lassoo around his thoughts.

When Father Jack found in Conal's eyes a remoteness and a lonely puzzlement, he had not been wrong. Conal, always a dreamer, kept his aspirations and his doubts remote from public eyes, partly because he feared they'd sound ridiculous to others of his age. But there lingered within him, stronger than any youthful lusts from which he was not free—however little any girl or woman had a hold on his heart, and however much the lecherous wits mocked him as a 'confirmed bachelor'—stronger than any youthful ambition to win wide fame in the world, a fancy that sorted well with much that the Father had said; though heavily hung around and hampered with doubts, it was a dream of self-commitment to some superbly unselfish course. This aspiration, hopeless as it seemed in the privacy of his mind, did not necessarily involve much religion. In imagination he was a neophyte, say, of some extremely noble order of Templars or Knights Hospitallers; only rarely a discalced friar like the Carmelites, and never, never, a Carthusian or Trappist vowed to loneliness and silence.

But, whatever it might be, this desire was inflammable stuff easily set alight by a similar desire like the Father's. And for several minutes after Father Jack had disappeared Conal, with his detective story on his knees, cast himself as a member of the Father's new Anglo-Indian Order and experienced a spell of joy and excitement, as of one born anew and in possession of a peace that passes understanding; he could recognise this as akin to the experience called 'conversion' but knew well enough, from many instances in his past, that the bright flame would quickly burn itself out.

Conal's religion in these days was still a matter of trust and hope as the Bishop had counselled; it was no full and stable orthodoxy. He went regularly to the conventual church of the Cowley Fathers ('Cowley Dads' in College parlance) between the Iffley and Cowley roads. He loved their crenellated and pinnacled church, and the approach to it through the Fathers' garden where a riot of flowers on either side of the path welcomed the visitor every inch of his holy way. He loved the ballet-like drama of their High Mass and, while on the Bishop's advice he prayed in harmony with such faith as was his, he wished always that he could enlarge this faith to encompass all that this magnificent service implied. He had made for himself a prayer at Mass which he could never tell aloud to any man, and it was, 'However dim and blind my faith, O God, let me so order my life that I am worshipping thee aright and doing thy will.'

Often, like other undergraduates, he sat happily with the Fathers in their Guests' Common Room and discussed with them his doubts and difficulties. What he rejoiced in was their complete toleration and understanding. His greatest obstacle to a full faith, he would tell them, was still the vengeful and retributive face of Christianity, the hell-fire doctrine which had so torn him to pieces when he was only twelve years old. He recreated for them a picture of Miss Merriweather demanding in the Drood Place Parlour, apparently with delight, that every hell-fire damnation, reported as the actual words of Christ, must be believed for ever as it stood; and he was greatly helped by one Cowley Father who, apparently untroubled by Miss Merriweather, said, 'Don't worry. Just do what a bishop told you: trust your own trust, and that, I'm pretty sure, is the belief—or will become the belief—that without Christ and his Father of Love, life isn't worth living, or death worth dying.'

Even more than these words from this father, which called up all his agreement, fervent agreement insusceptible of denial, a robust and uncompromising sentence from another father, one of the youngest, Father Roden Perceval, who looked far too boyish, too near his diaconate, to have donned the title, 'Father', remained for ever in his memory as comfort and easement. 'I believe you're right, my boy,' the father said. 'There's no dodging the fact that there's plenty of sternness as well as great love in Our Lord's words; I'm sure he meant to disturb the complacent or self-righteous people to their very depths; but on the other hand I am equally certain it's time to stop for ever the mouths of those blasphemers who call it "sentimental" to declare that the monstrous infliction of eternal pain on any creature is inconsistent with God's love. After all, didn't our Lord laugh at James and John, when they wanted to call down fire from heaven, and nickname them *Boanerges* or "Sons of Thunder"? Whenever you're worrying about the Faith, my dear man, meditate on this for fifteen or twenty minutes: "If God's Love is absolute, all the rest follows."'

'You mean?'

'I mean, the whole Faith follows. How could he offer to sacrifice himself less, both Body and Blood, than many a poor human lover might do for his beloved? Think of it. Think of it. Work it out.'

'If I work it out, Father, for fifteen or twenty months, the one thing I never arrive at is eternal retribution.'

'But, my dear boy, what do we know about eternity? Suppose it has nothing to do with time and space but is a single stillness, a Now with no Before or no After, but some other dimension which our mere spacio-temporal minds can never imagine? Who knows? Who knows?'

Such words as these were often a lamp for his feet, if less than unclouded daylight all around.

With these memories in his mind, and with his spell of 'conversion' burning out, he took up his detective story again, abandoning the difficult world of reality for the facile country of fiction. He had not adventured much further in this entrancing land when someone else came hurrying over the lawn to accost him. This was Robbie Cawdor, his closest college friend, who had been a freshman with him and had rooms next to him in the New Buildings. Robbie, like everyone else on the lawns, had a book in his hand. But it was no scholarly work; it too was a novel and one which, seemingly, he wanted to introduce to Conal.

While Conal was tall and slim Robbie was short and plump, with the result that wags called them Don Quixote and Sancho Panza, an appellation less than apt because Conal, though tall, was neither long enough nor lean enough, and Robbie, though short and stocky, was not round or podgy enough. Robbie was a Scot from Fettes so it was fitting that the book he was carrying should be by Sir Walter Scott and about a Scot. It was *Quentin Durward*. With it, and with a digit holding open one place, he burst upon Conal.

'Conal!' he called. 'Conal!'

'Oh God!' Conal sighed, annoyed by this snatching of him from a pleasant absorption.

'Conal ... Quentin ... Gillie.' Robbie stressed each name when he arrived at Conal's side. 'It's just ludicrous for you to go on arguing that you're no' a Scot.'

'I'll certainly go on arguing I'm no' a Scot,' Conal retorted, imitating the deliberate Gaelic in Robbie's words.

'Mebbe ye will. Mebbe ye will. Aye, Ah've nae doot ye will. And that'll no' mak' it true.'

'Father contends that we've a bit of Irish in us. That's why he called me Conal.'

'Och—Ah've nae use for "Conal"—and what the hell's the sense of claiming Irish blood when you can be a full-blooded

Highland Scot? Have some sense, chum.' The Gaelic had collapsed. 'Who wouldn't be a Highlander if he could? Wasn't it Sir Colin Campbell who said when he saw that the relief of your Lucknow would be the toughest job ever, "We shall need Highlanders for this"?'

'And a damn-silly remark too,' said Conal.

'No. Just plain sense. "Gillie" is a Highland word, to begin with. And then there's Quentin. You admit that your old man and all his forefathers have been Quentins. Why?'

'I don't know.'

'No, you don't. So I'll tell you. "Quentin's" been a Scottish name for centuries, and your father's father, or some earlier bloke, knowing that he was a Scot, decided that this was an honour that should be established for ever. And look here.' He opened his book at the chosen place. '*Quentin Durward*. The hero's a Scot, and why did Scott call him "Quentin"? And why should there be an exact description of you in it?' He picked up the wreck of Father Jack's chair and sat in it to read. 'He must have foreseen your existence by precognition or necromancy. I believe in necromancy.'

'You would.'

'Well, just listen to this. "The age of this young traveller might be about nineteen or twenty, and his face and person which were very prepossessing——" '

'Thank you,' said the listener with a nod.

' "—prepossessing, but did not belong to the country in which he was now a sojourner. His dress was very neat and arranged with the precision of a youth conscious of possessing a fine person.... Although his form had not attained its full strength he was tall and active, and the lightness of his step showed that his pedestrian mode of travelling was pleasure rather than pain—" if that isn't you forever walking over the hills, I don't know what is. "His features without being quite regular were frank, open and pleasing, while his bright blue eye had an appropriate glance for every object of interest—" especially a pretty girl, I would suggest. All the time I was reading this I saw you. I mean to say, the guy's you to the life.'

'The only trouble about that is that it might apply to almost anyone of nineteen or twenty.'

'No, it's you. Exactly. And who was that black beard I saw you talking to so earnestly?'

'That,' said Conal sharply, as one putting a frivolous puppy in his place, 'was a highly distinguished scholar from Eton and Balliol who is preparing to give his whole life to India.'

'A missionary?'

'A missionary at present, but he's proposing to be far more.'

'Anglican?'

'Anglican certainly.'

'Well, I hope he's a Catholic and not just "Broad" or "Low". And still less "High". Spare us from "High".'

'He's more of a Catholic than you'll ever be. If he succeeds in what he hopes to do he'll be professed as a religious, taking vows of poverty, chastity and obedience. I can't see you vowed to any of these; certainly not to the first and the last, and I'm not comfortable about your devotion to the second.'

They were now on Robbie's favourite subject—his current obsession. A Scottish presbyterian by upbringing, he was a convert to Anglicanism in its most picturesque and romantic presentations; in other words, he was now almost more ultramontane in his loyalties to a 'One Holy Catholic and Apostolic Church' than the Holy Father himself. These were the years of impassioned and deeply enjoyed hostilities among young Anglo-Catholics—Oxonians especially; did not the Oxford Movement spring from Oriel? —between the 'Sarum' or 'English Users' of ecclesiastical ceremonial and the 'Roman' or 'Romanisers'. Conal was Sarum and Robbie Roman, and their battles, warm always and often contemptuous, were probably the stoutest root of their mutual affection.

The Sarum Users had their Prophet ('The Blessed St Percy', as Robbie called the Rev. Percy Dearmer, lately vicar of a small red church near Primrose Hill) and their Book, his popular and best-selling *The Parson's Handbook*. The Roman Users studied only in the missals of Catholics across the Channel. But in whichever army you enlisted you were known as a 'Spike'—so long as you were not just 'High'—and you loved your enemies because they were spikes too. You and your opponents were at one in your bottomless contempt for the 'Prots' (Protestants). The *casus belli*, however furiously fought over, didn't amount to much more than whether you had two candles on the altar (Sarum) or six (Roman)—clearly Canon Patrice's predecessor at Wedgery had leaned towards Sarum—and whether the celebrating priest wore an English chasuble or a Roman.

Within a second of referring to the condition of Father Jack's Catholicity, *Quentin Durward* was forgotten and the obsessive topic had overrun the field.

'Indian vesture?' Robbie asked. 'Mean to say he'll abandon the traditional vestments worn by the Catholic Church all over the world?'

'Worn by one part of the Catholic Church,' Conal corrected, 'but not in this country which quite justifiably has its own uses.'

'Only used by a semi-heretical party in this country, thank God,' Robbie amended in his turn. 'My view is that the practice of you Sarum users is an insult to the Holy Spirit.'

'I beg your pardon?' Bewilderment, shock, incredulity here—or a pretence of them.

'Of course it amounts to a betrayal of the Holy Spirit. The Sarum or English chasuble was only found by rubbing brasses, many hundreds of years old, in Old Sarum or somewhere, and what do you suppose the Holy Spirit was doing in those hundreds of years? Was he asleep instead of directing the Church in all it should do?'

'No,' said Conal, 'I think it more likely that his interest in ecclesiastical vestments was but slight. Or, even more likely, that he happens to be an artist and can see that the English chasuble, falling into lovely oval folds, is far more beautiful than your square Roman one which looks more like a sandwich-man's board than anything else. Perhaps after three or four hundred years, which are less than a minute in his sight, he decided to wake up the Church to something beautiful it had lost. Anyhow the Cowley Dads, so far as they go, have their six candles——'

'So far as they go. That's the trouble,' Robbie worried. 'Like you, I've talked with them, but only once, thank you. For me they were all too ready to play with the Prots.'

'They're wonderfully Liberal, if that's what you mean.'

'Liberal. Liberal.' Robbie spoke the word as if it were an offence in his mouth. 'Why in some ways they're almost modernists.' For this word 'modernists' he dropped his voice almost as if it were a word best not spoken in Catholic ears, or, if spoken, breathed low. 'I've been to their High Mass, but if you want to see how High Mass should really be celebrated you should come to St Gabriel's, Archangel.' The name of this church was St Gabriel's, Oxford, but Robbie, with his need for everything to be at its most picturesque always spoke of it as St Gabriel's, Archangel. 'Why don't you come with me there? I found the Cowley Dads High Mass pretty Protty.'

Pretty Protty! This of the Cowley Fathers! This of their High Mass! Conal, grimly grinning, wondered on what Himalayan peak of Anti-Protestantism Robbie now stood. He felt it would certainly be exciting to see the church of Robbie's heart's desire. 'I'll come with you one Sunday, Rob. Before Term ends.'

'Good,' said Robbie. 'Then you'll really see something.' And they settled for Sunday week.

3

Before that day Conal took his favourite walk along the range of hills between Thames and Cherwell of which the highest peak was Shotover Hill, nearly six hundred feet. He never climbed these hills without remembering the Sussex Downs and the summits of Wedgery and Beachy Head. Below him in the valleys the Oxfordshire countryside—instead of the Weald—was vested in the glories of late May and early June. On this golden afternoon the meadows were yellow with charlock; the woodlands had their bluebell carpets; and all the hedgerows were laden and drooping with the white blossom of may. Beneath his feet, in turf as thick and comforting as a towel, the wild thyme and milkwort were pink and blue everywhere, and the cats-ear and buttercups yellow. Overhead were larks and swifts and swallows. And once a flock of starlings.

Much of this he remarked with pleasure, but generally he was climbing like a sleep-walker because he was dreaming, first, of old Dr Balder and the Bishop, and then thinking of all that Father Jack had said, and of the strange happy spell it had cast upon him. It had been a transitory spell, comparable only, he thought, with the tall Bishop's gentle rehabilitation of his Christianity, or much of it, walking at his side eight years before. Everything the Father had outlined had seemed to fit exactly with that amount of Christianity in which he could firmly, fully, and happily believe. 'That saffron girdle round the habit of our brothers, British and Indian, will be *our* answer to the British guns at Amritsar.' Something like that Father Jack had said, and Conal's heart had leapt in agreement—an assent that was at once a conviction and a joy in the certainty of the conviction. And the Father had gone on, 'We British, instead of being the highest caste of all, higher than the very highest of the multiple Hindu castes, will be level with the lowest, and one with the untouchables.' And again for Conal there was the leap of joy and peace in his certainty that this was the ultimate expression of Christian *practice*, even if the total Catholic faith which fathered it was not yet totally his. For a moment in imagination he *was* one of those saffron-girdled brothers and exultant in being so; but it was a joyous imagination which he could not sustain. His head shook as he walked on.

High Mass at St Gabriel's was at eleven o'clock and from half-past ten Conal was sitting in his favourite place under the city wall, and waiting for Robbie Cawdor, his mentor and dragoman, to come and fetch him. Robbie was soon in sight, hastening towards his disciple. As before, he had a book in his hand but it was no stout volume of Walter Scott's; it was a tiny black book, small as book could be. He came yelling, 'Cruachan! Cruachan!'

'I beg your pardon?' Conal queried.

'Cruachan. The war-cry of the Campbells of Cawdor. I've been reading it all up. We're a sept of the Campbell of Cawdor Clan. We trace our origin from Sir John Campbell, son of the second Earl of Argyll who married in 1510 the heiress of the last Thane of Cawdor, descendant of Macbeth, King of Scotland. Granted that the Campbells are just about the most savage and disreputable of the Clans, and that Macbeth is no great credit to us, but it's nice to know. The Castle and Keep of the Campbells of Cawdor is as Highland as it can be, just south of the Moray Firth.'

'You don't say so!' Conal mocked.

'I do. I certainly do. And look at this tie. Look at my tie.'

Conal looked at the tie: a tartan with a black and green base, crossed by red and blue lines. 'Very aristocratic,' he allowed, while thinking that for so ardent and extreme a Catholic as Robbie, all this talk with its social boasting was no mood in which to approach High Mass at St Gabriel's, Archangel.

But Robbie trumpeted further, 'That's our tartan. I found it at Clutman's in the High, who've got all the ties in the world. Our crest is a swan proper, crowned, or. And our badge is fir club moss, whatever that may be, with bog myrtle. I must find out all about you Gillies. I feel sure your clan is far more respectable though probably far less interesting than ours.'

'And what may that book be? The pipe-music of the Cawdors?'

'Oh, dear no. This is for you today, so that you can see what a Mass really ought to be. It's Father Stanton's *Catholic Prayers*. It'll enable you to follow every movement in the sanctuary and to say the proper prayers.'

'Oh, thank you,' said Conal.

'Not at all.' Opening the book at a page he put it into Conal's hand. The page was headed 'Mass and Holy Communion'. Conal took it, shut it, and together they set off, leaving the Campbells behind, suitably lost by the mediaeval wall.

The June morning was grey and dull, and a light rain began to fall drearily, so that the church, when they entered it, with the six candles alight on the High Altar and the other candles distributed all over reredos, sanctuary and choir, while nave and aisles were left in the half-dusk of a dull day, did seem a paradisal retreat, one half sombre, and the whole engagingly impressive—after the uninspired and meaningless day without.

Conal kneeled in a pew by the side of Robbie, who made an extravagant sign of the cross over brow and breast while his lips muttered just audibly, but plainly intended for Conal to hear, 'In the name of the Father and of the Son and of the Holy Ghost.' A glance at Father Stanton's book showed Conal that this was the right way to begin.

The church, though in an Oxford slum, was filling fast with well-dressed and prosperous-looking people, the men going to pews on the right of the nave, the women to those on the left. At the back some eight rows were left for men, women and children together. Conal looked over his shoulder to see families occupying these pews, and Robbie, observing his glance, cocked his thumb backwards, grinned and said, 'Yes. That's the Mixed Bathing.'

Conal was surprised to find that, while he was not on the side of the Romanising extremists, he was longing for the church to fill to its walls. It was always good to watch a triumph. And the triumph was granted him. Soon there was not an empty seat anywhere and many people were standing. Outside, in the forecourt of the church, people were gazing over or between the heads of those standing thick within the West doorway.

As the church clock gonged eleven, the choir, men and boys,

but without any clergy, came in a silent procession from the sacristy to their stalls. One minute, and they were followed by a small procession: two taper-bearers escorting an acolyte holding a small vessel, a priest—or layman—in a magnificent and mysterious vestment, and then the Sub-deacon in his tunicle, the Deacon in his dalmatic, and the Priest in a golden cope.

'Please?' Conal begged of his instructor, not knowing what all this was about. He knew what the eucharistic vestments were and that the Celebrant should be in a chasuble, not a cope.

'The asperges,' said his instructor in a whisper.

'And that vessel?'

'The holy water vat, of course.'

'And the magnificent priest—if he is one—in front of the celebrating clergy? Who's that guy?'

'The Ceremoniarius, of course.'

When the procession had arrived before the altar, all knelt and the Deacon handed an instrument to the Priest.

Conal's glance at Robbie sought elucidation.

'The aspersorium,' Robbie whispered.

'Oh I see. Thank you. Asper...?'

'...sorium,' Robbie completed.

The Priest, taking this aspersorium, intoned the opening of an antiphon, 'Thou shalt purge me with hyssop, O Lord, and I shall be clean,' which the choir took up from him and sang beautifully, 'Thou shalt wash me and I shall be whiter than snow...' while the Priest, still on his knees, sprinkled the altar thrice, and, rising, sprinkled the other clergy.

All stood; and the Priest, accompanied by Deacon and Sub-deacon, sprinkled the choir, and then came down the nave to asperge the congregation, those on the Gospel side first as the procession went westward, and those on the Epistle side as it returned to the sanctuary.

Robbie looked happily towards Conal, proud of all that his pupil was seeing, while the three priests in the sanctuary went to the sedilia, Deacon and Sub-deacon helping the Priest change his golden cope for a chasuble; and themselves pulling on their maniples, after which all returned to the pavement before the altar.

The High Mass began.

It did not seem greatly different from anything Conal was accustomed to at the church of the Cowley Fathers, though the ceremonial was often more elaborate. At the beginning the Deacon presented his biretta to the Ceremoniarius as if it were a prize, and with both hands received the Priest's biretta, kissing the Priest's hand and giving this all-highest biretta to the Ceremoniarius, who thereupon received the Sub-deacon's biretta with a grateful bow and finally placed all three birettas in their proper places on the sedilia; at which satisfactory conclusion Robbie, who was a good Rugger scrum-half, well used to passing the ball to his three-quarters, grinned at Conal and said, 'Okay. All touched down.'

The Ceremoniarius returned to the lowest of the sanctuary steps and knelt.

The Mass could go on.

It went on. The priests, other than the Celebrant, moved with hands held immobile before their breasts in the traditional posture of prayer, palms pressed to palms, and thumbs over thumbs. Their faces stayed as expressionless as the carven features of statues, so that they themselves might be seen as no more than impersonal instruments through which God wrought his miracle of the Mass. For the same purpose the Celebrant was keeping his voice low, expressionless and speedy in 'the blessed mutter of the Mass'.

At one point Conal had an opportunity to whisper to Robbie that he didn't like the short cottas of the acolytes with their deep lace fringes, which the Blessed St Percy had described in his book as 'approximating to ladies' underwear' but much preferred the long apparelled albs of the English Use, among the most beautiful vestments in the world. Robbie condemned them in a whispered syllable: 'nightgowns.'

For the rest of the service, a pageant as beautiful, dramatic and significant—nay, far more significant than any stage could bear because it affected to deal with the great Reality and not with fiction—did heighten in Conal, who loved the ancient ceremonies, though he could have done with less than this, his longing to accept the Faith in its entirety; and he did at the moment of the Elevation of the Host when the sanctus bell rang thrice and the thurifer incensed the Host with three double swings—and again at the Elevation of the Chalice, the bell ringing thrice, the chains of the thurible ringing with it, and the eight acolytes lifting their torches in honour of the Elevation, he did say again his secret prayer that, however dim or blinded his faith might be he might manage to worship aright, and do God's will.

He said it with the deepest longing ever when the performance was at its most beautiful, visibly, sensuously (because of the oriental fragrance of the smoke ascending before the altar) and audibly when the choir were singing softly, *'Agnus Dei, qui tollis peccata mundi....'*

In Latin? Conal turned his face towards Robbie that he might read the surprise in it. But Robbie's head was buried in his arms along the pew's top, and Conal knew that all his frivolities and beloved disputations were laid aside, and his worship now was a minor ecstasy and as earnest and true as that of any other worshipper, far holier than he, in this dense congregation. He brought his face back to the priest bowed over the sacred elements on the altar, and thought, 'If *Kyrie eleison* in Greek, why not *Agnus Dei* in Latin?'

'Agnus Dei, qui tollis peccata mundi, miserere nobis. Agnus Dei, qui tollis peccata mundi, dona nobis pacem'; and then, never more softly:

> 'Let all mortal flesh keep silence,
>   And with fear and trembling stand;
> Ponder nothing earthly-minded,
>   For with blessing in his hand,
> Christ our God to earth descendeth,
>   Our full homage to demand.'

And yet, when the whole majestic service was over and the celebrating priests had departed to the sacristy, and all music was at an end, and only one priest in a humble black cassock was in his stall, who very quietly—indeed hardly audibly—responded to the Angelus bell in the tower, 'The Angel of the Lord declared unto Mary'; and the congregation, none of whom had moved from their places, joined him in this homely, quiet salute of gratitude for the Incarnation, 'And she conceived of the Holy Ghost. Hail Mary, full of grace, the Lord is with thee, blessed art thou amongst women, and blessed is the fruit of thy womb...' Why the great contrast between the stupendous service and this softly murmured congregational prayer stirred in Conal the deepest feelings he had known yet—feelings, however, that were, as usual, a blend of almost certain 'Conversion' with yet unslakeable Doubt, he did not know. All he knew was that he longed to believe every word of this, at least.

So much did Robbie with all his absurdities and flippancies and his extravagant hopes of Romanising a stubborn and self-satisfied Anglican Communion achieve for Conal. It was a milestone, if only a small one, in his journey.

4

Conal went down from Oxford in mid-summer of the following year. He remained with the Sheridans through the autumn months so as to return to India and Gondapore at October's end when the heat was cooling and the rains over—though heat was never stifling nor rains unendurable on the Deccan plateau, where the climate was more sensible than anywhere on the plains.

Early in the summer he learned that he had got a Third in Greats, while Robbie, who had never given much thought to tedious sessions in the examination Schools (which he called obscenely 'Stools'), had got a Fourth in Modern History, after a few weeks of work.

Conal's parting with the Sheridans, probably for ever, was much more poignant than anything he would have imagined in his boyhood, for Marjorie, now twenty-one, had grown from 'a rather objectionable little beast' into this tall girl of some beauty, much social charm, and even considerable sense; and Lizetta had been treating Conal more respectfully, and even deferentially, since he'd ceased to be a child in a school cap and become a tall young man at Oxford. Living so long with Marge as a sister there'd been no possibility of his falling in love with her, but there was a great friendliness now between them. Inconceivable a dozen years ago, but Marjorie without doubt had tears in her eyes as, following Lizetta, she pressed a long strong kiss on each of his cheeks in her goodbye. These unexpected tears of Marge at their parting were perhaps the strangest pleasure he would carry home to his native India.

It was wonderful to be on the P. and O. twenty-thousand-ton *Karachi*, with one's eyes ever ahead for the Mediterranean and Port Said and the Canal, and thence into the Arabian Sea. And at last to anchor within the embrace of Bombay Harbour, that splendid lagoon, twenty miles wide and sheltered by its mountains from monsoon and storm. Surely nowhere else in the world, thought this exile returning, was there such an approach from the sea.

And then to dock and land ashore, one's feet on Indian soil, and to hurry to a spacious chamber in the towering Taj Mahal Hotel. From which one hurried out into the noisy streets to revisit, after years of absence, many a place of childhood memory, and to rejoice in a traffic so different from, say, Piccadilly, because it was often a torrent of bullock carts, horse-drawn landaus, cyclists in plenty, gharries, rickshaws, holy men nearly naked with their burdens on their heads and walking in the middle of the roadway instead of on the pavements, and yes, here at last—perfecting the picture—an elephant padding unworried through it all because he—or she—was larger and more undamageable than anything or anyone else.

Here was India. The India of his birth and boyhood which, as with his father, had so much of his heart. Wedgery and Slings and all the Downs of Sussex seemed a world away.

Eager for Gondapore and his old home, he left Bombay the next morning, taking train for Gondapore, and for all the first of the hundred-mile journey, as the train found its difficult way up a broken slope through the Ghats, he was looking out at their forested peaks, measured in thousands of feet rather than hundreds, and comparing them with the gentle Downs.

At Gondapore his father and mother were sitting in the station-house verandah, with their fine new Sunbeam car waiting outside. His father, in a tussore silk suit, sat with his topee on his knees. He was not at all as he had looked for several years in his son's imagination. Slim then, he was now full-bodied; his hair plentiful then was now thin to baldness, except for thick wings over either ear, and they were grey. There was a new roll of flesh under his chin, and the only thing that was quite unchanged was the sparkle of benevolence and laughter in his eyes.

His mother had changed much less; if anything she seemed slimmer, her face as rounded as ever and only slightly more lined.

His father drove the Sunbeam; drove it fast through the narrow crowded streets, past the bazaars, and past the shrines and temples in this city of orthodox Hinduism. As he drove Conal said, 'I nearly got my greatest friend at Oxford, Robbie Cawdor, to have a shot at the I.C.S. but I'm afraid he's too lazy. How he got a Fourth in History I simply don't know. The Examiners must just have been tired.'

'Well, I've got another friend for you,' said Mr Gillie. 'From Oxford and with a good degree. About your age. Must have gone down the term you went up. He particularly wants to be your friend.'

'Why? Who is he?'

'Tell you all about that later,' said his father with a mischievous smile. 'Let's get home first.'

Plainly there was some mystery here, and some unspoken reason why his father was racing home to the old bungalow as if longing for his son to see it. Unlike many Collectors his father had not been moved to another District, so the bungalow was the boy's old familiar home.

And now they were swinging into its compound through the mango grove to the domestic garden, and there the bungalow was. But how different. How splendidly different. In shape it was the same as he remembered it in childhood: a wide hip-roofed bungalow standing on a podium some five feet high, with a dozen steps leading up to the verandah which encompassed all four sides of it. But the tiles of the roof—surely grey long ago—had become crimson tiles sun-faded into pink, and all the rest of the building under the eaves—verandah piers and railings, corridors and window casements had been painted a lively green, only those parts that looked into the sun having paled at the sight of it. Tropical plants which he remembered as small—or did not remember at all—were now massive and lofty. The flowers that bordered the entrance drive were as brilliant as flowers in the East can be. Two *malis* were at work among them, and the quiet in the compound after the noisy street set free the mind to detect and savour the jasmine scents.

'Yes,' laughed his father, 'we have more servants now to brighten things up. We've built new quarters for them and a new go-down. Now come and look inside.'

Inside the bungalow Conal found that all the passages and

rooms which in his boyhood had been humbly covered in Chinese matting were now paved with red tiles, and that his bedroom was in a new extension with windows that sought the breeze from every side.

When that evening Conal changed out of his shorts and open shirt into his dinner kit—as all the Sahibs did, not necessarily for social reasons but because the daytime sweats enforced it—he found that his parents were on the verandah, sitting there while the evening cooled and the sun sunk behind the trees in a crimson and saffron sky. He was about to sit beside his mother, two seats from his father, but she rose and said, 'No. *Between* us on the first night home after fourteen years.'

In the big room behind them the servants were preparing a special dinner to honour his homecoming—a kind of *burra khana* ('very formal occasion') as Mr Gillie with happy laughs insisted on calling it.

Seated between them, Conal began at once, 'Now who and what is this Oxford friend you're reserving for me?'

'He's Mohandas Chandra,' said his father, and said no more, only looking towards his son with a teasing smile.

'He is, is he?' Conal asked this in the same mocking tone.

'No less.'

'Then I take it he's a Hindu. Would I be right?'

'Yes, he's one of the Hindus at their best. Not of Brahman caste, but of some sub-caste very near it. *Bania*, I think. But that isn't the point. He's just a splendid fellow.'

'And he came to England to graduate at Oxford?'

'Yes, just as his father did before him. New College had been his father's college and the old boy was determined his son should go there too. So he sent him to England when he was about fourteen to live with an English family—one's heard of this before—and be crammed by a tutor for four years. A bright lad, he ended with a Second in Greats.'

'Hell! A second! Are you sure I'm good enough for him? A second is quite Something.'

'And,' Mr Gillie pursued, piling on the shocks, 'he's a barrister-at-law. He kept his terms and ate his dinners, and everything else you have to do, though, as a Hindu, unable to eat meat, I imagine he could enjoy only the bread, potatoes and greens. But that didn't seem to disqualify him, and he was duly called to the Bar.'

Here Conal put a question with assumed carelessness because he wasn't ready yet to discuss with his parents his religious hopes and doubts, 'Is he a Christian?'

'Almost as nearly as a Hindu can be. There was a time when he wavered between Hinduism and Christianity, or, as he says, "between the Gita and the Sermon on the Mount", but that exercise at Amritsar where a few hundred of his brothers were mown down rather slackened the pull towards Christianity.'

'Who can wonder?'

Mr Gillie shrugged. 'I think he achieved a synthesis to his own satisfaction, some synthesis between the two which enables him to remain loyal to Hinduism. His father has been a devoted follower of Gandhi ever since the 1890s. A coeval of Gandhi's, he met him in Bombay and more or less fell down and worshipped everything he stood for—non-violence, passive resistance, civil disobedience, *ahimsa*, and the whole bag of tricks. Hence his boy's name.'

'Why hence?'

'Isn't Mohandas Gandhi's—I'd almost said "Christian name"— Gandhi's first name?'

'That's something I never knew. Does anybody know it?'

'Not many, I daresay. He's "The Mahatma" to everybody now. But old man Chandra regarded the Mahatma, and still does, as his own special *guru*, and Mohandas goes all the way with his father, if not a little further. Like father, like son, the boy is one of those gentle, humane, and courteous Hindus, fully accepting *ahimsa*, which means that one must never hurt a single living creature. It's getting on for my thirty-second year in India, and I've never ceased to be amazed that the Hindus can be the most gentle and amiable race on earth when they're not being the most mur- derous.'

'We can murder too.' Conal was seeing the strewn corpses on the Jallianwala Bagh.

His father trapped the allusion. 'Yes, alas ... but we did censure the General, deprive him of all command, finish his career for him.'

'More applauded him.'

'Here too. And still do.... However.... Mohandas is one who

212

would never, never, countenance murder or massacre.... There are reasons why I not only want him to be your friend but even more perhaps—much more—for you to be *his* friend.'

'What reasons?'

'You'll see. You'll see.'

At this interesting stage the butler appeared from the big room, bowed, and said to his mistress as to the hostess, 'Lady Sahib, the dinner is served.'

So they went into the living-room and took their places at the long table. The meal-to-be was certainly no *burra khana*, for it was but a family festa with no guests. As Mrs Gillie said, 'Daddy wanted it to be a *burra khana* with heaps of guests to welcome you, but I insisted that it should be ourselves alone.' So Mr Gillie sat at the head of his table with wife on one side, son on the other, and the table stretching into a wilderness. But if there were no guests, there were more servants than diners. Around the table ever active, were the butler, the assistant butler, the *hamal* (houseman) and the 'boy', known as the man of all work. Fervently waited on by these deferential servants, Conal could not fail to be marking the contrast between all this dignified ceremonial—now that his father was a big man in India—and the humbler meals at the Sheridans' home in Chelsea with one parlour-maid attending—usually a transient figure, so great the servant trouble, and so small the patience of Lizetta as a housewife.

The dishes themselves were worthy of any *burra khana*: hors d'oeuvres, soup, fish, prawn curry, chicken pilau, and a roast sirloin which must (Conal thought) grieve the souls, while whetting the appetites, of these servants if their Hinduism was orthodox. Every dish was perfectly prepared, because the cook was a Goan, 'and Goans,' Conal's father declared with only small exaggeration, 'are the finest cooks on earth.'

'Lord, what a meal!' said Conal.

'Lord, what an occasion!' said his father.

During the meal Conal tried to reintroduce the subject of Mohandas Chandra, but his father evaded it with a grim smile. 'No. Mo'mo shall speak for himself.'

Mo'mo? Very intimate then was the friendship between his parents and this young Indian, little older than himself.

5

It was not difficult for a Collector's son, with a fair degree from Oxford, to find a job in Gondapore and so to live with his parents in their bungalow. There had been established in Gondapore the Imperial Victoria College in 1878, two years after Disraeli had proclaimed Victoria Empress of India. It was at first a school for boys and girls but the girls had long since been transferred to a new school at Radalpur. Conal had not been three weeks in his parents' home when one of the masters at the College was invalided home, and since the present headmaster was a Father Greatrex of the Cowley Fathers, it was almost inevitable that Conal, with affectionate recommendations from the Mother House in Oxford, should stroll into the vacancy.

The school had about a hundred boys of almost every class, race, and religion, some well-to-do who paid well, some poor who could only pay small fees or none. Since ruled by the Cowley Fathers, it was Anglican Christian with an Anglo-Catholic face, but the Fathers with their characteristic tolerance seldom attempted any conversion of their students because the price of 'breaking caste' would be so great and the consequences for Brahmins, Kshatryas and others too menacing. They hoped that the best of these students could see the whole of Christian practice in their Bhagavad Gita, as summed up in a famous Gujarati stanza :

> But the truly noble know all men as one,
> And return with gladness good for evil done;

and that one day, perhaps, they might discern that a birth at Bethlehem had been the one supreme avatar or Incarnation.

With the poorest boys the school had a wonderful record. Coming often from squalid homes, they had been shaped into self-respecting citizens, getting jobs in Government service, railways, police, post office, army, industry, and even Holy

Orders, a few being priests in Anglican churches. Their old Hindu world of poverty, idolatries and absurd superstitions was forever behind them. This record sat well with Conal's mood in these days, secret to himself but at play with a tremendous dream, unattainable perhaps, which had been with him ever since Father Jack tossed the seeds of it into his heart, sitting with him in New College Garden.

For the first time Conal and Mohandas were sitting in the garden between the mango grove and the open area with the many flowerbeds, where *malis* were again at work. The cool of November was now around them, very welcome, very kind. Mohandas' young face was as completely Aryan in its features as that of any young Englishman home from a month of broiling sun-bathing by the sea: narrow straight nose, thin-lipped mouth, tapering chin. His body had the smallness, slimness and grace of so many Indians. Only his hair was a boot-black, his skin a dark coffee-brown and the shaven beard, had he allowed it to grow, would have been of the same black silk as his hair, so that by mid-afternoon the flush of this beard on chin and lips made his face dark indeed. Conscious of his dark skin he made a joke of it in almost his first words; but Conal perceived that the joke was a symptom of distress.

'When they asked my mother, Would she have her coffee black or white,' he said with a laugh, 'the silly girl answered "black, please".'

Instantly Conal comforted him. 'Nothing of the sort, Mo'ho. She said, "Black with quite a little cream. Thank you." And she got exactly what she asked for, Mo'ho.'

The affectionate nickname, though Conal had got it wrong, was designed to show Mohandas that Mr Gillie, the Collector Sahib's son, was going to tread in his old man's steps and treat Mo'mo as in every way an equal. This friendliness enabled Mo'mo to speak from his heart. 'I love England. I shall always love her. From the moment I arrived there everyone—the family I lived with, my young tutor, the people in every shop or in the pubs— treated me as no different from themselves. I couldn't believe that they were the same people as the British here. And it was just the same at Oxford. I made friends there who regarded me as one of themselves—while here I'm only a "native", and that's a word that's little better than "nigger". Do you wonder that I shall love England and Oxford for ever, Conal—may I call you that? I was nine years in England and I never once heard the word "wog" or "nigger". But perhaps I was just lucky.'

'No,' said Conal, 'that's England, when she's at home, except for the fools.'

'Not here, not here,' Mohandas sighed. 'In England I was a graduate and a barrister, here it's "wog". Only the other day one of your Civil Servants, meaning to be funny perhaps, said to me at the door of the Club, "What are you doing here, Wog?" Can you believe it? Just as if I was a low-caste Babu clerk.'

Conal immediately saw and corrected the inconsistency here. 'For Father and me there's no difference between a Babu clerk and you or any other of your countrymen. He's not a "wog" any more than you or the highest Brahmin are. Dad argues that there can't be any basic difference between most Indians and the English. We're the same in blood and bone, Aryans and Indo-Europeans, the only difference being that when we migrated from Central Asia or somewhere your lot went into the hot lands and got brown; ours into the cold and got pink. Aren't the bones of our faces the same? Aren't your girls exquisitely slim and slender in their saris, with their silky black hair? *Your* black hair is silky and I wish my brown stuff were too, but in most things we're the same—whether your mother liked her coffee black, brown or white.'

'I love your father,' said the ingenuous and amiable young man. 'Absolutely love him. And it's he that's saving for me my love of England, which is precious to me. It was terrible to return from Oxford where I had so many friends—really loving friends—to Gondapore and find your British speaking to me as if I were a well-liked dog to be patted and given bones, but a lesser animal nonetheless. I hadn't been here a week before they'd taught me my place again. Never more for me the happy comradeship of Oxford. Never more. There I was a guest to be made much of and laughed with; now I'm a serf again.'

'No, no,' Conal expostulated, but Mohandas hurried on. 'Then

I met your father. This may be my own country, but I think—you see I know and love your New Testament—I think he remembered the words, "I was a stranger and you took me in", because he made me come in and dine with him—not made me stay out on the verandah as the other Sahibs do—and he asked me to go for long walks with him. God, how is it that you English, so human and kind in your own land, can become so pompous and arrogant and insulting over here? But not your father; he brought his English kindness with him.'

Conal nodded, saying only, 'Yes, that's Father.'

'In Oxford I walked side by side with my white friends, but only yesterday a Colonel Sahib looked at me and it was a look that said plainly "Get off this sidewalk, Wog. Indians don't walk on the same pavement with me." I slipped off into the roadway—there was nothing else to do—but I was thinking of the pavements at Oxford where I walked side by side with my friends: the High, the Broad, St Giles, Folly Bridge—there was no difference between us there—and New College Gardens. Your and my New College Garden under the city wall.'

This reminded Conal of Father Jack, and he told Mohandas, because it was so apt to what he was saying, all about the Father's plans for an ashram in which the British would be the brothers of Indians—no showing them 'who was master' as at Amritsar, but enacting only—for Mohandas had mentioned his love of the Gospels—'Whosoever will be great among you, let him be as your servant.'

Mohandas was full of applause for this plan of Conal's friend, but it all lay in the future, and he wanted to get back to Conal's father. 'Do you know, your father has walked arm-in-arm with me—deliberately, I know—and he sometimes takes me into the Continental Club where normally I should be avoided and left alone, but with him, the Burra Sahib, anybody—everybody—speaks to me as if I were no different from Them. He takes me there on purpose for this, I can see. We're not fools, we Indians; we see.'

'Come on, Mo'ho,' said Conal, getting up from his chair, 'let's go for a long walk together, arm-in-arm.'

*   *   *

Conal talked often with his father about his revulsion from this Master-race treatment of any Indian whose skin was brown, and never mind if he was a graduate from Oxford and a barrister-at-law. 'I can't stand a single ounce of it,' he said.

'Nor I,' his father agreed, but with a hopeless humping of his shoulders. 'I discourage it all I can, but it's rather like sweeping back the Atlantic.'

'That of course I understand,' said Conal, happy in this sympathy between himself and his father.

'We're not all the same,' Mr Gillie comforted him. 'There are quite a few of us who've developed a fanatical love for India and the Indians. An astonishing thing, Conal, the capacity of some English to fall hopelessly in love with Eastern countries and Eastern peoples. (We *are* a little mad, I suppose.) They can be either men or women. There was Gertrude Bell, and Hester Stanhope and Doughty and then St John Philby, and now this fellow Lawrence, all lost in love of the Arabs; and we've got several here who've given the whole of their hearts to the Indians. Father Jack is obviously one of them, and I think I'm another in a minor sort of way.'

'Me too,' Conal vigorously avowed. 'Not half!'

'And Mohandas is the opposite side of the penny. He's fallen in love with England as we with India.'

'With England when she's at home, yes; but not when she's sitting in New Delhi, or, worse, in Gondapore.'

Nodding in some agreement with this, Mr Gillie suggested, 'Well, we must save all we can of his love for England, you and I'; and Conal muttered, 'God help me to do so.'

Father Jack's ashram did not lie so far in the future as Mohandas supposed. Indeed, it was already an embryo in the womb of time. In the very year of Conal's return to India Father Jack, as an experiment, had begun a communal life with five young Indian Christians in a small bungalow, part of a mission compound at Miri, some sixty miles from Gondapore, allotted to them for this adventure. Though not as yet adopting anything like the full Rule of a Friary, they lived as friars might, dressed in the white home-woven cassock, the khaddar, with its saffron girdle. They lived above—or below—all the customs of caste or class in India or Britain. One of them wore the full saffron robe of a sannyasi, that is to say one who had been long professed as a 'religious', taking the full vows, and who now, like any friar of old, travelled among the poor and the outcastes, preaching Christianity and trusting solely to God's gift of hospitality in the hearts of men for bed and board—though bed is hardly the word since Father Jack and his Indian brothers slept in Indian fashion on mats on the earth. To his tiny group—himself and the five Indians—Father Jack gave the name, Christa Seva Sangha, 'Society of the Servants of Christ'. Their Rule, if such it could be called, since they were not yet recognised or blessed by their Bishop, was summed up in the words of Christ, 'By this shall ye know that ye are my disciples if ye have love to one another', and by a deliberate elaboration of St Paul's words, 'Where there is neither Greek nor Jew, circumcision nor uncircumcision, Barbarian, Scythian, bond nor free, Hindu nor Moslem, British master nor Indian servant, but where Christ is all and in all'.

Conal, taking his father's car, drove out once to visit their home at Miri, longing to meet Father Jack again and see all that he was getting up to, and to talk again about their talk in the garden of New College. He came home bursting with enthusiasm to his parents. 'It's truly wonderful what they're attempting. I don't think I've ever been so impressed with anything before. It's far above anything I could ever do. Every week they go out to a leper asylum and cheer them all up and make friends of them all. That's not for me. Outcastes, yes; every time, but lepers? No. No, thank you.'

'Nor for me,' sighed his father.

'It's rather pathetic to see Jack as the only Englishman while there are five Indians. There ought to be at least as many British as Indians, but it's early yet, and he believes that others will come to join him, even perhaps from England. I'd like to write home to some Oxford lads and make them see his vision and come out and help him.' As he said this he remembered Robbie saying carelessly that he was 'thinking of taking Orders', and he could see that Robbie's idea was to become an Anglican priest in a lace-fringed cotta, Romanising the poor old C. of E. or censing its altars in a splendid Roman chasuble; certainly not an Indianising priest in Indian garments, vowed to a stark asceticism. 'Their work, while awaiting recognition, is carried on in the villages of the Ahmadnagar district, alike among the caste people and the outcastes, with especial favour for the outcastes. They're breaking caste fearlessly, and damn-all what happens. These wretched outcastes live in mud huts severely separated from the main bodies of the villages for they're not allowed to enter the temples or drink from the village wells, but must earn their livelihoods as scavengers for people of caste who could not touch them without being polluted. According to caste, an untouch- able must stand at least sixty-four feet away from a Brahmin lest he should pollute him. To me this is all howling rubbish. Plain bilge; and I'm with anyone who'll get shut of it for ever.'

'So am I,' said his father, 'but it'll take a hundred years, and more, to get shut of it for ever.'

'And meanwhile,' Conal ran on ardently, 'the Sangha's made it clear that any untouchable would be welcomed as a brother. The very word "untouchable" is now unmentionable in the Sangha; any quondam untouchable, whether scavenger, sweeper or whatnot, has now his new special name'—he stated it tri- umphantly: ' "Child of God." '

Father and Mother listened with interest, his mother asking most of the questions and at times shaking her head, if not in disapproval, in some doubtfulness; his father mainly silent and uncommitted, but with his eyes fixed upon his son, as if with some private concern.

Christa Seva Sangha was formally established and blessed by the Bishop of Bombay in St Barnabas' Church at Miri; St Barna- bas being the Sangha's patron, the Son of Consolation who sold his land for the poor. Father Jack was elected its Acharya, or Superior, and the Rule, for the present, kept simple and informal to allow for modifications or perhaps in time for sterner and stricter vows. In its simplest statement it was *bhakti*, or 'devotion', expressed by prayer, meditation and study, in that order, and by daily ministry to sick and poor. Of these occupations priority was given to the first two, prayer and meditation, for the Sangha accepted the motto given to the Cowley Fathers by their Founder fifty years before: 'the great matter is to get the match well alight before you try to kindle the fire.'

None of the brothers, except the one, were fully professed as yet, not even the Acharya; 'poverty' or 'sharing all things in common' was the only vow. There was, for example, one brother who was married, but he and his wife, living in a small house apart from the others, accepted poverty and shared all. Just as the brothers wore the saffron girdle or saffron robe of India so all the language of the Sangha was in Indian dress: a postulant was a *mumukshu*, a novice a *sadhak* and a professor a *sannyasi*.

'Indian dress? Indian dress?' Mohandas spoke with a mocking laugh. 'Why, my God, Conal, one day in my first weeks home, when I had work in the Courts at Calcutta—it was a Sunday, and feeling more than half a Christian, I thought I'd go to the cathedral ... But....'

He and Conal were sitting on the verandah of the Gillies' bungalow. It was the day after the Bishop's inauguration of Christa Seva Sangha, and Conal, aglow with enthusiasm, had been describing the ceremonies to him. Since the Feast of St Barnabas occurs in early June, this was an evening when they could feel in the air around them, now dense and sultry, the approach of the monsoon rains. They knew the monsoon would be on them at any moment. At any moment they might hear the rains advancing upon them like an invading army. But the parched earth before their eyes, swinging up its dust into the winds, or sending its dust-devils dancing along, did not regard the approaching monsoon as an enemy but as friend and saviour. It was thirsty for salvation. As the dusk deepened into dark the fireflies above the mango grove lit their thousand lamps brilliantly as if to welcome what was coming.

Mohandas, wavering as ever between the Gita and the Gospel, quoted with laughter after hearing all that had happened at Miri, 'Almost thou persuadest me to be a Christian ... *But....*' and he told his story about Calcutta and its cathedral. 'More than half a Christian, I thought I'd go to the cathedral—the cathedral, mark you—and, fool that I was, I went along in my latest Indian dress of which I was rather proud. I was refused admittance. I was turned away at the door. By some verger or other.'

'No!' Conal exclaimed incredulously. 'That's impossible. It was some fool.'

'Fool or not, he expressed something about the attitude of most British in India—you Christians included. The fellow was an Indian himself and I told him what I thought—not in anger because I happen to believe the Mahatma to be the perfect Christian when he insists that we're to overcome our enemies, not by violent anger but by love, saving their faces whenever we can. He agreed with all I argued but just shook his head sadly and said, "I know; I know; but you realise what some of the Sahibs would say." I did. I realised well but, trying to be Christian and forgive, I went home, got into European dress, and came back. Then nobody turned a hair when I walked into the cathedral. So much for your Indian dress.'

'But, Mo'ho, the Sangha's Indian dress is designed to declare the very opposite of all this, and the Bishop himself blessed and approved it.'

'Yes, but, my dear Conal, there are other missionaries in India, and they are slightly different. Listen. The other day three friends of mine from dear Oxford, who'd just arrived to take up their jobs in the I.C.S., were driving all round the place to see everything and they asked me to come with them in their car. They hadn't been here long enough to know that I was no longer their equal but a despised native. Among other places they visited a mission station—yes, and this was in your Ahmadnagar district, not many miles from your Christa Seva Sangha. The missionary in charge asked all three of them into tea. He—he left me out on the verandah.'

'He couldn't have meant to,' Conal protested. 'He couldn't *possibly*. It was just thoughtlessness—forgetfulness.'

'Oh no, it wasn't. Because when they were sitting down to tea, they said, "Where the hell's Mohandas?" And the missionary said, "Why? Did you want him to come in?" They said, "Of course! What the hell!" And he answered, "Well, certainly I'll have him in. But it's not usually done, you know."'

Conal's heart was so belaboured by this story that at first he couldn't speak then he said only, 'I simply can't believe it. It's horrible.'

Smiling, almost as if to comfort him, Mohandas submitted, 'But he was only speaking the truth! It's *not* usually done. What appals me most is the speed with which your English girls, when they come out here, learn what's done and what isn't done, and accept it all as if it was some local Indian curry. It was in my hearing at a bridge party only a few months ago—a party for "bridging" the gap between British and Indians, given by a grand Commissioner like your father—that I overheard a girl, not much more than twenty, saying, "I can't understand any boys coming to India now that they're giving top jobs to Indians everywhere. Why, at any moment you may have to take your orders from a wog...." Yes, Conal, a wog.'

Conal shook his head, shrugged his shoulders, spread his hands —all gestures of despair—and could only say at last, 'Oh, I wish I could do my bit to break it all down. I'd give anything to do it.' Trying to laugh, he flung back at Mohandas his own scriptural quotation, 'Almost thou persuadest me to be a Christa-Seva-Sangha-wallah.'

At that moment the rain was on them. A great wind like a preliminary barrage stormed ahead of the rain; Conal leaned forward in his chair and said only, 'It's coming'; and then the rain fell like a single curtain from sky to earth. You could almost see and smell and hear the starved earth welcoming it: it threw forth a pleasing smell of dry soil soaking and of water flooding; the mosquitoes and flies littered the air above the rain-washed pools; the frogs croaked and the crickets chirped in a general welcome. Conal and Mohandas ran from the invading rain into the bungalow where they could hardly speak any more for the rain cataracting on to the roof.

It was in light-hearted mockery that King Agrippa said to St Paul, 'Almost thou persuadest me....' and Conal with Mohandas had pretended to be doing the same. But in some secret place of his heart it was not a jest—or it was less than a jest. For long now, for three years, he had been in virulent, implacable revolt against the memory of Amritsar and its 'Crawling Order'; against much that his father reported to him about the attitude of all too many of his fellow magistrates towards their native underlings; against much of this deportment which he could now watch for himself; and finally—and most persuasive of all—against the insults heaped daily upon an alumnus of his own college at Oxford.

Mohandas had come again to him with perhaps the most horrific story of all.

'What do you think, Conal?' he had demanded. 'Yesterday I was sitting in the Poona train when a bunch of your English Tommies got into my carriage. They were very young and newly arrived in India, I think, but they'd learned their lesson about how to treat the natives. They looked at me and said, "We can't sit with *him*, can we?" and prepared to get out. But one of them said, "No, bugger it all, *we* don't do the getting out. It's *him* that's got to do that." And they ordered me to get out. I refused like hell. They agreed, after some sort of arguing, that they couldn't get out for me, and sent for a station official. He, if you'll believe it, was an Indian, a fellow countryman, but he said he could do nothing and I had better get out. And one of the Tommies said to him—but perhaps he was the platoon's comic man who had to be funny—but what do you think he said?'

Conal waited in silence for the information.

'He said to the official, "Look here, cock. We can't sit here with a savage."'

Conal, defeated, said only—and after a pause, 'Mo'ho, I apologise for all my countrymen. I do with all my heart.'

Mohandas, appeased a little by this gentle answer, decided that it was his turn to comfort Conal. '"Savage" was the word; I was an untouchable; but I got out of the carriage realising that it was partly our fault. We invented untouchability and demonstrated it to the world; and now the very least of our conquerors—your half-illiterate Tommies—can make us drink the wine we've brewed for others. We deserve it. We just deserve it,' he said bitterly. 'We've dubbed one-fifth of our people as untouchables. So I didn't trouble to say I was not a savage, I was a barrister-at-law from the Middle Temple and an Oxford graduate——'

'With a better degree than I ever got,' Conal put in as a little balm.

'—I got out of the carriage and since most of the other compartments were filled with British soldiers, I travelled home in the luggage van.'

Conal's violent and enduring revolt against this sort of British behaviour made him ponder whether, in some way or other, he could support Father Jack's dramatic repudiation of it all before the eyes of India and the world. Christa Seva Sangha, small though it might be at present with the Acharya himself as the only Englishman in it, was yet—Conal could not lose this conviction and at times did not wish to do so—a true and splendid Answer, the one Christian Answer. He would wonder, as the days went by, if, though his faith was still less sure than any of the C.S.S. brothers, he could declare himself a 'kind of postulant' for the Sangha, a postulant implying no more than one who was testing himself to learn if he had a vocation. And would it be possible, he wondered, to stay, while a postulant, living in his parents' home and continuing to teach in his school. After all, the C.S.S. was still an inchoate and amorphous creation, and there was the precedent of the Franciscan tertiaries who continued living in the world as civilians but secretly obeying a Rule of prayer, simplicity of living, and labours for the advance of Christianity and the brotherhood of mankind. All of which had the best of his heart.

And in the end, after days and days of inconclusive pondering, days and nights of longing to declare before the world where he stood, the evening came when he drove out to Father Jack's ashram, still trailing clouds of doubt, but—as he put it to himself —'rather madly happy'—and actually offered himself as a postulant on these oddly irresolute terms. Father Jack accepted them at once, and there and then, on that very evening, they went out together, and secretly, to St Barnabas Church, where the C.S.S. had been inaugurated; and alone in its little chapel, the Father, as Acharya, within the sanctuary rails, and Conal kneeling before them, this postulancy was confirmed in the briefest and simplest service of question and answer.

'Do you wish,' the Acharya asked, 'to be admitted as a Mumuk-shu of Christa Seva Sangha?'

'I do.'

'Will you live according to the Rule which will be given you?'

'I will.'

'Almighty God, who has given you the will for this life and work, give you the grace faithfully to fulfil the same.'

Then they both, one on either side of the rails, knelt for silent prayer, after which the Acharya rose and, raising his hand, said over Conal still kneeling, 'Conal Quentin Gillie, I admit thee as a Mumukshu of the Christa Seva Sangha' and, laying both hands on his head, said, 'The Lord bless thee and keep thee in all thy ways.'

That was all. As side by side they walked away from the chapel and the church, Father Jack touched Conal's elbow affectionately and said, 'Bless you and welcome, Brother Conal.'

Brother Conal? The Acharya was addressing him, though only a tentative postulant, as one of his brothers! This was either a flattering pleasure or a signal for doubt; he could not say which: he was still not certain that he had a real vocation; whether, in the ancient words, this postulancy was *ex Deo, per hominem*, or *ex necessitate*. Certainly not *ex necessitate*. Hardly *ex Deo*. Possibly *per hominem*—via Father Jack. Nevertheless, leaving aside the doubts, he smiled and said in the same humour as the Acharya, 'Thank you, Reverend Father.'

At least this was all that was visible. Conal, overcome by shyness, still fettered by doubt, and in the strange way of a reserved public-schoolboy rather ashamed of it all, told nothing of this to anyone, not even to his parents, but went on with his customary life at home and at the school, while trying, unseen by anyone, and with some difficulty, to do all that a postulant was expected to do.

6

So vague and indefinite was this position of Conal as a postulant,
so much a secret between him and Father Jack, that it demanded
no terminal date by which a decision must be reached; and
month followed month with Conal moving slowly, if at all, from
his stance as a Doubting Thomas. All that happened was that,
whenever possible, he went out to the ashram to see what the
brothers were now doing and to chat with the Acharya.

They had now moved from their two rooms in the mission
bungalow at Miri to another mission bungalow at Junnar, an old
town under the Western Ghats, which the Church Missionary
Society, a protestant, evangelical body, had most tolerantly placed
at their disposal. A year here, and they moved to—of all places—
an ancient Mohammedan tomb, empty of its original occupant—
or occupants—and converted it into a humble home. This was still
in the Ahmadnagar district. Their membership had increased
slowly; they were now a community of twenty members, one-half
British, one-half Indian. And then the wonderful thing happened.
There was interest and discussion in England about this unusual
sangha in India, not all of it approving, but some money was
collected for them and one generous lady, unable to think with
any happiness of them dwelling like ghosts in a tomb, sent them
a thousand pounds so that they could buy an adequate site and
doubtless build with their own hands a proper home. They had
always had their eyes on Poona as the best site for their ashram,
and with this momentous gift, this manna from Heaven, they
bought five acres of land on the outskirts of the great city.

Poona had been the Mahratta capital in the days of the Peshwas; it was now the centre of the Bombay Presidency and in the
hot months the headquarters of its Government; and besides
being the chief military station in the Deccan, it had its university
and colleges of every kind—art, agriculture, medicine, law—with
its student population running into many thousands.

So now the Sangha went into tents. Their home was now a muster of tents on their precious new site. 'Get you into your tents and into the land of your possession' was the Acharya's happy command in the voice of Joshua. These tents were now their cells and, emerging from them throughout a period of eight months, through cool season, hot season and rains, they set about erecting the ashram of their dreams.

It could be described as a three-winged bungalow of the simplest fashion, built round three sides of a large open court. Like all bungalows in India it was verandah'd, but the verandah along the three wings was the plainest imaginable, a march of low concrete piers supporting a flat concrete roof. Behind this narrow verandah were the cells, small rooms partitioned from one another by walls of white sackcloth. Outside these cells the colonnaded verandah served as the Cloisters.

They planted orange and cypress trees to make a garden, and —perhaps most important of all—built one great circular platform raised only a few inches from the ground, in the midst of the spacious forecourt. This was to be the stage for the two great moments of worship, known in India as *sandhya*, when the two brief twilight periods, at dawn and at dusk, are given to meditation, prayer, and praise, the worshippers sitting in whichever semicircle faces the rising or the setting sun. The *sandhya* might be styled the Half-light Watches which swung Night into Day, Day into Night.

Many times through these eight months of building Conal, who had now his own car, an old black Ford, one of the celebrated 'tin Lizzies' that had done their service in the Great War, came to help a little in the work, unrecognised as a postulant by any except the Acharya. Several times he brought Mohandas with him, and together they enjoyed the building, often merely for the fun of it, though in Conal's secret heart (besides the fun) the more he helped, the fonder he became of the brothers, especially the Indians, and the more he wondered if he was slowly building a decision within himself.

But most unexpected of all things was this: it was Mohandas who completed for Conal the building of this private ashram within himself; Mohandas who erected the king-post which held tie-beams and rafters together. Wholly unknown to Conal,

Mohandas had not only been indulging an amateurish pleasure in the business of building; he had been enjoying many a talk with those brothers who were Hindus like himself and many serious discussions with the Acharya. Ever 'more than half a Christian', he began to wish he could be a whole Christian and one of them. It was likely too that the humiliations to which he had been subjected were driving him fast towards a sangha which existed to cry defiance and shame upon them all. Like many other of the finest Hindus he had their immemorial drive towards *bhakti* and self-immolation, and he came much faster than Conal, his friend, towards his own decision. Conal, going into Mohandas' room, had often observed with some wonder the picture of Christ along with the picture of Gandhi, and by the side of Mohandas' bed a crucifix. Beneath the crucifix was a plain little prie-dieu that might have come from a monk's cell. Mohandas had now persuaded himself that the Gandhian and the Christian dogmas were much the same, ringing truths in his heart he could never deny. Anyway, without a word to Conal or to anyone else he—just as Conal had done—offered himself as a postulant. A postulant for the present, and no more. With all an Indian's love of dramatic symbolism he begged the Acharya formally to admit him as a postulant on the day in April which was the anniversary of Amritsar. The General of Amritsar fame with his 'Crawling Order' had commanded Indians to prostrate themselves or be publicly whipped, and Mohandas in an ironic response fell to his knees before the altar in the tiny chapel which the brothers had now built in their new ashram; and he was accepted as a postulant in the same secret way, and on the same secret terms, that had shrouded Conal's acceptance.

So great, however, was Mohandas' joy in this admission that only a few days later he told Conal all about it.

And Conal, astonished, for nothing could have been further from his imagination, but filled with a delight still barely credible, revealed to Mo'ho—proudly—that he himself had been a postulant for nearly a year now.

And day after day thereafter, the more he gave thought to this extraordinary and extreme Christian triumph with Mohandas, and the more he knew, in every region of his soul and mind, that the Christian, and for that matter the Gandhian, proclamation that the only successful resistance to evil was by its opposite—by non-violent love for the enemy and a fearless suffering for the truth as one saw it—was the one whole, absolute and irresistible truth, so he came nearer and nearer to *his* final decision. Here was the same Conal who day and night had worried over Christian dogmas at Wedgery under the Downs. And at last, not without the deep inner peace that came always with such resolves, he decided that he was going to lead his friend Mohandas from in front: he would now go forward and offer himself to Father Jack as a novice. The joy—or ecstasy, for it seemed no less—was so full that he felt sure it could never be wholly undone. He had sense enough to know that such moments of ecstatic conviction could fade—but not always—and what was one to do but trust one's present certainty—had not the Bishop said something like this?—and act upon it? Else would he delay for ever between two opinions. Act while one opinion only possessed the field, and while you could believe nothing but that it would be in possession for ever.

Soon—tomorrow—he must disclose all to his parents. It would be a formidable task, and his heart began to hammer at the prospect of it—but the sooner the better; he would tell them tomorrow —in the evening when their day's work was done.

7

October now, and though the great rains were not over, the evenings were pleasant and cool under the verandah awnings, and Conal knew that Father and Mother would be enjoying the brief Indian twilight in their deck-chairs before the living-rooms windows.

He went out to them there. As so often before, his father moved to another chair that Conal might sit between him and his mother.

To lead the way into what was going to be so difficult a confession Conal began by some easy references to Mohandas. 'You've heard about Mohandas, I suppose? He's tired of being treated almost as an untouchable by some of us, and he's become a Christian. A full-fledged Christian.'

'You don't surprise me in the least,' said Mr Gillie, innocent of what was to come. 'The greatest of all Hindus, the Mahatma himself, to whom Mo'ho's old man was so devoted, proclaimed to all India that if untouchability was to be an inalienable part of Hinduism, he'd advise Hindus to embrace Christianity. I've always rather suspected that this would happen with Mo'ho. I'm not sure I don't prefer your version of his name. Deeply religious Hindus tend to go the whole way at last—in one direction or the other.'

'He's gone rather more than the whole way,' said Conal, advancing step by step. 'He's now one of Father Jack's postulants.'

His mother spoke. 'Oh, I think that's wonderful news. They're doing wonderful work, Father Jack and his brothers. One more Indian for them. Splendid!'

This seemed to open for Conal the difficult door—if only for a little way. 'Perhaps I ought to have told you before, Mother, that they accepted me for a postulant about a year ago.'

'*What?*' His mother swirled round in her chair, and her word was almost a cry. 'Oh, *no*! No, no. Conal, what are you saying? Conal...?'

Mr Gillie had not spoken. He was only staring; his face a picture of surprise at issue with shock. The surprise—or shock—left him for the present void of speech. Meantime, to ease his mother's distress, and at the same time to ease his approach to a yet more shocking avowal, Conal said, 'A postulant only, Mummy. That doesn't necessarily mean that one's finally committed.'

'Then what on earth does it mean?'

'Only that you're willing to test yourself and see if you're really any good for something more. It doesn't mean that you'll go the whole way.'

Mr Gillie spoke at last, but all he could manage to say was, 'Why have you never told us anything about this? You've never said a word.'

Conal fiddled with his fingers, interlacing them and then grasping one hand, and now the other. 'It's silly but I think I was half ashamed of it. I was both happy with it and worried with it, so I got into the habit of keeping quiet about it. I thought I'd tell you when I'd decided something.'

'Decided? Decided, have you? Decided what?'

Conal saw that, in a stumbling nervousness, he'd come too quickly upon the evening's confession. To evade it, he stayed silent, but Mr Gillie persisted. 'You've been deliberating with yourself for a year, and now you've decided upon a course; is that it?'

Feebly Conal answered, 'Yes, I suppose so. I think so.'

'And it is?'

'That I'm prepared to become a novice, if Christa Seva Sangha'll have me.'

The word 'novice' had so obviously deepened their shock that he hastened to lessen it. 'But even this doesn't finally commit one. A novitiate can last another year or more. It's not an end.'

But Mr Gillie was too shrewd a man to be pacified by a skilful piece of discounting like this. 'Oh yes, Conal, it is nearly always the final decision. A novitiate is a preparation, not a testing. You've had your period of testing as a postulant.'

Since there was no deceiving his father, Conal accepted this as the usual truth, shrugging and admitting weakly, 'Well ... I suppose so.'

At which his mother burst in, 'Oh Conal ... Conal ... you mustn't do this. You're *not* to do it. Please, *please* don't. It's different for Father Jack. He's already a priest and a missionary.'

'There are other laymen now in the C.S.S.,' Conal reminded her. 'Both British and Indian laymen. I'm disposed to be another. That's all.'

His mother was now in tears. 'Don't think I don't admire Father Jack and all he's doing, but you must know that everybody is amazed by it, and many of them disapprove of it; he Eton and Balliol and yet for all practical purposes "gone native", wearing Indian clothes and eating only Indian food and walking about barefoot and all that sort of thing. They say he——'

But Conal interrupted, impatiently. ' "Going native" is no disreputable phrase for me, if natives are behaving nobly.'

His mother was not to be diverted by any such comment, even if she heard it.

'I'm all for the fine work he does among Indians; it teaches them to give up stealing and lying and to live honestly so that it's easier for us to associate with them, as you and Father and I have always tried to do. But for that it's not necessary to go native.'

Conal's answer was instant. 'I don't need to go native, I am one.'

'You?'

'Yes, wasn't I born in India? And thanks to our magnificent British class system which is almost as bad as India's caste to which we feel so superior, I'm quite a little looked down upon in the Club by those who are British-born.'

'That's absolute nonsense,' she insisted. 'Your father and mother are British.'

'Of course it's nonsense. And it exists. The British-born here look down upon the country-bred like me; the country-bred look down upon the half-breeds, and so on, down and down. I'm quite prepared to be done with it all.'

His father, halting somewhere between the two disputants, now took the side of his wife. 'Conal you *are* exaggerating. You were not country-bred. Didn't I send you to England to be educated there? What you're saying *is* an exaggeration.'

'Perhaps a little, but not entirely. And, anyhow, I have no use any more for any of it.'

'Nor have I,' said Mr Gillie. 'I never have. When I first came to India thirty years ago I was given a book telling us how to treat the Indians. It told us that we must be firm and dignified so as to win their submission, but must let them know clearly who was in charge. It explained to us which Indians could be allowed a chair and which must remain standing and which must take their shoes off their feet in our presence. I felt my first distaste for all this before I'd landed at Bombay.'

'Good, Father.' The happy compliment sprang from Conal. 'Good.'

'I don't know that it was any credit to me. I was simply not made that way. And I'm glad that you're not made that way. But this is a tremendous step.'

'Of course it is, Father. And that's why I've been doing battle with it for a year. And I think I know where I am now. Father Jack at New College told me all about the fifteen hundred bodies on the Jallianwala Bagh and declared that, as far as he was concerned, the Church wasn't, like the Priest and the Levite, going to pass by on the other side. And everything in my heart, and soul, then and there, told me that he was speaking the truth for me too. That was three years ago.' Conal was now aroused to an excitement and had forgotten all about sparing his parents. He cared only to pour out the bottled-up but maturing vision of these past years. 'And for the last year I've been asked to witness the ghastly humiliations of a good Oxford friend, Mohandas. I like Mohandas; he's one of the best, and if we're not massacring him and his like, we're robbing them of their dignity as men; we're stripping them of their rights as the true citizens of this country; we're wounding them deeply—and I've had enough of it. It's quite simple really. Like Father Jack, I've no desire to be their master; I'm just their neighbour; and I'm not going to pass by on the other side.'

His mother who had heard some of this outburst but not all, for she was tethered to her own objection, snatched at the weapon of pathos. 'Surely I have some little influence with you—my only son?'

'Enough influence to have kept me silent for a year.'

'But not now?'

'No, Mother.'

'And you won't—say, for a few months so that we can talk it over—postpone this decision you've come to?'

'I shall not.'

'Not for your mother's sake?'

'No. In the end one has to decide this alone. It is decided.'

She was in tears and could hardly speak, but she did manage to say, 'Do remember that your father is now a Deputy Commissioner and if the neighbours think that his son—almost all of them think that Father Jack's Sangha is made up of agitators for India's Independence—if they think that a Commissioner's son is with all these, many of them won't speak to us any more.'

This was an argument so unacceptable to her husband that he did not hesitate to say, 'Darling, I'll cheerfully do without speech from anyone who reviles my son.'

'Thank you, Father.'

Conal waited and then to his mother said, 'I'm sorry, Mother, but I'm afraid I must admit that I'm now wholly on the side of Independence.'

But again his mother, perhaps fortunately, had not listened. 'All my friends say they've no use for British who seek to please Indians by trying to look like them instead of staying honestly themselves.'

'And there may be a strong temptation for them to say that sort of thing because at the back of their minds they want the Indians to know their place and keep their heads low. I don't. One doesn't cease to be English by trying to draw closer to our Indian friends—and brothers.'

Mr Gillie, tolerant and peace-loving, suggested, 'Perhaps both ways are sensible and have their uses.'

Now it was Conal who was not properly listening, because he was disappointed that his mother had not heard his dramatic pro-Independence declaration, which had been intended as a healthy shock for her. He repeated it. 'I'm all for Independence.'

'What? ... You mean ... ?' She had got it now, and, unable in her bewilderment, to find natural words, dropped into those formal phrases, familiar to her from Official Pronouncements.

'You mean you side with those who want to overthrow Britain as the Paramount Power and His Majesty as the King Emperor?'

'Nothing less.' A voice out of the past was now speaking in Conal's mind. It was saying, 'Be yourself. Think for yourself and never mind what other people want you to say.' And he was seeing a little pit in Wedgery's quiet churchyard with the ashes of Dr Balder being lowered into it. 'Decide for yourself and live your own life. Go your own way fearlessly.' Still from these old ashes spoke their wonted fires.

'Mother, I've really decided what I'm going to do. I mustn't go on pretending I haven't. I shall offer myself as a novice tomorrow.'

'Oh, no. No, you can't. You can't be going to do that.'

' 'Fraid so, Ma.' He tried to bring the matter down from her tragic level to something that savoured of comedy. 'A visitor asked Father Jack if it was true that all those in the Sangha were agitators for Independence and he answered, "Alas, no, I only wish they were."'

But Mrs Gillie was determined to remain on her tragic heights. 'I'd hoped to see you married to some nice girl and then I'd be able to see my grandchildren. I was longing for grandchildren. But now all that's gone for ever. And you won't be able to live with us any longer.'

'Well, Mother, I *am* marrying a rather beautiful and seductive half-caste in her Indian sari. Her name is Christa Seva Sangha, and a charming name too. And it doesn't mean some final break with you and Dad. I could come and see you often. The C.S.S. isn't an enclosed order. It's an enormously active order. Out in the world, fighting. If I'd married your nice girl, I'd have had to live in another bungalow than this. And what's our ashram but another bungalow?'

Useless. Mrs Gillie was not allowing a hand to take hers and help her down from emotional heights. 'And your father and I'll soon be going home to England, while you remain for ever in India.'

'Yes, perhaps, but there's nothing in our Rule against furloughs in England. We should just bring our Rule along with us. With our luggage.'

Still not wanting to hear any sense like this, she just said,

'I'd thought perhaps we'd all go home together,' and with her tears falling fast, she hurried from the verandah—and from the complexities and cruelties of Life which had exploded there.

Conal in his chair dropped his shoulders sadly, and raising his palms, let them fall to his knees again, hopelessly. His father twisting an unlit cheroot round and round, stayed silent too. Till, having lit the cheroot and started to smoke it, he said, 'Conal, I've worked now thirty years in India and learned to love the Indians. Or most of them, anyway. And I want you to know that, for my part, I'm happy and proud at what you propose to do.'

Conal looked down upon his fingers. 'Thank you for saying that. I felt you would understand.'

'I understand.' Then to avoid sentimentality his father swung towards levity. 'I'll help your mother. It's always been said, and I'm afraid it's rather true that it takes a man from England about two years to learn his natural superiority to an Indian, but it only takes a woman six months. And, once the dears have got the disease, it's incurable.'

Conal felt too that it was time to remit seriousness and laugh at himself. 'I sometimes wonder how far what I'm doing now results from a sermon by Canon Patrice about *Athanasius contra mundum*. It certainly seems contrary to most of the feminine *mundum*.'

'Who's Canon Patrice?'

'I've told you a hundred times: the extremely Low Church Rector, but very decent sort, at Wedgery. And on the other hand I sometimes wonder if there isn't an element of defiance of the good Canon in my ending up in so Catholic a monkery as the C.S.S.' He returned a little way towards sadness. 'I suppose poor Mum thinks I'm throwing my life away.'

'If she does,' said his father, 'I'll try to persuade her that it would do the world and humanity no harm if more and more young men threw their lives away into these brotherhoods of love and service.' With a laugh he added, 'Didn't you tell me that somebody once said to you, "A single friar in his habit is more convincing than a thousand sermons"?'

'Yes, it was the Bishop. On the Downs.'

'Well, there's something in it, I suppose.'

8

'There's not a hope in hell, Brother Conal,' said the Acharya, 'of our ridiculous little chapel holding the crush of people who want to be present at your admission as a novice. Half the world wants to come. First, there are your parents and all their friends, and all their household of servants who want to come along and see what's being done to their young Sahib. Then of course there are all our twenty brethren. Then there's Mohandas and all his friends. His parents being earnest disciples of the Mahatma, have accepted willingly, if not cheerfully, what he proposes to do, and have given it their blessing—and, I understand, the Mahatma's. I know it was your idea that you and Mohandas should be admitted side by side, but I'm afraid I had to overrule that. I ruled that his novitiate must last many months longer, and he quite understands. But he's a nice lad, and his friends are far too many; and they're all coming along. However, you'll have another postulant at your side, another convert from Hinduism, old Rajendra Behala. The two of you will be admitted together and clothed as sadhaks. And all his friends will be there! But where, Brother Conal; where? I forgot to say that there'll also be lots of the people we've worked amongst, people of all castes, along with their children—perhaps even a cured leper or two. And where do we put them? You're a bright lad, Brother Conal. Tell me what to do.'

Conal, as so often, shrugged, raised eyebrows, spread palms, and grinned. 'Thank God, it's your funeral, Reverend Father.'

'We'll have to borrow some other church in Poona. . . . I had one very bright idea, and that was to conduct a full pilgrimage of us all to Bombay Cathedral. It's only a hundred and twenty miles away, and a nice walk over the Ghats. And the Bishop loves us. Didn't he bless us and start us going? He fully approves of us, which is more than you can say of some of our holy fathers in

Poona. But I suppose a hundred and twenty miles over the Ghats would be a bit steep for some of us. . . .'

But two days later, when Conal was again at the ashram, the Acharya greeted him with a triumphant proclamation. 'It's solved. It's all solved. God is good. *Laus Deo*. And *Deo gratias*, and all the rest of it. God and the Cowley Fathers. Your old friends, the Cowley Fathers. They seem to regard you as one of their protégés. They've offered us their church, the Church of the Holy Name, just about the loveliest church in Poona.'

It was no delighted exaggeration of Father Jack's to describe the Cowley Fathers' Church of the Holy Name as perhaps the loveliest in Poona. Outside it appeared a plain red building but within it was magnificent: a large basilica of cold, white beauty, with tall white Ionic columns marching beneath the arched clerestory windows towards a high altar of patterned marble, enclosed and crowned by an imposing baldaquin. Paved with marble, its former part was empty of chairs, a great, clean, cold space between the columns, since Indians sit cross-legged in their temples or churches. But of late years the westward half of this great shining floor, so burnished and glistened that it mirrored the tall pillars to one-half of their depths, as might a pool in utter stillness, chairs had been placed for European worshippers who could thus look over the heads of all cross-legged Indians in front of them.

And today, for the admission and clothing of Conal and Rajendra the Indian children and their parents or other Indians sat in front of all, and the many Europeans behind, while the Sangha brethren in their long white saffron-girdled cassocks stood on either side of the sanctuary steps. Behind these, robed, but merely as well-wishers, or perhaps we might presume to call them con-celebrants, stood a few Cowley Fathers. The two suppliants for admission, one brown, one white, one middle-aged and one young, Rajendra and Conal, stood before the steps; and after the reading of an Epistle, the Upacharya (Father Jack's deputy) led them before the Acharya standing on the altar pavement.

The two suppliants knelt.

And the Upacharya began, 'Reverend Father, Rajendra Behala and Conal Quentin Gillie—' it had been Conal's request that the Hindu's name should come first—'humbly desire to be admitted on probation to Christa Seva Sangha that thereby they may be the more enabled to advance the glory of God and the spread of his Kingdom.'

The Acharya lifted his face to address the brethren on either side of him. 'Brothers, these are they whom we propose to admit to the degree of sadhak in Christa Seva Sangha for, after testing them, we find not otherwise but that they may be ready and suited to be admitted thereunto. Nevertheless, if there be any among you who know any cause or hindrance why these persons should not be so received, let him come forward now and declare what that cause or hindrance is.'

In the small formal silence while the Acharya waited lest anyone should speak Conal's mind flew back into the past and saw all that old scene in the church at Wedgery when Canon Patrice had been instituted and inducted as its Rector: Sir Harman Drood saying to the Bishop seated behind the altar rails, 'Right Reverend Father in God, I present unto thee this godly and well-learned man to be admitted to the Cure of Souls in this our parish. . . .' and the Bishop making his slight inclination towards the presenting patron; Lizetta and Marjorie in the former pew, and Lizetta melting into a stream of tears, for no other reason than that the words were beautiful.

Before he could remember more he heard the Acharya asking them, 'Do you wish to become sadhaks in Christa Seva Sangha?'

Both: 'I do.'

Other questions followed. Among them, 'Will you try to live according to the Rule of the Sangha?'

'I will so try by the help of God.'

'Will you so long as you remain a sadhak of Christa Seva Holy Word?'

'I will, by the help of God.'

'Will you seek to minister to others, particularly the sick, the sorrowful, and the needy?'

'I will so seek, by the grace of God.'

'Will you so long as you remain a sadhak of Christa Seva Sangha count all that you possess as belonging to the Sangha and gladly serve God without payment or reward?'

'I am so determined.'

After a promise of obedience in all things lawful came the Acharya's blessing. 'May God who has called you to this degree, and given you a ready will to serve him, grant you strength to carry out that which you have undertaken in his Name, and prosper your work with fruitfulness.'

Before their final admission Father Jack desired all the congregation to pray in silence for them; and in the silence Conal remembered the silence at Wedgery's All Hallows and the *Veni Creator Spiritus* following it. When this present silence, a dozen years later, was over the Acharya took the right hand of each and said, 'I admit thee as a sadhak of Christa Seva Sangha——'

(—the Bishop reading the Deed of Institution while the new Rector held its seal in both hands. '*Accipe meam curam et tuam.*' The panels of Droods long dead on the transept walls: 'Sir Eudo Drood of Drood Place, Died 1771 ...' 'Lady Aurelia Drood....' Isidora ... the Bishop....)

And just as that same Bishop had laid his hands on the newly instituted Rector, so the Acharya was now laying his hands on each of these two new novices and saying, 'The Lord keep thee in the light of His Presence. The Lord preserve thy going out and thy coming in from this time forth for evermore.'

Next the Acharya presented to each his habit, the long white khaddar cassock, with the words, 'The Lord put off from thee the old man and his deeds, and put on the new man, which after God is created in righteousness and true holiness.'

For one minute, and during a silence, Rajendra and Conal followed the Upacharya into the vestry and there put on these habits; then returned, clothed, to the Acharya, who presented each with his saffron girdle, saying, 'I gird thee with the girdle of humility for the ministry of Jesus thy Lord, and of his brethren in the world....' The Upacharya, as his Superior said these words, helping each to tie the girdle about himself.

Accipe meam curam et tuam.

Mother, father and Mohandas were gone with all their friends after maternal kisses which Conal declared with laughter were no final parting but merely an *au revoir*. And now he was alone with his new family. It was late in the afternoon when the parents left, so that the day was approaching its hour of *sandhya*; that twilight worship so ancient among the Hindu religious that no one for centuries past had learned its roots.

Conal had more than once shared as a guest with the Sangha in its evening *sandhya*, but now he walked out with the brothers as one of them to the great circular platform in the ashram's garden which was designed for this watch and worship during the two twilights. All the brothers and a few guests sat themselves in a semi-circle on that half of the platform which looked towards the last of another day's sun. As they sat there the sun was losing a little, but only a little, of its warm incandescence and suffering the invasion of a night's first cool airs. The day's glare was now tempered to the eyes and one could look at the sun.

At first the whole gathering in its semi-circle watched in silence, with no movement except that of one brother in the centre of the platform who was sprinkling grains of incense on a brazier of glowing embers, so that the sacred scent of incense smoke mingled pleasantly with the rich scent of the evening's cow-dung fires in the villages around. Neither the incense nor the dung-scent defeated in this last haze the jasmine of an Indian garden. All three blended together, Conal thought, into the very breath of India.

The western sky to which all looked was now a bright orange steadily fading into amber, till it deepened into the sapphire velvet of an Indian night, sparkling with ever more and more stars, while the fireflies, as always, sprinkled their own local darkness with their own tiny stars.

And there the congregation sat, an arc of simple citizens, brown and white, Indian and European, all facing a giant sun as it sank and all accepting each other with a mutual courtesy and regard.

At first they had watched in a silence rather like that of a Quakers' meeting attempting communication with the Unseen, but now, in the twilight's after-image, they sang a famous Marathi song, accompanied by one Indian guitar and a beating of its rhythm by one brother on an Indian drum. Conal knew well its translation:

Be thou at hand, O Lord;
  Then, though my board be piled
With wealth of daintiest fare
  Or bitter herbs and wild,
If thou do but accept me now,
  Unfailing rest alone art thou.

During the silences and the singing Conal felt his heart swelling
and throbbing with a sense of joy to think that here he was—here
he sat—having really given himself to the two things that had
hung about and embraced him since childhood; the one a boy's
unbroken love for India and the Indians, the other a love or
faith in Christianity that had been many times broken and
tormented. This great happiness in his heart now was, he could
see, like the exultation of 'being in love'—in love with what he
had done; and such a reasonless exultation—or exaltation—
must diminish inevitably into a quiet, daily, tempered love, but
he could not believe tonight that it was a love which would pass
and not endure. This was a peace and stillness that would know
many a break in the future—many a doubt and many a conflict
—for no life is peace for ever.

Mohandas, still, by the Father's order, no more than a postulant,
sat by Conal, the novice's side. Because of the songs it was not
easy for him to talk with Conal, but he did say in a low voice,
'This must be the most marvellous twilight for you.'

'I am very happy,' Conal allowed, but said no more.

'The most marvellous in your life,' continued the ebullient
young Indian. 'As it will be for me when the day comes. I'm just
living for it.'

'It's a twilight before many new days, during which all manner
of things may happen. And who can tell what will happen in the
end?' Conal said with a half-smile, faintly correcting a forecast
too ready and easy. 'I am very happy now.'

But Mohandas had to continue, uncorrected. 'There will be only
one more remarkable, and that'll be the twilight after we've been
fully professed.'

'Yes, I hope I shall be as happy then. I believe I shall.'

Their murmurs, lost in the chanting, displayed the difference between an over-expansive young Indian and an under-stating young Englishman.

At one time during the chanting of another *bhajan* or Indian lyric which he could not so easily translate he fell to wondering again who had played the greatest role—and how—in those distant Wedgery days which had so torn him apart—the greatest role in setting his feet upon the path that had brought him to this strange platform under Indian stars. Was it Canon Patrice in his study and his pulpit, or the Bishop on the Downs, Miss Merriweather with her congenial acclamation of the Wrath to Come, or that jovial old Dr Balder, with his 'Decide on your own beliefs. Go your own way.' He was inclined to give the answer to the tall, imposing and so kindly Bishop, but this might be because such an award seemed the most fitting—and yet it was true that no word had ever been more memorable in his life than the Bishop's smiling suggestion to a prep-schoolboy that the Church, for all its two thousand years of life, might still be in its prep-school stage, because men were stubborn and resistant stuff for the spirit to work in. 'But he goes on; he goes on; and he wins in the end.'

Or had there sounded an even more potent voice than any of these in an Oxford garden? 'Crawl, you Indians. Or be publicly whipped.'

Mohandas and Rajendra sat on either side of him. They sat cross-legged in Indian fashion but each had a hand in Conal's.

From these memories he was suddenly recalled by the Acharya's voice leading them in a final prayer inherited from centuries beyond anyone's sight: '*Asatoma sadgamya; tamasoma jyotir-gamaya;* From falsehood bring me to truth; from darkness to light.' And every man in that semicircular throng responded through the new darkness, '*Shanti.* Peace.'

*   *   *

AD
D.J.R.
uxorem dilectam et auxilium
cum amore et gratiis
hic ultimus auctoris
libellus